Praise for *Girl Online*

"Sugg's obvious understanding of the complexities and pitfalls of the online world, coupled with her sensitivity to adolescence, make for a compelling and satisfying coming-of-age tale in the digital age."

—*Booklist*

"*Girl Online* left us wishing adorkable, quirky Penny was our BFF (especially if the package included her amazing best friend Elliot!) because who doesn't love a sweet, adventure-filled NYC love story? No one, that's who! A must read for fans of *Dash & Lily's Book of Dares*, *Invisibility*, and *Suite Scarlett*."

—*Justine Magazine*

"Fun and relatable while also having a positive message."

—*The Independent* (UK)

"A sweet story . . . sugary as a frosted cupcake. . . . The charm of *Girl Online* is the message that growing up doesn't have to mean leaving childish stuff behind."

—*The Telegraph* (UK)

I have this dream that, secretly,
all teenage girls feel exactly like me.

And maybe one day, when we realize that we all feel the same,
we can all stop pretending we're something we're not.

That would be awesome.

But until that day, I'm going to keep it real on this blog
and keep it unreal in "real" life.

Girl Online

ZOE SUGG

The First Novel by Zoella

Keywords
PRESS
—
ATRIA

New York   London   Toronto   Sydney   New Delhi

ATRIA PAPERBACK
An imprint of Simon & Schuster, Inc.
1230 Avenue of the Americas
New York, NY 10020

Instagram competition winner: Amy Walker

First Keywords Press/**ATRIA** PAPERBACK edition August 2016

Keywords Press/**ATRIA** PAPERBACK and colophons are trademarks of Simon & Schuster, Inc.

For information about special discounts for bulk purchases, please contact Simon & Schuster Special Sales at 1-866-506-1949 or business@simonandschuster.com.

The Simon & Schuster Speakers Bureau can bring authors to your live event. For more information, or to book an event, contact the Simon & Schuster Speakers Bureau at 1-866-248-3049 or visit our website at www.simonspeakers.com.

Manufactured in the United States of America

10 9 8 7 6 5 4 3 2 1

Library of Congress Cataloging-in-Publication Data has been applied for.

ISBN 978-1-4767-9745-8
ISBN 978-1-4767-9976-6 (pbk)
ISBN 978-1-4767-9746-5 (ebook)

I want to dedicate this book to all the people who made this possible. The people who have subscribed to my channel, watched my videos, and read my blog, whether that was in 2009 or yesterday. Your support means the absolute world to me. There are no words to express just how much I love every single one of you—without you this book would not be in your hand.

One year ago . . .

Hello, World!

I've decided to start a blog.

This blog.

Why, you might ask?

You know when you shake a Coke can and then you open it and it explodes everywhere? Well, that's how I feel right now. I have so many things I want to say fizzing up inside of me, but I don't have the confidence to say them out loud.

My dad once told me that I should start writing a diary. He said that keeping a diary is a great way of expressing our innermost thoughts. He also said it would be great to look back on when I was old and that it would "really make me appreciate my teenage years." Hmm, it's obviously been so long since he was a teenager, he's forgotten what it's actually like.

I did try, though—writing a diary. I managed about three entries before I gave up. Most of them went something like this:

Rained today; my new shoes got ruined. Jenny contemplated skipping math. She didn't. John Barry got a nosebleed in science because he poked a pencil up there. I laughed at him. He wasn't impressed. It was awkward. 'Night.

Not exactly Bridget Jones, right? More like, "can't be bothered."

The thought of writing stuff to myself in a diary seems a bit pointless really.

I want to feel like someone, somewhere, will be able to read what I've got to say.

That's why I've decided to give this blog a go—so that I have somewhere I can say exactly what I want, when I want and how I want—*to someone*. And not have to worry that what I say won't sound cool or will make me look stupid or lose me friends.

That's why this blog is anonymous.

So that I can be totally me.

My best friend Wiki *(that's not his real name, by the way—I can't give his real name or this won't be anonymous)* would say that the fact that I'm having to be anonymous in order to be myself is an "epic tragedy." But what does he know? He's not a teenage girl with anxiety issues. *(He's actually a teenage boy with parental issues but that's a whole other story.)*

Sometimes I wonder if it's *because* I'm a teenage girl that I have anxiety issues. Let's face it—there is a lot to get anxious about.

Top Ten Reasons for Teenage Girls Getting Anxious

1. You're supposed to look perfect all of the time

2. This coincides with your hormones deciding to go bonkers

3. Which leads to the spottiest time of your entire life *(making number 1 totally impossible!)*

4. Which also coincides with the first time you've had the freedom to buy chocolate whenever you like *(making number 3 even worse!)*

5. Suddenly everyone cares about what you wear

6. And what you wear has to look perfect too

7. Then you're supposed to know how to pose like a supermodel

8. So you can take a selfie of yourself in your outfit of the day

9. Which you then have to post on social media for all your friends to see

10. You're supposed to be wildly attractive to the opposite sex *(while dealing with all of the above!)*

Please picture me giving a dramatic, heartfelt sigh at this point.

But surely I can't be the only teenage girl who feels like this?

I have this dream that secretly all teenage girls feel exactly like me.

And maybe one day, when we all realize that we all feel the same, we can all stop pretending to be something we're not.

That would be awesome.

But until that day, I'm going to keep it real on this blog. And keep it unreal in "real" life.

I'm going to say what I want to say, and it would be really cool if you *(whoever you might be)* join me.

This can be our very own corner of the Internet where we can talk about what it truly feels like to be a teenage girl—without having to pretend to be something we're not.

I also love taking photos *(don't you just love the way photos are able to freeze special moments in time forever? Beautiful sunsets, birthday parties, salted-caramel cupcakes with thick frosting . . .)* so I'll be posting lots of them too. But there won't be any selfies obviously, for anonymity reasons.

OK, well I guess that's all for now. Thank you for reading *(if anyone actually has been reading!)*. And let me know what you think in the comments below.

Girl Online, going offline xxx

★ Chapter One ★

Present day . . .

> Hey, Penny, did you know that William Shakespeare is an anagram for "I am a weakish speller"?

I look at the text from Elliot and sigh. In the time I've been watching the dress rehearsal for *Romeo and Juliet* (three hours of my life that I will *never* get back), Elliot has bombarded me with hundreds of random texts about Shakespeare. He's supposed to be doing it to relieve my boredom but, seriously, does anyone really need to know that Shakespeare was baptized in 1564? Or that he had seven siblings?

"Penny, could you get a shot of Juliet leaning out of the trailer?"

I quickly grab my camera and nod to Mr. Beaconsfield. "Yes, sir."

Mr. Beaconsfield is the Year Eleven drama teacher. He's one of those teachers who likes being "down with the kids"—all gelled hair and "call me Jeff." He's also the reason our version of *Romeo and Juliet* is set in a Brooklyn ghetto and Juliet is leaning out of a trailer rather than a balcony. My BFIS (*Best Friend in School*), Megan, loves Mr. Beaconsfield, but then, he does always cast her in all the lead roles. Personally, I think he's a little creepy. Teachers shouldn't want to hang out with teenagers. They should want to mark books and stress about school inspections and whatever else they get up to in the staff room.

I go up the steps at the side of the stage and crouch down beneath Megan. She's wearing a baseball cap with SWAG printed on the front and has a thick fake-gold chain with a huge fake-gold dollar sign dangling from her neck. There's no way she'd be seen dead in that outfit anywhere else; that's how much she loves Mr. Beaconsfield. I'm about to take a picture when Megan hisses down to me: "Make sure you don't get my spot."

"What?" I whisper back.

"The spot on the side of my nose. Make sure you don't get it in the picture."

"Oh. Right." I shift to one side and zoom in. The lighting from this side isn't the best but at least the spot isn't visible. I take the picture, then turn to leave the stage. As I do, I glance out into the auditorium. Apart from Mr. Beaconsfield and the two assistant directors, all of the seats are empty. I instinctively breathe a sigh of relief. To say I'm not very good with crowds would be a bit like saying Justin Bieber isn't very good with the paparazzi. I don't know how people can actually perform onstage. I only have to go up there for a couple of seconds to take a photo and I feel uneasy.

"Thanks, Pen," Mr. Beaconsfield says as I hurry down the steps. That's another cringe-fact about him—the way he calls us all by a nickname. I mean, seriously! It's okay for my family but not my teachers!

Just as I get back to my safe spot at the side of the stage my phone bleeps again.

Oh my God, Juliet used to be played by a man back in Shakespeare's day! You have to tell Ollie—I'd love to see his face! ☺

I look up at Ollie, who is currently gazing up at Megan.

"But, soft! What light through yonder window breaks?" he says, in the worst New York accent ever.

I can't help but sigh. Even though Ollie's dressed in an even worse costume than Megan's—making him look like a cross between a *Jeremy Kyle* guest and Snoop Dogg—he still somehow manages to look cute.

Elliot hates Ollie. He thinks Ollie's really vain and calls him the Walking Selfie, but, to be fair, he doesn't really know him. Elliot goes to a private school in Hove; he's only seen Ollie when we've bumped into him on the beach or in town.

"Shouldn't Penny take a picture of me in this scene too?" Ollie asks, when he finally gets to the end of his speech. He's still talking in his fake American accent—which he's been doing ever since he got the part. Apparently all the top actors do it; they call it "method acting."

"Of course, Ollz," says Call-Me-Jeff. "Pen?"

I put down my phone and run back up the steps.

"Can you make sure you get my best side?" Ollie whispers at me from beneath his cap. His one has STUD printed on the front in black diamante.

"Sure," I reply. "Er, which side is that again?"

Ollie looks at me like I'm crazy.

"It's just so hard to tell," I whisper, my face flushing crimson.

Ollie continues to frown.

"Because they both look good to me," I say, desperation setting in. Oh my God! What is wrong with me?! I can practically hear Elliot shrieking in horror. Thankfully at this point, Ollie starts to grin. It makes him look really boyish and way more approachable.

"It's my right side," he says, and turns back to face the trailer.

"Is that—er—your right, or mine?" I ask, wanting to make double sure.

"Come on, Pen. We haven't got all day!" Mr. Beaconsfield calls out.

"It's *my* right, of course," Ollie hisses, looking at me like I'm demented again.

Even Megan's frowning at me now. My face burning, I take the picture. I don't do any of my usual things, like checking the lighting or the angle or anything—I just press the button and stumble out of there.

When the rehearsal is finally over—and I've learned from

Elliot that Shakespeare was only eighteen when he got married and he wrote thirty-eight plays in total—a group of us head to JB's Diner to get milkshakes and chips.

As we reach the seafront, Ollie starts walking along beside me. "How you doin'?" he says in his fake New York drawl.

"Um, OK, thanks," I say, my tongue instantly tying itself in knots. Now he's out of his Romeo gangster gear, he looks even better. His blond surfer-dude hair is perfectly tousled and his blue eyes are sparkling like the sea in the winter sunshine. To be honest, I'm not entirely sure if he's my type—he may be a little too boy-band-meets-athlete perfect—but it's so unusual for me to have the undivided attention of the school heartthrob that I can't help feeling embarrassed.

"I was wondering . . ." he says, grinning down at me.

Instantly my inner voice starts finishing his sentence: *What do you like to do in your spare time? Why have I never properly noticed you before? Would you like to go out with me?*

". . . if I could take a look at the picture you took of me? Just to make sure I look OK."

"Oh—er—right. Yes, OK. I'll show you when we get to JB's." It's at exactly this moment that I fall into a hole. OK, it's not a big hole and I don't actually disappear inside it or anything, but I do catch my foot and end up tumbling forward—making me look about as attractive and sophisticated as a Saturday-night drunk. That's one thing I hate about Brighton, where I live. It seems to be full of holes that exist just for me to fall into! I style it out and luckily Ollie seems not to notice.

When we get to JB's, Ollie dives straight into the booth next to me. I see Megan raise her eyebrows and I instantly feel like I've done something wrong. Megan's very good at making me feel this way. I turn away and concentrate on the Christmas decorations around the diner instead—the swirls of green and red tinsel, and the mechanical Father Christmas who yells, "Ho, ho, ho!" every time someone walks past. Christmas is definitely my favorite time of the year. There's something about it that always calms me. After a few moments, I turn back to the table. Luckily, Megan's now absorbed with her phone.

My fingers twitch as the inspiration for a blog post pops into my head. Sometimes it feels as if school is one big play and we're all supposed to perform our set roles all the time. In our real-life play, Ollie isn't supposed to sit next to me; he's supposed to sit next to Megan. They aren't actually dating or anything but they're both definitely on the same rung of the social ladder. And Megan *never* falls into holes. She just seems to glide through life, all glossy chestnut hair and pouting. The twins slide into the booth next to Megan. The twins are called Kira and Amara. They have non-speaking parts in the play and that's kind of how Megan treats them in real life—as extras to her lead role.

"Can I get you guys anything to drink?" a waitress says, arriving at our table with a pad and a grin.

"That would be awesome!" Ollie says loudly in his pretend American accent, and I can't help cringing.

We all order shakes—apart from Megan, who orders a mineral water—and then Ollie turns to me. "So, can I see?"

"What? Oh, yes." I fumble in my bag for my camera and start scrolling through the pictures. When I get to the one of Ollie, I pass it to him. I hold my breath as I wait for his response.

"Sweet," he says. "That looks really good."

"Ooh, let me see my one," Megan cries, grabbing the camera from him and pressing at it wildly. My whole body tenses. Normally, I don't mind sharing things—I even give half my advent-calendar chocolates to my brother, Tom— but my camera is different. It's my most prized possession. It's my safety net.

"Oh. My. God. Penny!" Megan shrieks. "What have you done? It looks like I've got a mustache!" She slams the camera down on the table.

"Careful!" I say.

Megan glares at me before picking up the camera and fiddling with the buttons. "How do I delete the picture of me?"

I grab the camera back from her a little too forcefully and one of her false fingernails catches on the strap.

"Ow! You've broken my nail!"

"You could have broken my camera."

"Is that all you care about?" Megan glares at me across the table. "It's not my fault you took such a terrible picture."

In my head an answer forms itself: *It's not my fault you made me take it that way because you've got a spot.* But I stop myself from saying it.

"Let me see," Ollie says, grabbing the camera from me.

As he starts to laugh and Megan glares at me even harder, I feel a familiar tightness gripping my throat. I try to swallow but it's impossible. I feel trapped inside the booth. *Please don't let this be happening again*, I silently plead. But it is. A burning heat rushes through my body and I can barely breathe. The pictures of movie stars lining the wall all suddenly seem to be staring down at me. The music from the jukebox is suddenly too loud. The red chairs too bright. No matter what I do, I can't seem to control my own body. The palms of my hands go clammy and my heart starts to pound.

"Ho, ho, ho!" the mechanical Father Christmas by the door calls. But he doesn't sound cheery anymore. He sounds menacing.

"I need to go," I say quietly.

"But what about the picture?" Megan whines, flicking her glossy dark hair over her shoulder.

"I'll delete it."

"What about your milkshake?" Kira says.

I take some money from my purse and put it on the table, hoping they don't notice my trembling fingers. "One of you guys have it. I just remembered I have to help my mum with something. I need to get home."

Ollie looks at me and for a second I think he actually looks disappointed. "Will you be in town tomorrow?" he asks.

Megan glares at him across the table.

"I guess so." I feel so hot it's making my vision blurred. I need to get out of here, now. If they keep me trapped in this booth for much longer, I'm certain I'm going to pass out. It takes everything I've got not to yell at Ollie to get out of my way.

"Cool." Ollie slides out of the booth and hands me my camera. "Maybe see you around then."

"Yes."

One of the twins, I can't tell which, starts to ask if I'm

OK, but I don't stop to answer her. Somehow, I make it out of the diner and onto the seafront. I hear the shriek of a seagull followed by a shriek of laughter. A group of women are tottering toward me, all spray tans on high heels. They're wearing Barbie-pink T-shirts, even though it's December, and one of them has a string of learner plates around her neck. I internally groan. That's another thing I hate about living in Brighton—the way it's invaded by stag and hen parties every Friday night. I dart across the road and head down to the beach. The wind is icy and fresh but it's exactly what I need. I stand on the wet pebbles and stare out to sea and wait until the waves, crashing in and rolling out, coax my heartbeat back to normal.

Chapter Two

For most girls, coming home to find your mum posing on the stairs in a wedding dress would be a freakish occurrence. For me, it's the norm.

"Hello, darling," she says, as soon as I come in the front door. "What do you think?" She leans on the banister and throws out an arm, her long auburn curls cascading over her face. The wedding dress is ivory and empire line and has a border of lace flowers around the neck. It's really beautiful but I'm still feeling so shaken up, all I can do is nod.

"It's for the Glastonbury-themed wedding," Mum explains, coming down the stairs to give me a kiss. As usual she smells of rose and patchouli oil. "Don't you love it? Doesn't it just scream flower power?"

"Mmm," I say. "It's nice."

"Nice?" Mum looks at me like I'm crazy. "Nice? This dress isn't just nice—it's—it's majestic—it's divine."

"It's a dress, dear," my dad says, coming out into the hall. He grins at me and raises his eyebrows. I raise my eyebrows back. I might look more like Mum but personality-wise I am much more like Dad—way more down to earth! "Good day?" he asks, as he gives me a hug.

"OK," I say, suddenly wishing that I was five years old again and I could just curl up on his lap and ask him to read me a story.

"OK?" Dad steps back and looks at me carefully. "Is that a good OK or a bad OK?"

"Good," I say, not wanting to create any more drama.

He smiles. "Good."

"Will you be able to help out in the shop tomorrow, Pen?" Mum asks, looking at herself in the hall mirror.

"Sure. What time?"

"Just a couple of hours in the afternoon, while I'm at the wedding."

Mum and Dad own a wedding-planning business called To Have and to Hold and it's based in a shop in town. Mum started the business after she gave up her acting career to have my brother, Tom, and me. She specializes in quirky themes. She also specializes in trying on all of the wedding dresses she stocks—I think she misses wearing costumes from her acting days.

"How long till dinner?" I ask.

"About an hour," Dad says. "I'm making shepherd's pie."

"Awesome." I grin at him and start feeling a bit more human. Dad's shepherd's pie is amazing. "I'm just going upstairs for a bit."

"OK," Mum and Dad say in unison.

"Ha! Jinx!" Mum cries, kissing Dad on the cheek.

I go up the first flight of stairs, and past my parents' bedroom. As I reach Tom's room I hear the thudding beat of hip-hop. I used to hate hearing his music all the time but now that he's at uni I like it, because it means he's home for the holidays. I've really missed him since he's been away.

"Hey, Tom-Tom," I call as I walk past his door.

"Hey, Pen-Pen," he calls back.

I go to the end of the landing and start climbing another flight of stairs. My room is at the very top of the house. Even though it's a lot smaller than the other bedrooms, I love it. With its sloping ceilings and wooden beams, it's really cozy and snug, and it's so high up I'm actually able to see a dark blue line of sea on the horizon. Even when it's dark out, just knowing the sea's there makes me feel calmer inside. I light the string of fairy lights draped over my dressing-table mirror and a couple of vanilla-scented candles. Then I sit down on my bed and take a deep breath.

Now that I'm back home it finally feels safe to think about what happened in the diner. It's the third time something like this has happened to me now and I can feel a ball of dread growing in the pit of my stomach. The first time it happened, I'd hoped it was a one-off. The second time, I hoped it was just bad luck. But now it's happened again . . . I shiver and wriggle under my duvet. As my body starts to warm up, I have a random flashback to when I was a little kid and Mum used to make me a tent out of blankets to play in. I'd lie inside the tent with a stash of books and my torch and read for hours. I loved having a little hideaway from the world. I'm about to close my eyes and snuggle deeper under the duvet when I hear three loud knocks on my bedroom wall. Elliot. I throw off the duvet and knock back twice.

Elliot and I have been next-door neighbors our entire

lives. And we're not only next-door neighbors but next-door-*bedroom* neighbors, which is seriously cool. We invented our wall-knocking code years ago. Three knocks means, *Can I come over?* Two knocks means, *Yes, come over right now.*

I get up and quickly scramble out of my school uniform and into my snow leopard onesie. Elliot hates onesies. He says the person who invented them ought to be hung upside down from Brighton Pier by their shoelaces, but then Elliot is seriously stylish. Not in a fashion slave way; he just has this knack of putting really random things together and making them look great. I love taking photos of his style.

As I hear his front door slam, I quickly look in the dressing-table mirror and sigh. I pretty much sigh every time I look in the mirror. It's like a reflex action. *Look in the mirror—sigh. Look in the mirror—sigh.* This time, I'm not sighing at my freckles and the way they cover my face like the speckles on a Mini Egg—I can't really see them in the candlelight. This time, I'm sighing at my hair. How come when the sea breeze messes up Ollie's hair it looks super-cute but when it messes up mine it looks as if I've stuck my fingers in a plug socket? I quickly pull a brush through my curls, but this only makes them go even frizzier. It's bad enough that my hair is red—Elliot insists that it's strawberry blond (it's definitely more strawberry than blond)—but at least if it was permanently sleek like Megan's that would be something. I give up with the brush. Elliot won't care. He's seen me when I had the flu and wasn't able to wash my hair for a week.

I hear the doorbell go and Mum and Elliot talking. Elliot will love the wedding dress. Elliot loves Mum. And Mum loves Elliot—my whole family does. He's practically been adopted by us, to be honest. Elliot's parents are both lawyers. They both work super-hard and even when they're home they're usually researching some case or other. Elliot's convinced he was switched at birth and sent home with the wrong parents. They just don't get him at all. When he came out to them, his dad actually said, "Don't worry, son, I'm sure it's just a phase." Like being gay is something you can grow out of!

I hear Elliot's feet pounding up the stairs and the door flies open. "Lady Penelope!" he cries. He's wearing a vintage pin-striped suit and braces and a bright red pair of Converse—this is him dressing down.

"Lord Elliot!" I cry back. (We spent most of last weekend watching *Downton Abbey* box sets.)

Elliot stares at me through his black-rimmed glasses. "OK, what's up?"

I shake my head and laugh. Sometimes I swear he can read my mind. "What do you mean?"

"You look really pale. And you're wearing that hideous onesie. You only wear that when you're feeling depressed. Or you have physics homework."

"Same thing," I say with a laugh, and sit down on the bed. Elliot sits next to me, looking concerned.

"I—I had one of those weird panic things again."

Elliot puts his wiry arm around my shoulders. "No way. When? Where?"

"JB's."

Elliot gives a sarcastic snort. "Huh, I'm not surprised. The decor in there is vile! Seriously, though, what happened?"

I explain, feeling more embarrassed with every word. It all sounds so trivial and silly now.

"I don't know why you hang out with Megan and Ollie," Elliot says, when I reach the end of my tale of woe.

"They're not that bad," I say lamely. "It's me. Why do I keep getting so stressed about stuff? I mean, I could get it the first time, but today . . ."

Elliot tilts his head to one side the way he always does when he's thinking. "Maybe you should blog about it."

Elliot's the only person who knows about my blog. I told him right from the start because (a) I can trust him with anything, and (b) he's the one person I can totally be myself with, so there's nothing on the blog that he wouldn't already know about.

I frown at him. "Do you think? Wouldn't it be a bit heavy?"

Elliot shakes his head. "Not at all. It might make you feel better to write about it. It might help you make sense of it. And you never know—maybe some of your followers have gone through the same thing. Remember that time you posted about your clumsiness?"

I nod. About six months ago I blogged about falling head-first into the wheelie bin and my followers went up from 202 to just under 1,000 in a week. I've never had so many shares. Or comments. It turns out I'm definitely not the only teenage girl born with a clumsy gene. "I suppose so . . ."

Elliot looks at me and grins. "Lady Penelope, I *know* so."

15 December

Help!!

Hey, guys!

Thanks so much for all of your lovely comments about my pics from Snooper's Paradise—I'm glad you love its quirkiness as much as I do.

This week's post is really difficult to write because it's about something really scary that's happened to me—*is* happening to me. When I first started this blog, I said I was always going to be completely honest here, but back then I had no idea **Girl Online** would take off the way it has. I can't believe I now have 5,432 followers—thanks so much! Although the thought of opening up to you all about this is terrifying, Wiki reckons it might make me feel better, so here goes.

Some time ago, I was in a car crash. It's OK—no one died or anything. But it was still one of the worst experiences of my life.

My parents and I were driving back home and it was one of those rainy nights when the water seems to be coming straight at you like a wave. Even when my dad had the windscreen wipers going at about 100 miles per hour it didn't seem to make any difference. It was like driving through a tsunami. We'd just gotten onto a dual carriageway when a car cut right in front of us. I'm not exactly sure what happened next—I think Dad tried to brake and swerve—but the road was so wet and slippery we skidded into the central reservation. And then our car actually spun over!

I don't know about you, but I've only ever seen this happen in movies. And in the movies, right after the car turns over, it usually blows up or a lorry plows into it or something, so all I could think was: *We're going to die.* I kept calling out to Mum and Dad, not knowing if they were OK, and they kept calling out to me, but I wasn't able to get to them. I was trapped, on my own, upside down, in the back.

Thankfully, we didn't die. A really nice man saw what happened and stopped his car to help us. Then, when the emergency services got there, they were really lovely too. We were driven home in a police car and sat up drinking sugary tea under duvets on the sofa until the sun came up. And now everything is pretty much back to normal. My parents don't really talk about the accident anymore, and we have a brand-new non-mangled car sitting in the driveway. Everyone keeps saying to me, "You're so lucky you didn't get hurt." And I am. I know that. But the thing is, even though I didn't get any cuts and bruises on the outside, it feels as if something inside of me has broken.

I don't even know if an accident like that can cause this, but I keep having these weird panicky moments. If something stresses me out and I feel like I can't escape, I start feeling like I did when I was trapped in the car. I go all hot and shivery and I feel like I can't breathe. It's happened three times now—so I'm really scared that it's going to keep on happening. And I don't know what to do.

I hope you don't mind me writing about this. I promise I'll get back to my usual self next week. I promise there'll be loads of really yummy pics from Choccywoccydoodah! But if any of you have been through anything like I've just described, and you have any tips on how to make it stop, pleeeeease post them in the comments below. It's bad enough being *the Clumsiest Person in the Universe*. I don't want to be the panickiest too!!

Thank you!

Girl Online, going offline xxx

Chapter Three

The next morning I wake up to the usual chorus of seagulls squawking. Fingers of pale wintery light are creeping in through the gaps in the curtains. This is good. Recently I've been waking up so early it's still been dark outside.

Elliot was right—writing the blog post really did help. I wrote it after he went home last night. At first it felt a bit awkward and cringey, but after a couple of sentences, all the thoughts and feelings I've been bottling up about the accident just flowed out of me. Once I posted it, I didn't do my usual thing of waiting to see if it got any comments or shares. I felt so sleepy I just closed my laptop and went to bed.

As my body slowly adjusts itself to the fact that it has to wake up and deal with a whole new day, I rub my eyes and look around my bedroom. Mum and Dad joke that they didn't really need to wallpaper my room because pretty much every inch of wall is covered with photos. When I ran out of space recently, I started clipping pictures onto a line and stringing it like bunting over my bed. Most of these photos are of Elliot messing around on the beach, playing dress-up in his vintage clothes. There's also my favorite photograph of Mum, Dad, and Tom, all sitting around the tree last Christmas morning, with steaming mugs of coffee nestled in their hands. I love capturing these special little moments in time. This picture also reminds me of the moment just after: when Mum spied me hiding with my camera around the corner and called me over to join them on the sofa and we all started singing a really silly version of "We Wish You a Merry Christmas." This is one of the things I love the most about photos: the way they can help you capture and relive moments of happiness forever.

I take my phone from my bedside table and turn it on. There's a few seconds' silence before it starts going crazy with email alerts. I go to my inbox and see that it's crammed full of notifications from my blog. There have been loads of comments overnight. I pick my laptop up from the floor and open it, my heart pounding. Even though I've been running Girl Online for a year now, and even though my followers are really lovely and always post really positive things, I still have this crazy fear that one day it might all go wrong. What if they thought my post last night was too much—too heavy?

But it's fine—in fact, it's way better than fine. As I quickly scroll through the comments, I see words like "thank you," "brave," "honesty," and "love" popping up again and again. I take a deep breath and start reading them properly. And what I read brings tears to my eyes.

Thank you for sharing this . . .

It sounds as if you're suffering from panic attacks. Don't worry, I get them too . . .

I thought I was the only one . . .

Now I know I'm not alone . . .

You're bound to be shaken up after the accident . . .

Thank you for your honesty . . .

It will get better . . .

Have you tried relaxation techniques?

You're so brave for sharing . . .

On and on they go until I feel as if I'm wrapped up in a toasty-warm blanket of love. In a way, it's nice to know that "panic attacks" are an actual thing and not just my mind going crazy. There are things I can do to help myself feel more in control. I make a mental note to look them up later.

Downstairs, I hear my parents' bedroom door opening and the soft thud of footsteps across the landing. I smile as I think of my dad on his way to make "Saturday Breakfast." Elliot and I always give my dad's "Saturday Breakfast" capital letters and speech marks because it is such a major event. I don't think there's a pan in the house that goes unused as he whips up bacon, three kinds of sausages, hash browns, and all kinds of eggs, with grilled herby tomatoes on the side and a stack of the fluffiest pancakes ever. My stomach starts rumbling just at the thought.

I knock on the wall five times—code for *Are you awake?* Straight away, Elliot knocks back three times—*Can I come over?* I knock back twice to say that he can. Now my whole body feels as if it's grinning. Everything's going to be OK. My panic attacks will go once the shock of the accident wears off. I'll feel back to normal again soon. And in the meantime it's "Saturday Breakfast"!

"Poached eggs or scrambled, Elliot?" Dad looks at Elliot expectantly. He's wearing his usual Saturday-morning chef-ing gear: grey hoodie and sweatpants and a blue-and-white stripy apron.

"How are you scrambling them?" Elliot asks. In any other context this would be a pretty stupid question but not when it comes to my dad—he's known for being able to scramble eggs in about two hundred different ways.

"Wiv some finely diced onions and a sprinkling of ze chives," Dad replies in a fake French accent. He talks in a fake French accent a lot when he's cooking—he thinks it makes him sound more chef-like.

"High five!" Elliot says, holding his hand up. Dad high-fives him with a wooden spoon. "Scrambled please."

Elliot is wearing his pajamas and dressing gown. His dressing gown is silky and covered in a dark burgundy-and-green paisley pattern. He looks like he's stepped straight out of an old black-and-white movie. All that's missing is a pipe. I pour myself a glass of juice just as Tom trudges into the room. Further proof that Dad's "Saturday Breakfast" is awesome—it actually gets Tom out of bed before 9 a.m. on a weekend day. Whether or not he is actually awake is another matter.

"Morning," Elliot says just a little too loudly—for Tom's benefit.

"Hmm," Tom grunts, slumping into a chair and plonking his head on the table.

"Caffeine for Mister Tom," Elliot says, pouring him a mug of rich, dark coffee from the cafetière.

Tom lifts his head just enough to take a sip. "Hmm," he grunts again, his eyes shut tight.

There's the most gorgeous smell of sizzling bacon coming from the stove. I start buttering myself a slice of bread to take my mind off my hunger. I think I might actually be about to drool.

"Hello! Hello!" Mum cries, wafting into the room.

She's the only one of us who's actually dressed, as she's going off to open the shop as soon as she's finished eating. As always, she looks stunning. She's wearing an emerald-green shift dress that goes perfectly with her auburn curls. Whenever I wear green, I have the horrible feeling that I might look just like a walking Christmas decoration, but Mum always manages to style it out. She walks around the table, kissing each of us on top of the head. "And how are we all this fine December morning?"

"We are all just tickety-boo, thank you," Elliot replies in his poshest voice.

"Splendid!" Mum replies in an even posher voice. She goes over to Dad and kisses him on the back of his neck. "It smells amazing, darling."

Dad spins around and grabs her in a hug. We all avert our eyes. I guess it's good that my parents still get on so well—that they don't sit in bitter silence for hours on end like Elliot's—but sometimes their PDAs are a little bit cringey.

"Are you still OK to help Andrea out in the shop this afternoon?" Mum asks, coming to sit next to me.

"Of course." I turn to Elliot. "Do you fancy a trip around the Lanes this morning?"

Tom immediately groans. He hates anything to do with clothes and shopping—which is probably why he's currently wearing a vile orange football top and red pajama bottoms.

"Of course," Elliot replies. Elliot is most definitely my soul brother.

"And a trip to the 2p machines on the pier?" I add hopefully.

"Of course *not*," Elliot replies with a frown. I flick him with my napkin. As Mum gets up to fetch some maple syrup from the cupboard, Elliot leans in close to me and whispers, "OMG, your blog last night was amazing. Did you see all the comments?"

I nod and grin, feeling stupidly proud.

"I told you it would go down well," Elliot says smugly.

"What went down well?" Mum asks, coming back to the table.

"Nothing," I say.

"The *Titanic*," Elliot says.

Two hours later, Elliot and I are on the end of the pier playing the 2p game.

"I'm sorry," Elliot says, raising his voice over the sound of ringing slot machines, "but I just don't see the point of this dumb game. At. All."

I insert another coin and clench my hands together as I watch the tray of coins slide forward. The coins on the edge of the tray quiver—but stay put. I let out a loud sigh.

"I mean, it's a bit like Myspace, isn't it? Or porridge? There's just no point to it!"

I insert another 2p and start singing "la, la, la" inside my head to drown out Elliot's moaning. The truth is he loves to hate the 2p game as much as I love to play it. The tray slides forward and at first it looks as if I've lost again. But then one of the coins hanging over the edge drops and this sparks an avalanche. I clap my hands for joy as a load of coins clatter down into the tray.

"Yes!" I cry, hugging Elliot just to annoy him even more.

He frowns at me but I can tell from the way his eyes are twinkling behind his red-rimmed glasses that he's trying really hard not to grin.

"I've won!" I scoop the money from the tray.

"So you have." Elliot looks down at the coins in my hand. "Twenty whole pence. What on earth are you going to do with such a life-changing sum?"

I tilt my head to one side. "Well, first I'll make sure that my family is all taken care of. Then I'll buy myself a mini convertible. And then I think I'll buy my good friend Elliot *a sense of humor*!" I shriek with laughter as I dodge his play-punch. "Come on; let's check out the Lanes before I have to start work."

The Lanes are my favorite part of Brighton—apart from the sea of course. Their labyrinth of cobbled streets and quaint little shops make you feel as if you've turned a corner and journeyed two hundred years back in time.

"Did you know that the Cricketers' Arms used to be called the Laste and Fishcart?" Elliot says, as we walk past the old pub.

"The Last Fishcart," I say, absentmindedly, as I watch a

girl walking toward us. She's wearing an amber trilby hat with a full-length printed jumpsuit. She looks amazing. I instantly want to take a picture, but I'm a second too late and she disappears around the corner.

"No, not the Last Fishcart—the Laste *and* Fishcart," Elliot says. "A laste is the measurement they used for ten thousand herrings—back in the day when Brighton was a fishing village."

"All right, Wiki," I say with a grin.

Elliot truly is a walking, talking Wikipedia. I don't know how he manages to store so much random info in his head. His brain must be the equivalent of a six-terabyte hard drive. (A six-terabyte hard drive is currently the biggest hard drive in the world—another random fact I learned from Elliot!)

I feel my phone vibrate in my pocket. It's a text from Megan. I instantly think of what happened yesterday in JB's and my mouth goes dry. But her text is surprisingly friendly.

> Hey, are we still on for tonight? Xoxo

I'd totally forgotten about tonight. Earlier in the week I'd suggested we have a sleepover like we used to. I was partly joking, and partly trying to get our friendship back onto its old, easier ground, when everything seemed so blissfully uncomplicated.

"Who is it?" Elliot asks as we make our way past one of the Lanes' many jewelry shops. The window curves out from the front, as if it is literally bulging with trays of silver neck-laces, bracelets, and rings.

"Megan," I mutter, hoping Elliot won't hear—or won't care.

"What does *she* want?" he says.

My heart sinks. "Oh, just to see if we're still on for tonight."

Elliot stares at me. "What's happening tonight?"

I look down at the cobbled street. "I asked her to come over for a sleepover."

"A sleepover? Er, hello, we are in Year Eleven now."

I look at him, my face flushing. "I know. I didn't think she'd want to come, to be honest."

"So why did you ask her?"

"I thought it would be fun," I reply with a shrug.

"Hmm," Elliot says. "About as much fun as a night in with my parents, which is what I'm now doomed to."

"I'm sorry." I link arms with Elliot. He's wearing his vin-tage woolen coat. It feels all warm and snug.

"Never mind," Elliot says with a sigh. "I've got a massive history project to finish by Monday so it's probably best I stay in. Hey, did you know that the house over there used to be the Sussex and Brighton Infirmary for Eye Diseases?"

That's one of the things I love the most about Elliot—he can never stay cross for more than about ten seconds. If only all friends could be like that!

We walk past Choccywoccydoodah, just as a couple is coming out, bringing with them the sweet smell of cookies baking.

"Shall we pop into Tic Toc for a hot chocolate?" I ask. I still have half an hour before I have to be at the shop.

"Er, shall the moon rise tonight?" Elliot says theatrically. He opens the door and waves me in.

Inside the café is steamy and warm. There is no denying Tic Toc does the best hot chocolate in Brighton. And Elliot and I ought to know, we've conducted a scientific survey into it. As Elliot checks out the cakes on the counter, I sit down at a table and quickly text Megan back.

Sure. Come round about 8 Px

"OMG!" Elliot says as he gets back to the table. "They've got a new flavor cupcake!" His eyes are as wide as saucers. "Raspberry and Mocha."

"Oh wow."

"Do you want one?"

I nod. Even though I'm still pretty stuffed from breakfast I *always* have room for a cupcake.

"Cool. I'll go and order."

As Elliot heads back to the counter I lean back in my chair, letting the warmth of the café seep into me. Then the door opens and a boy walks in. I recognize him immediately as Ollie's older brother, Sebastian. Ollie comes strolling in behind him. I grab the menu card and pretend to study it, hoping that he won't see me and they'll go and sit in the far corner. But then I hear the chair at the table next to me being scraped back on the wooden floor.

"Penny!"

I look up and see Ollie grinning down at me. There's no denying it—his grin is puppy-dog cute. He sits down in the chair next to me. Across from him, Sebastian stares at me coldly. Sebastian is two years older than us and he's one of the most popular—and arrogant—people in sixth form. He's also a regional tennis champion. Rumor has it he once told Andy Murray he ought to work harder on his backhand. I can believe it.

"What do you want?" he asks Ollie tersely.

"Can I get a chocolate milkshake?" Ollie says.

Sebastian scowls at him like he's just asked for a cup of vomit. "Seriously? Please don't tell me you want sprinkles and a flake too?"

Ollie nods, and it's the first time I've ever seen him look embarrassed.

Sebastian shakes his head and sighs. "You're such a kid."

"All right. I'll have a coffee then." Ollie's cheeks are bright red now. It's weird seeing him so unconfident. I feel really sorry for him.

Sebastian goes over to the counter and queues up behind Elliot, and I start panicking about what Elliot will do when he sees our table has been crashed by the Walking Selfie.

"It's so strange bumping into you like this," Ollie says, taking off his scarf. "I just texted Megan about half an hour ago asking for your number."

"Really?" My voice comes out in a squeak. I cough and try again. "Why's that?" My voice now sounds as deep as a man's. I look down at the tablecloth and wish that it would magically come to life and wrap itself around me to hide my shame.

"I was going to ask you if you fancied meeting tomorrow lunchtime?"

I glance at Ollie, wondering if maybe I haven't woken up yet and everything that's happened so far has just been a dream. I pinch my leg under the table to check—a little too hard.

"Ow!"

Ollie looks at me, concerned. "What's wrong?"

"Nothing, I . . ."

"You looked like you were in pain."

"I was. It was—it —" I rack my brains for some kind of explanation. "I think I've been bitten."

"Bitten? By what?"

"Er. A flea?"

NO! NO! NO! NO! NO! my inner voice yells at me.

Ollie moves away slightly in his seat.

"I mean, i-it wasn't a flea," I stammer. "Obviously! I don't have fleas or anything—it just felt like . . ."

I shift uncomfortably and the leather padding on my chair makes a loud noise. A loud farting-type noise.

"That wasn't me—it was my chair!" I yelp. Why, oh why, did I have to sit in the chair with some kind of built-in whoopee cushion? I shift again, trying to make the same noise, to prove to Ollie that I didn't just break wind, but now, of course, my chair remains deadly silent.

Ollie stares at me. Then he sniffs—he actually sniffs the air with a pained expression on his face. Oh my God—he thinks I farted. He thinks I have fleas and I farted! I start praying for an asteroid to hit the café, or for the zombie apocalypse to start—anything to make Ollie forget what has just happened.

"Oh no! Is that the time?" I say, not even bothering to look at my watch or my phone. "I have to go. Have to get to work." I stumble up from my chair.

"But what about tomorrow?" Ollie says.

"Yes. Absolutely. Text me." Finally, I say something that doesn't sound insane. That actually sounds quite cool. But then, as I gather up mine and Elliot's coats, I trip on my scarf and crash into a waitress carrying a tray of toasted paninis. Cutlery is sent clattering to the floor and a terrible shocked silence falls upon the café. I can feel everyone's eyes burning into me. Somehow I make it over to Elliot without any further disaster. "We have to go," I hiss at him.

"What?" He frowns at me. "But what about our food?"

"Get it to go and bring it to the shop. There's been an emergency. Thank you. Bye."

And, with that, I fling his coat at him and stumble out onto the street.

Chapter Four

It takes about two hours for my cheeks to return to their normal temperature. Elliot thought the whole thing was hilarious. He even said I should have told Ollie, "Better out than in"! But he doesn't understand. What happened today was the closest I've ever gotten to being asked out on a date by someone I have an actual crush on. I bet in the All-Time History of Dating no girl has ever told a boy who has just asked her out that she has fleas—and then farted! Or at least sounded as if she farted. That has to go down as the worst response *ever*!

From my seat behind the counter, I look around To Have and to Hold. Andrea is over by the rails of dresses helping a young woman decide between a Barbie- and a Cinderella-themed wedding. The young woman's fiancé is sulking in an armchair in the corner after being told we don't do a Grand Prix theme. It's only about three o'clock but outside the light's already beginning to fade. The shoppers rushing by look grim-faced and wind-swept. I'm glad I'm in here, even if I am working. To be honest, coming to the shop doesn't ever feel much like working. Mum has created such a beautiful space it's more like coming to a fairy grotto, what with the twinkling lights and the scented candles and the music. I reckon we must be the only shop in Brighton—if not the UK—to play background music on a vintage record player. But the crackling of the needle on the vinyl really adds to the atmosphere, especially with our playlist of soulful love songs. It's impossible to leave To Have and to Hold without feeling all warm and melty inside. Unless of course you've just told the boy you've had a crush on for the past six years that you might have fleas.

To take my mind off "Flea and Fart Shame," I decide to go and check the window display. Every couple of weeks Mum changes the display to feature our newest theme. At the moment it's *Downton Abbey* so the bridal mannequin in the window is wearing a white ruffled long-sleeved dress with a collar so high it looks more like a blouse. I notice that the brooch on the collar has gone slightly askew so I climb into the window to adjust it. When I turn around to go back, I see a couple outside looking at the display. The woman is gazing at the bridal gown and although I can't hear what she's saying I can definitely lip-read that it's "Oh my God!"

As I walk back to the counter, the bell over the door jangles and the couple walks in.

"It's the cutest thing ever!" the woman says in a strong American accent.

I look at them and smile. "Hello, can I help you?"

They both smile back at me—their teeth are as perfectly straight and dazzling white as the keys on a piano.

"Yes, we were just wondering if you cater for international weddings?" the man asks.

As they reach the counter, I'm hit by a waft of after-shave. But it's not the cheap stuff that Tom wears before a night out in town; it smells more subtle and spicy. It smells expensive.

"Well, I'm not exactly sure," I tell him. Mum has organized some weddings abroad before. But they've always been for friends. I'm not about to lose her a potential client, though. "What was it you were interested in?"

"We're supposed to be getting married right before Christmas," the man says. He must see the shocked look on my face because he continues: "Yes, *this* Christmas, as in just over a week away! But we just this morning heard that our wedding planner has other commitments . . ."

"He ran off with the bride from the last wedding he organized!" the woman exclaims.

I fight the urge to grin. That's exactly the kind of story that Elliot and Tom would find hilarious. "Oh dear," I say.

"It's so stressful," the woman says. "Especially as we're here in the UK on business so we're not able to meet with any other wedding planners back home."

"We were thinking of calling the whole thing off," the man says.

"But then we saw your adorable display in the window," the woman continues. "I just love *Downton Abbey* . . . we're all in love with it in the States."

"And so we were wondering if maybe we could hire you guys to take over our wedding," the man says.

"It would be so cute," his fiancée says.

The man sulking in the armchair mutters something.

"Of course," I say quickly. "My mum's the manager of the business but she's out at the moment. Can I take your details and get her to give you a call when she gets back?"

"Sure. I'm Jim Brady." The man hands me a business card. It's one of those expensive ones where the writing is embossed and the card is really thick and silky smooth.

"And I'm Cindy Johnson—soon to be Brady," the woman says with a smile, handing me an equally expensive-looking card.

"Obviously we have the venue booked already so you guys would just need to do the styling," Jim says.

"We're getting married at the Waldorf Astoria in New York," Cindy adds. From the expectant way she's looking at me I'm guessing that's a very good thing.

"That's lovely," I say with a smile.

"Oh, y'all have the cutest accent!" Cindy turns to Jim, her eyes wide. "Honey, if we do have a *Downton Abbey* wedding maybe we should say our vows in British accents." She turns back to me. "Wouldn't that be adorable?"

I smile at her and nod. "Yes, absolutely."

The sulking man in the armchair looks at me and rolls his eyes.

"Why did the chicken cross the road, roll in mud, and cross the road again?" Dad asks me as soon as I walk into the living room.

He and Tom are both sprawled on the L-shaped sofa, munching on a huge bowl of popcorn with football blaring away on the TV. This is what always happens when they're left home alone together.

"Please don't ask him," Tom says, looking up at me with pleading eyes. "You'll regret it till your dying day."

"No, she won't," Dad replies quick as a flash. "Pen shares my refined sense of humor—good job one of my offspring does." He pats the sofa next to him and I go and sit down. He's right; we definitely share the same sense of humor. Whether it's refined is another story.

"I don't know—why did the chicken cross the road, roll in mud, and cross the road again?" I say, grabbing a handful of popcorn.

"Nooooo!" Tom wails, burying his head under a cushion.

"Because he was a dirty double-crosser!" Dad and I look at each other and start buckling over with laughter. From beneath his cushion, Tom howls.

"How was it down at the shop?" Dad asks, as soon as we've pulled ourselves together.

"Pretty quiet," I reply, and I see a flicker of worry cross Dad's face. With most people choosing to get married in the summer, winter is always our quietest time, but this year it's even deader than usual. "Oh, but I did get an American couple asking if we could do their wedding in New York. They seemed pretty serious too."

Dad raises his eyebrows. "Really?"

"Yes, they want a *Downton Abbey* theme. But they need it mega quickly. They're meant to be getting married just before Christmas but their original wedding planner ran off with the bride from his last wedding."

Now it's Tom's turn to start laughing.

"What's the joke?" Mum says, coming in the door and taking off her coat.

"Why did the chicken cross the road, roll in—" Dad begins.

"No!" Tom yells. "That wasn't the joke. The joke was why did the American couple have to call off their wedding?"

Mum looks at us all like we're crazy. She looks at us like this a lot.

"Because their planner ran off with the bride from his last wedding." Tom starts cracking up again.

Mum sits down next to me, looking even more puzzled. "What's he talking about?"

I tell her about Cindy and Jim. "They're getting married in a hotel called the Waldorf Astoria," I add at the end.

Mum and Dad's eyebrows do a synchronized lift.

"The Waldorf Astoria?" Dad says dreamily.

'In New York," Mum says, looking equally dreamy.

"Yes. I've got all their details here." I hand Mum Cindy's and Jim's business cards. "They asked if you could call them as soon as possible. I know we don't normally do international weddings but I thought it was best to let you talk to them. I hope I did the right thing."

Mum and Dad look at each other and then they both grin at me.

"Oh, you did the right thing, darling," Mum says, hugging me to her.

As Mum and Dad start chatting about the Waldorf Astoria, the text alert goes off on my phone. It's Elliot.

> OMG—my dad just asked me if I've got a girlfriend yet!!! Thinking I might have to hire a team of cheerleaders to spell it out for him. Enjoy your sleepover with Mega-Bitch :P

I quickly type a reply.

> Either that or you could get Choccywoccydoodah to ice it on a cake for him. And thank you— I think ;) Pxxx

Almost immediately my phone goes off again. But this time it's from a new number.

> Hi, Pen, do you want to meet tomorrow at Lucky Beach? About 12? We could have lunch . . . Ollie x

I stare at my phone in shock. Even though I am the Clumsiest Person in the Universe, and even though he thinks I might have fleas and a chronic wind problem, Ollie wants to meet me! For lunch! At a proper restaurant! Oh my God . . . I think I've just been asked on a date!

Chapter Five

If there's anything guaranteed to wipe the probably-just-been-asked-out-on-a-date smile off your face, it's the sight of one of your best friends sitting on your bed, staring sullenly into space like she's about to keel over and die from boredom. Since Megan got here, twenty minutes ago—or it could be twenty days, it feels that long—everything I've suggested we do has been greeted with a bored shrug or a tight-lipped "no thanks." What was the point in her coming over if she's just going to sit and sulk all night? And then I get it. This must be my punishment for what happened at JB's last night. She obviously still hasn't forgiven me for breaking her fingernail. I internally groan. What was I thinking, asking her over? How could I have possibly imagined it would be like our sleepovers used to be?

Megan and I have been friends since our first day at secondary school, when our teacher sat us next to each other. I'll be honest: at first this friendship was formed out of fear. I'd spent the entire summer holiday worrying that no one would want to be my friend and I'd be destined to spend SEVEN

YEARS drifting from classroom to classroom alone. But it wasn't long before our friendship changed from desperate to genuine and all of my fears faded away.

My favorite memory of me and Megan was when we were twelve and my dog Milo had just died. (Milo dying is not my favorite part—obviously—that was one of the worst things that *ever* happened to me.) But, when she found out, Megan came around to my house with a little goody bag of gifts, including a poem she'd written about Milo called "Cutie Paws" and a framed photo of me chasing him around the park. That's how she used to be—kind and caring. But then she got into acting and it totally changed her—especially when she got her first TV role. Megan calls it a TV role but actually it was for a TV advert for GlueStick. She had to stick two pieces of card together and smile at the camera and say, "Wow, it's so sticky!" She was only on-screen for about five seconds but the way Megan talks about it, it's as if she'd been cast in the lead role of a movie. And ever since then it's like she thinks she's better than everyone else. Including me. Now, every time I'm with her I feel as if I'm being interviewed for the job of best friend and I spend the whole time dreading I'm going to say or do the wrong thing. Like right now.

"So . . ." I say. "What would you like to do?"

"Dunno." Megan looks around the room and her gaze comes to a rest on one of the photos on my wall. "Oh my God! Why have you taken a photo of a stone?"

I get a weird squirmy feeling in the pit of my stomach. The photo is of a snowy-white stone with three holes in it.

According to Elliot, stones with holes in them always used to be considered lucky charms. "It's a lucky stone," I say.

"Why's it lucky?" Megan stares scornfully at the picture.

"Because it has holes in it. Fishermen always used to take them on their boats with them, to keep them safe."

Megan smiles a tight little smile. "You're so quirky, Penny!"

Usually, I like the word "quirky." But whenever Megan says it about me it sounds like the worst thing in the world and it makes me want to punch her. I hug a cushion to me and sigh. I can't face an entire night like this. I have to do something to rescue the situation.

"Do you want to do face masks?" I ask hopefully. "I've got a couple of those strawberry peel-off ones we used to use."

Megan shakes her head. "No thanks."

I glance at the wall and wonder if Elliot is sitting on his bed too. It feels horrible thinking that he might just be a couple of feet away from me and yet I'm trapped here—unable to see or talk to him—in this Sleepover from Hell.

I'm about to ask Megan what she'd like to do again when she kicks off her shoes and wriggles back on the bed.

"What was up with you yesterday in the diner?" she asks, staring pointedly at her missing false nail. "Why did you act so weird?"

I think about coming up with an excuse. Then I remember my last blog post and how good it felt to open up about my panic attacks. I haven't mentioned them at all to Megan. But maybe it will make things a bit easier between us if I'm honest.

I take a deep breath. "You know I was in that car accident with my parents a while ago?"

Megan looks at me blankly for a second. "Oh, yeah."

"Well, ever since then, I've been getting these weird panic attacks and I feel just like I did when I was trapped in the car. Like I get all kinds of hot and feel as if I can't breathe and—"

"Oh my God, do not talk to me about getting panicked!" Megan interrupts. "I can't believe there's only two days till the school play. I am so scared I'm going to mess up."

"You won't mess up. You're the best one in it."

"Really?" She looks at me, widening her chocolatey-brown eyes. "It's just so much pressure, though, knowing that the success of the show is riding on my shoulders. Jeff said that I remind him of a young Angelina Jolie, which is, like, super-cute of him but it just makes the pressure even worse."

"Right. Well, I'm sure you'll be fine." I feel a sour mixture of anger and hurt. Yet again, she has turned the conversation back on herself—even when I was trying to tell her something private and serious.

"I'm so glad I have such great chemistry with Ollie," Megan continues. "Jeff says we're like Angelina Jolie and Brad Pitt in that movie they did together—you know, when they first fell in love." Megan looks at me and gives me another of her tight little smiles. "Ollie tells me everything, you know."

I feel a bit sick. "Oh, so you—you know about tomorrow then?"

She frowns. "What about tomorrow?"

My face instantly flushes. "He's asked me to meet him for lunch."

It's almost as if I can see the cogs in her brain whirring as she processes this information. Clearly she didn't know. Clearly Ollie doesn't tell her everything after all.

"He's asked to meet you? Where?" She's still smiling but it's so forced it looks as if her jaw might crack from the strain.

"At Lucky Beach around midday."

"What? Just you?"

There's something about her shocked expression and the way she says "just you" that makes me really mad. I know that Ollie is way out of my league in the stupid School Leagues of Attractiveness and General Greatness but if a boy has asked you out for lunch, shouldn't your friend be happy for you instead of gaping at you like a goldfish? Unless . . .

"Do you like Ollie?" The question pops out before I have time to censor it.

Megan looks at me coldly. "Of course I like Ollie."

"No, I mean, *like* like?"

Megan throws back her head and gives a fake little laugh. "No, of course not. He's way too young for me."

I stare at her and all I can think is, *Who are you?* Megan might have been one of my closest friends for six years but right now it's like I don't know her at all.

★··*Chapter Six*··★

If *The Guinness Book of Records* ever wants to feature the World's Worst Ever Sleepover they need to get in touch with me. Seriously. I wake up while it's still dark—never good on a Sunday—and lie there sending psychic messages to Elliot through the bedroom wall. When we were little, we used to try to have the same dream when we went to sleep. We thought that because we slept right next door to each other it would be possible, like we could float up into one giant dream bubble hovering over our houses. *I've had the worst night ever*, I try telling him.

Megan is still fast asleep on the other side of the room on the sofa bed. As I look at her, a new blog title composes itself in my head—CAN YOU OUTGROW YOUR BEST FRIEND?—and all of my hurt and anger at Megan starts welling up inside of me, dying to spill out. It's so frustrating when this happens and I'm not able to actually write anything. Once, in the middle of a math exam, I got this awesome idea for a blog—at the time I was certain it would be the funniest, most interesting blog I'd ever written. I'd come up with a really clever title and everything. But then I got lost in a sea of algebra and when I came out of the exam the only letters I could think of were x and y. I still can't remember what that blog post was supposed to be about.

Scared of losing my current idea, I take my phone from my bedside table and burrow under my duvet. I'd put my phone on silent when we went to sleep last night—at eleven thirty!!! Now I see that Elliot sent me a text at just gone midnight.

> How's it going with Mega-Boring? Are you missing me?! My project is making me want to poke my eyes out with a pencil. I mean, seriously, who needs to know about the Corn Laws? Why does corn even need a law?!

I start typing a reply.

> Worst sleepover EVER! So bad I was already asleep when you sent your text!!! I think there needs to be a Corn Law and the law should be that hot buttery corn on the cob should be served with every meal. I MISS YOU SO MUCH!!!

Almost as soon as I've sent the text I hear a faint knocking on the wall. One knock, followed by four, followed by three:

I—love—you. I'm about to knock back when I hear Megan groan.

"What's that knocking noise?"

"I don't know," I lie.

"Is it that boy next door?"

Megan has met Elliot loads of times; there's no way she doesn't know his name. This fact makes me hate her even more.

"I don't know why you hang out with him," she continues. "He's so weird."

I lie on top of my arms to stop myself from leaping out of the bed and bashing her over the head with a pillow.

"Could I have some coffee?" she asks.

"Yep." Even though she just insulted my best friend and even though she totally ruined last night and even though I want to kill her with a pillow, I'm so grateful for an excuse to get away from her for a few minutes that I leap out of bed and pull on my dressing gown.

Down in the kitchen, I find Dad sitting at the table, drinking a mug of tea and reading the paper. He's an early bird just like me. His hair is still ruffled from sleeping and his chin is covered with a grey shadow of stubble.

"Hey," he says when he sees me. "How's the sleepover going?"

I look at him and raise my eyebrows.

"That good, huh?"

I nod, then go and turn the kettle on. A few weeks ago, when we were making a spag bol together, I told Dad that Megan and I hadn't been getting on very well.

"Dad?"

"Yes."

"Do you think that it's possible to outgrow a friend?"

He smiles and nods. "Oh yes. It happens all the time, especially at your age when you're changing so much." He gestures at me to sit down next to him. "Did I ever tell you about Timothy Taylor?"

I shake my head.

"He was my best friend all through junior school. We were as thick as thieves. But then, when we got to secondary school, he really changed and I just didn't want to hang out with him."

"Why? What did he do?"

"He started playing rugby!" Dad chortles. Dad is a total football nut and can't understand people who prefer rugby. "But seriously," he continues, "it wasn't just that. He started getting really full of himself too. I didn't have anything in common with him anymore."

"So what happened? Did you fall out?"

"Nah. Just drifted apart really. And we both found other friends we had more in common with. So don't worry about Her Ladyship." He nods toward upstairs. "You'll be fine—sometimes you just have to let people go."

"Thanks, Dad." I get up and kiss him on top of his head.

"No problem." He laughs. "Who knew I could be so wise so early—and on so little caffeine!"

When I get back to my bedroom, Megan is up and fully dressed. I internally cheer—hopefully this means she'll be going soon.

"Here's your coffee." I pass her the mug. She takes it but

doesn't say thanks. Instead she says, "So, what are you going to wear for your lunch with Ollie?"

I look at her blankly. In all of the stress of the Sleepover from Hell I hadn't given it any thought.

"If I were you, I'd go for a really casual look. You don't want to seem too keen. I'd lend you my hoodie but I don't think the color would suit you." She takes a sip of her coffee and smiles at me sweetly. "It's such a shame your hair's red. It doesn't really go with anything, does it?"

I realize there and then that for me to have any hope of actually enjoying my morning and looking forward to meeting Ollie, Megan has to go. Like, right now.

"I'm so sorry, but my dad's just told me that I need to help out with something down at the shop this morning."

Megan frowns. "On a Sunday?"

"Yes. So I'm afraid you're going to have to go."

Megan actually looks disappointed. "Oh, but I was going to help you get ready."

I force myself to smile at her. "It's OK, I can manage."

She looks at me and raises her eyebrows. "Are you sure?"

"Oh yes, absolutely."

It turns out that actually, when it comes to getting ready to meet Ollie, I can't manage at all. It's half an hour since Megan left and my room looks like a nuclear clothes bomb has gone off. In my desperate whirlwind of trying things on and ripping them off again, not a single inch of bedroom space has been left untouched by some random article of clothing. I look at the stripy tights dangling forlornly from the light fixture and sigh. What am I going to wear?!

I'm in a real dilemma. The kind that people write to advice columns about. Normally, if I'm having any kind of fashion crisis, Elliot is the first person I turn to, but I can hardly imagine him wanting to help me when Ollie's involved. I wander around my room sighing; even the sight of the sea on the horizon doesn't make me feel any better. Not when I've got to be down by the sea in one hour's time and I'M STILL NOT DRESSED!

Then a question forms in my mind. *What would I wear if it were just up to me?* I go over to the heap of clothes on the floor by my rocking chair and I pull out a black tea dress dotted with tiny purple hearts. I put it on with a pair of black opaque tights and look in the mirror. The dress is a perfect fit and makes my waist look really tiny. I'm about to pull on a pair of ballet pumps when that question pops into my head again. *What would I wear if it were just up to me?* I root around in the bottom of my wardrobe for my biker boots. Then I put on my black leather jacket.

"*Don't forget me!*" my camera seems to call out to me. I stuff it into my pocket. I learned long ago never to leave my camera behind. It was always on the days when I left it at home that I'd see the best photo opportunities ever. And who knows what photo opportunities I might get with Ollie . . . ? I instinctively blush as I imagine Ollie asking if I can take a picture of him and me together. Even though I hate selfies, I might not mind a couple's one . . . OK, so I might be getting a bit ahead of myself—but isn't it every girl's right to get a bit overexcited, when her biggest crush has just asked her out?

Chapter Seven

Of course, as soon as I get to the beach, my newfound confidence begins to slip. *What if he doesn't show up? What if it was all a prank? What if I trip just as he's about to kiss me? Oh my God, what if he kisses me?! He's not going to kiss you, you fool.* On and on, my inner voice spirals into near hysteria.

I decide to walk to the café along the beach so that I can get closer to the sea in the hope that it might calm me down a bit. *The pebbles are wet! You're going to fall over! You're going to fall over and end up with seaweed stuck to your bum, just like you did at Tom's birthday barbecue.* I slow right down. The sea is nice and calm and the winter sunshine sparkles on it like a sprinkling of glitter. I take in a deep breath of the salty air. And another. *What if a seagull poos on your head?!* "Shut up!" I mutter out loud but I look up quickly to check there are no gulls hovering. When I look back down, Ollie is standing a few feet in front of me.

"How did you get there?" is the first thing I can think to say.

"I walked," he says, looking at me weirdly. "Are you OK? You looked as if you were talking to yourself."

"What? Oh no, I was just—I was just—singing."

"Singing?"

"Yes, you know, like, a song."

"Yes, I know what singing is."

"Of course you do. Soz." *Soz?!!* Since when did I ever say "soz"?! I've been with Ollie for precisely ten seconds and already he must think I'm a singing, sozzing loony. This doesn't bode well for our lunch at all.

"Have you got your camera on you?" he asks.

"Yes," I reply, my heartbeat quickening—could he be about to ask for a photo of us already?! "Why?"

"I was just wondering if you could take a few headshots of me, down here on the beach. I could really do with some, you know, like arty ones for my profile online. And you're such an awesome photographer." He dazzles me with one of his megawatt smiles.

"Oh. OK." I don't know what to make of this. Surely this isn't the reason he invited me to meet him? No, he definitely said lunch yesterday. The photos must be an extra. Something he just thought of. I tell myself not to be so stupid and take my camera from my pocket.

"I was thinking maybe we could take some over by the pier."

"Sure."

As we start walking along the beach, a woman jogger passes us and smiles. I feel a surge of happiness. It must look to her as if Ollie and I are "together." If only it could feel a bit more relaxed and enjoyable. I search my brain for something interesting—and non-embarrassing—to say.

"So, you must be really proud of your brother."

Ollie looks at me blankly. "Why?"

"Well, with him being so good at tennis."

Ollie mutters something and stares out to sea. There's something about his serious expression and the way the light is falling on his face, accentuating his cheekbones, that would make an awesome black-and-white shot.

"Hold it right there," I say, turning my camera on.

"What?" Ollie frowns at me.

"Keep that expression and look out to sea again. It'll make a really cool picture."

"Oh, right." Instantly, Ollie's expression softens and he looks back at the sea. "How about this?"

"Perfect."

I zoom in and adjust the angle until I've got just the right shadowing on his face, then I take the shot.

"Let's see." He leans in to look at the camera display and our heads are so close they're almost touching. He smells of aftershave and peppermint. My heart starts pounding. "That looks really great." He looks at me and smiles. Up this close, his eyes are impossibly blue. I realize that if he wanted to kiss me right now he would barely have to move. We continue looking at each other for a second longer. "You're really good at this, aren't you?" he says, his voice softer than usual.

"Thank you." Embarrassed, I look away and the moment is gone. We carry on walking. Two more joggers run past us, their feet crunching on the pebbles.

"How about one of me lying on the beach?" he says. "You know, for something a bit different."

"Sure." A vision of us both lying on the beach wrapped in each other's arms pops into my head. My face instantly begins to flush.

Ollie scrambles down onto the stones. "How about if you take one from above me?"

"OK, that could be fun." I stand next to Ollie and try to take a shot but it doesn't quite work; it's not centred enough. "I think I'm going to have to stand right over you," I tell him.

Ollie looks at me and grins. I feel a weird tingling sensation shimmy up my spine. I carefully step one foot over his body so that I'm standing astride him. I look through the lens. He's grinning up at me.

"I hope you're not looking up my dress," I say jokily.

Ollie chuckles. "As if!"

For a brief moment I feel as if I've actually managed to achieve the impossible and have a humiliation-free flirtation. But then, just as I'm taking my bird's-eye shot of Ollie, the pebbles begin to give way and both my feet start sliding in opposite directions. I desperately try to keep my footing but this only makes it worse and suddenly I am sitting right on top of Ollie's stomach.

"I'm so sorry," I gasp, trying to scramble back up.

He catches hold of my wrist, laughing. "Don't be. It's hilarious. You're hilarious."

I look at him suspiciously. But he's not saying it the way Megan says, "You're so quirky." It actually sounds affectionate. "Thank you," I say.

"Oh my God! What are you doing?"

We both jump at the sound of Megan's voice. I turn to see her standing a few feet away, glaring at us. The twins are right behind her, grinning from ear to ear.

"I-I was just taking Ollie's picture," I stammer, my face going redder than a postbox, "and my feet slipped."

"Right." Megan keeps on glaring at me. I notice that she's changed out of the jeans and hoodie she was wearing when she left my house and is now wearing a skintight plum-colored dress with knee-high boots.

Somehow, I manage to clamber off Ollie without causing either of us an injury.

"What are you guys doing down here anyway?" Megan says, and she looks at Ollie pointedly. "I thought you were supposed to be going for lunch together."

"How did . . . ?" Ollie instantly looks embarrassed. "It was nothing major; I just wanted Penny to take some photos of me for my online profiles."

Megan turns to look at me and her smile actually looks triumphant. *See, I told you it wasn't a date*, it seems to be saying.

"Your photos are so good," Kira says, coming over to me.

"Yes," says Amara. "I loved that one you took of the old pier for your art project."

I smile at them weakly.

"So, where were you guys thinking of going for lunch?" Megan says.

Ollie shrugs. "Hadn't really thought about it, to be honest."

I stare at him, confused.

"We were just going to Nando's," Megan says sweetly. "Do you fancy joining us?"

"Sure," Ollie replies in a beat.

I instantly feel sick with anger and I kick out at the stones. One of them goes sailing into the air. I gasp in horror as I watch it sail straight into a passing West Highland terrier. It yelps in pain, and its owner—an old man with extremely bushy eyebrows—glares at me.

"I'm so sorry! It was an accident," I call over. *I'm just a walking accident*, I feel like adding. I can't even get angry without something excruciatingly embarrassing happening.

"Penny!" Megan says, scolding me like she's my mum. "That poor little dog!"

"Actually, I think I'm going to head off home," I say, fighting the urge to kick a stone at her.

"Oh really?" Megan can barely disguise her glee.

"But what about my pictures?" Ollie says, sounding really disappointed.

I can't even bring myself to look at him. "I'll email them to you later," I mutter.

"OK then, see you in school tomorrow," Megan says breezily.

As the twins call out goodbye, I bite down hard on my lip and start marching away from them across the beach. My head feels all tangled up in anger and confusion. But one thing I know for sure, without any shadow of a doubt, is that I've absolutely had it with Megan.

Chapter Eight

"Can you please, please, please promise me that you will listen to everything I have to say quietly and calmly, without making any catty remarks until I've finished?" I beg Elliot, now that I'm back home and have summoned him with the dire-emergency code of ten knocks on the wall.

Elliot leans back in the rocking chair and strokes his chin thoughtfully. "Does what you're about to tell me involve Mega-dull and the Walking Selfie?" he asks.

"Yes, but please can you not say anything rude about them until I've finished. And the phrase 'I told you so' is also banned."

Elliot looks aghast. "What, banned forever—or just while you're telling the story?"

"Forever."

Elliot sighs. "OK then, but you might need to gag me."

"Seriously!"

"OK, OK, my lips are sealed."

I sit cross-legged on my bed, staring down at the duvet, and recount my tale of woe, from the World's Worst Sleepover to Ollie's immortal words "It was nothing major."

"It was nothing major?" Elliot echoes as soon as I've finished. "I told—"

"No, don't say it!" I cry, covering my ears. "Honestly, I can't bear to hear it. I can't believe I actually thought it was a date!"

"And as for Mega-strumpet!" Elliot exclaims.

I frown at him. "Strumpet?"

Elliot nods. "It's a word Shakespeare invented to describe women of ill repute."

"Ah, I see."

"She really is vile," Elliot says, shaking his head in disgust. "I can't believe she crashed your lunch with Ollie. I told you—"

"Elliot!"

"OK, OK." Elliot puts his hands up in mock surrender. "I know what you should do," he says, grinning evilly. "You should Photoshop some spots and a hideous rash onto the Walking Selfie's pictures. Maybe an extra nose too . . ."

I look at Elliot and start to grin. I'm about to give him a huge hug when the unmistakable sound of a gong reverberates throughout the house.

"OMG! OMG!" Elliot leaps up and claps his hands with glee. "Family meeting!"

Our house is full of old theater props that my mum kept as keepsakes from plays she was in. One of them is a huge brass gong, which now lives in our hallway. When Tom and I were younger, we were always coming up with excuses to bang it, so in the end my parents made the rule that the gong should only ever be used to call a family meeting. I get off the bed and laugh at Elliot's super-excited expression.

"It's probably something really boring—like who wants turkey for Christmas dinner."

Elliot looks at me blankly. "Why would it be that? Everyone has turkey for Christmas dinner."

"Yes, but Dad was talking about cooking a goose this year."

Elliot pulls a horrified expression. "He can't cook a goose! That's gross!"

"Why?"

"I don't know—it just is."

I go over to the door with Elliot right behind me.

"*Rekao sam ti*," he whispers in my ear.

"What does that mean?" I say.

"I told you so, in Croatian. You didn't say I couldn't say it in Croatian," he shrieks as I poke him in the ribs.

"We want turkey," Elliot announces as soon as we walk into the kitchen.

Mum, Dad, and Tom are all seated at the table. Mum and Dad are looking all excited. Tom is slumped forward with his head resting on his arms.

"Eh?" Dad says to Elliot.

"For Christmas dinner," Elliot explains. "We want turkey, not goose. That's what this meeting's about, right? Christmas dinner?"

"Ah!" Dad says. "No. Actually, no it's not—although in a

way, I suppose it is, indirectly." He looks at Mum and raises his eyebrows.

Mum nods, then she looks at Elliot and gives him a sad smile. "I'm afraid you won't be able to come to us for Christmas dinner this year, Elliot."

"What?!" Elliot and I say in unison.

"We're not going to be here," Mum says.

"What?!" Now Tom has raised his head from the table and joined my and Elliot's chorus. We all stare at Mum in shock.

"What do you mean, we're not going to be here?" Tom says.

"Where are we going to be?" I stare from Mum to Dad and back again.

Mum and Dad look at each other and smile. "New York," they say together.

"No way!" Tom exclaims—but not in a good way.

I'm too stunned to say anything.

Elliot looks as if he might be about to cry.

"We've agreed to do that wedding," Mum says, smiling at me. "The *Downton Abbey* one—at the Waldorf."

"Oh. My. God." Elliot looks at me wide-eyed. "You lucky thing."

But the weird thing is I don't feel lucky. Instead, the back of my neck feels really hot and my hands go clammy. Going to New York would mean traveling by plane and right now I get freaked out enough at the thought of getting in a car. I don't want to go anywhere. I just need a nice normal family Christmas at home.

"I'm not going," Tom says.

"What?" Dad looks at him, shocked.

"Melanie is home next week. There's no way I'm going anywhere. I haven't seen her for months." Melanie is Tom's girlfriend. She's been away studying in France all this term. And, judging by the soppy updates he's been posting on Facebook lately, he is really pining for her.

"But you have to come," Mum says, looking really upset. "We're always together at Christmas."

Tom shakes his head. "If you want us to be together, you'll have to stay here."

"Tom," Dad says in a low warning voice.

"I don't want to go either," I say quietly.

"What—but . . ." Mum stares at me. She looks so upset it's horrible. "It's Christmas in New York! I thought you guys would jump at the chance."

"Yeah," Elliot mutters. "What's up with you?"

I look at him imploringly and finally see a flicker of recognition cross his face, like he's worked it out. He takes my hand and gives it a squeeze.

"Why do you have to work over Christmas anyway?" Tom says.

"Because we really need the money," Dad replies, and his tone is so serious that we all turn to look at him.

"It's been such a slow winter," Mum says. "This job is the answer to all of our prayers. They're paying more than we'd get for ten weddings in Britain. Plus our expenses." She looks at me pleadingly. "Are you sure you don't want to come?"

"I can't," I say. "I have to . . ."

"Do that English project," Elliot fills in for me. "The one that counts toward your final grade."

64 · Zoe Sugg

"Yes!" I say, giving him a grateful smile before turning back to Mum and Dad. "So I'm going to have to work flat out on that over the holidays. But you guys go. We'll be fine."

Tom nods too. "Yes. You guys go. We can always have Christmas together when you get back."

Mum looks at Dad. "I don't know. What do you think, Rob?"

"I think we need to think about it," Dad says. He looks just as upset as she does.

I feel terrible. I think about telling them the truth: that just the thought of having a panic attack trapped in a plane miles up in the sky is bringing me out in a cold sweat, but I can't. I don't want to worry them. There's no way they'd leave me if they knew what's been happening and then they'd miss out on the much-needed money. Them going to America and me staying here is definitely the best solution, but I can't help feeling sad inside. As my fear of the panic attacks gets bigger and bigger it seems to be making my world feel smaller and smaller.

17 December

Can You Outgrow Your Best Friend?

Hey, guys!

First of all, thank you SO much for all your lovely comments and tips on my blog about my panicky moments. Knowing they might be panic attacks weirdly makes me feel better. You guys are the best! ☺

Now, I know I said I'd blog about something a bit more lighthearted this time but something has happened that I really need to share with you . . .

When I was little I had a coat that I absolutely adored.

It was bright red and had shiny black buttons that were shaped like little roses.

It also had a furry collar and furry cuffs.

When I wore it I felt like a beautiful princess from a really cold faraway land like Russia or Norway (it's cold in Norway, right?).

I loved that coat so much I wore it everywhere, even when the weather started getting warmer.

And when the weather got too hot I refused to put the coat away in my cupboard. Instead, I kept it hanging on the back of my chair all summer so that I could still see it every day.

The second winter I had the coat it started to feel a little tight. But I didn't care because I couldn't bear the thought of life without it.

But by the third winter I'd grown so big I couldn't do the buttons up anymore.

When my mum told me I'd have to have a new winter coat I was heartbroken. But after a while I grew to love my new coat. Although it didn't have rose-shaped buttons or a furry collar, it was a beautiful shade of bluey green just like the sea. And after a while, when I looked at my old coat, the furry collar seemed a bit silly and it didn't really feel as if it was mine anymore, so I let my mum take it to the charity shop.

At the moment, when I'm with one of my best friends, it's like we don't fit anymore.

Everything she says feels mean and hurtful. Everything she does feels selfish and immature.

At first I blamed myself. I thought that maybe I was saying or doing something wrong.

But then I wondered if sometimes our friendships are a bit like clothes and when they start feeling uncomfortable it's not because we've done anything wrong. It just means that we've outgrown them.

I've decided that I'm not going to try to squeeze myself into a friendship that hurts me anymore. I'm going to let her go and just be friends with people who make me feel good about myself.

What about you?

Do you have any friends you think you might have outgrown?

I'd love to hear about it in the comments below . . .

Girl Online, going offline xxx

Chapter Nine

Normally, I like Mondays. I know, I know, I'm a freak! But I can't help it—I've always found the beginning of a whole new week kind of exciting. It's a chance to start all over again with seven fresh new days spread out in front of you—like a fun-sized New Year. But this Monday is different. This Monday is terrible and filling me with dread for FOUR reasons:

1. I've realized I've outgrown/hate my best (girl) friend.
2. I have to spend all day with this outgrown/hated friend, preparing for the play.
3. I also have to spend all day with the boy I've spent the entire weekend embarrassing myself in front of, preparing for the play.
4. It's the day of the play.

By the time I get into school, my heart has sunk so low I think I can actually feel it beating in my feet.

"Pen! So glad you're here!" Mr. Beaconsfield cries as soon as I walk into the hall. He's looking really flustered—he hasn't even remembered to put gel in his hair. His fringe is hanging limply over his forehead.

"Where are the others?" I ask, looking around the empty hall.

"They've gone up to the drama studio to do a final run-through while we—*you*—sort out the set."

I look up at the stage. "What's wrong with the set?"

"I'm afraid my graffiti-artist friend has let me down, so I need your help."

For weeks now Mr. Beaconsfield has been making a big song and dance about how he's got this street-artist friend who was going to come in and decorate our set to make it look more "ghetto." I should have known nothing would come of it. The closest Mr. Beaconsfield probably gets to the street is watching *Corrie*.

"What do you want me to do?" I ask as he hands me a carrier bag.

"Do some graffiti on the trailer and the back wall," Mr. Beaconsfield says as casually as if he's just asked me to sweep the floor. "I've got to get back to the others. Poor Megan is having terrible trouble remembering her final speech."

"Do some graffiti on them?" I look inside the bag. It's full of cans of spray paint. "What kind of graffiti?"

Mr. Beaconsfield looks even more stressed. "I don't know. Just do a few tags or something. You are supposed to be the set design assistant."

I frown. It's true that I'm supposed to be helping with the set design as well as be the official photographer but I never would have volunteered if I'd known it meant becoming some kind of Banksy. I mean, I did write I LUV 1D on a park bench three years ago . . . but I don't think that really counts.

"OK, I'm going to head up to the drama studio," Mr. Beaconsfield says, grabbing his clipboard from one of the chairs. "I'll come down to see how you're getting on at first break." And before I can say a single word he's scuttled off.

I look at the blank back wall of the set. This is crazy! If I go anywhere near it with a can of spray paint I'm going to wreck it and one thing I'm absolutely determined about today is that I'm not going to mess anything up. So I do what I always do in an emergency and I text Elliot. We know each other's timetables by heart so I know that he's in Latin. Elliot says his teacher is so old he actually spoke Latin when it was still a living language so hopefully he'll be able to text me back without being spotted.

HEEEEEEEELP!!! MY DRAMA TEACHER WANTS ME TO GRAFFITI THE SET—LIKE PROPER GRAFFITI!!! I THINK HE MIGHT HAVE LOST HIS MIND. PLEASE HELP ME BEFORE I LOSE MINE!!! WHAT SHALL I DO?!!!

I send the text and go up onto the stage and over to the pretend trailer. Maybe I could practice doing a "tag" behind it. Then if I mess it up no one in the audience will ever know and if I do discover that I miraculously have a latent talent for graffiti art, I can save the day—and the play.

I take one of the cans from the bag and flip off the lid. What would my tag be if I were a graffiti artist? I have no idea, so I decide to try drawing something instead. But what? What would people draw in a New York ghetto—that would go really well with *Romeo and Juliet*? Maybe some kind of broken love heart?

I cautiously press on the button at the top of the can. Nothing happens. I press a lot harder and a jet of bright purple paint shoots out. I try painting a heart but it looks just like a pair of butt cheeks. Thankfully, at that precise moment, my phone goes off. It's a text from Elliot.

STEP AWAY FROM THE SPRAY CANS!!!
You are a girl of many talents but painting isn't one of them ;) Don't you remember the picture you did of the Easter Bunny that time we were babysitting little Jennifer from down the road and how it gave her nightmares for months? Why don't you ask the lighting person if they can project one of your photos of street art onto the set? Remember the ones you took in Hastings? One of them would look great. PS my Latin teacher has just broken his false teeth biting on an apple!

As I read Elliot's text, I breathe a massive sigh of relief. I have a solution for the seemingly unsolvable and this fills me with hope. Maybe today won't be so bad after all . . .

And I'm right—the rest of the day goes surprisingly smoothly. The actors stay holed up in the drama studio with

Mr. Beaconsfield, frantically rehearsing, while Tony, the boy from Year Eleven who's doing the lighting, turns up to do a tech rehearsal and he's able to project one of my street-art photos onto the backdrop no problem. It looks amazing.

When I do finally see Megan, midway through the afternoon, everything's fine. Yet again, writing my blog seems to have helped me sort things out in my mind and now that I've accepted that I've outgrown her friendship, I feel under a lot less pressure. Even seeing Ollie again isn't too awkward. He and Megan are so nervous about the play, they're totally preoccupied going through their lines.

Just before curtain up, Mr. Beaconsfield calls us all together backstage. "You guys are going to be awesome," he says. "And, as my hero Jay-Z says, don't live life uptight—live up in the sky."

We all look at Mr. Beaconsfield blankly.

"Break a leg," he mutters. "Oh and, Pen, I'll need you to take one more photo for me at the end of the show, when the cast comes out to take their bow. Can you just nip onstage and grab a few shots?"

I feel a sudden flash of fear. This will mean going up onstage in front of a whole hall full of people, aka MY WORST NIGHTMARE. But then Mr. Beaconsfield races off to check that the videographer is ready to begin filming and the others all take their places backstage.

I fetch my camera from my bag and take my seat in the wings. It'll be fine, I tell myself. After all, it's not as if I have to remember any lines. All I have to do is go onstage, take a picture, and come off again. What's the worst that can happen . . . ?

Chapter Ten

The play runs without a hitch. Everyone remembers their lines and says them in exactly the right places, and even Ollie's accent doesn't sound too bad. By the time it reaches the scene where Juliet dies, I can actually hear members of the audience crying.

As Mr. Beaconsfield bounds backstage for the curtain call, he looks at me and grins. "Wasn't it amazing? Weren't they great?" he gushes.

I grin back at him. "They were brilliant."

"Don't take the picture until the whole cast has lined up for their final bow—including me," he whispers.

I nod and turn my camera on.

As the actors come out from the other side of the stage to take their bows, the applause builds, until it reaches a roar for Megan and Ollie. And even though Megan has made me want to punch, smother, and kick stones at her recently, I can't help getting swept up in the excitement of the moment. I'm really proud of her.

The applause is so loud now I can feel it vibrating through

my body. As the cast line up, Megan gestures at Mr. Beaconsfield to join—a scene they had carefully rehearsed earlier, despite Mr. Beaconsfield throwing his hands up and faking embarrassed surprise. I wait for him to reach the center of the line and then I make my way onto the stage. And even though I've been dreading this moment, it isn't that bad at all. The audience is so busy cheering the actors, I actually feel invisible.

Until I take a final step toward the center of the stage and the whole world seems to tilt on its axis. Only it isn't the world that's tilting—it's me, as I trip on the lace of my Converse and go staggering forward.

I can tell immediately that this isn't going to be one of those falls that I'll be able to style out. I'm falling too fast and at too sharp an angle and all I can think of is the camera in my hand. I mustn't break it. I can't let it smash on the floor. So I land about as awkwardly as possible, on my elbows, face-first. With my bum in the air pointing at the audience.

A shocked gasp, multiplied by about three hundred, echoes around the hall. The awful silence that follows is filled only by my inner voice asking, *Why does my bum feel so cold?* I glance over my shoulder and see that—to my horror—my skirt has flown up over my waist. A chorus of new whys fills my mind. *Why did I wear the skater skirt? Why did I take off my opaque tights backstage when I got too hot? Why, oh why, out of all the underwear that I possess, did I choose today to wear the most faded and frayed ones, covered in unicorns?*

I stay on all fours—paralyzed by a skin-crawling mixture of shock and horror. And then the audience starts to cheer again—but these cheers aren't like the ones before. These cheers are mocking and interspersed with wolf whistles and shrieks of laughter. I look up and see Megan glaring down at me. I see a hand reaching out to me. It's Ollie's. This makes me burn with embarrassment even more. I have to get out of there. I have to get off the stage. But instead of standing up and running, I make another terrible decision—I stay on all fours and crawl off. In slow motion. Or at least it feels like it. By the time I make it back into the wings, the hall is echoing with laughter. I stumble to my feet, grab my bag, and start to run.

I don't stop running until I get back home. I stagger into the hall, gasping for breath. I race up to my bedroom, avoiding all human contact inside the house, and collapse on my bed. I am so embarrassed—SO EMBARRASSED—that I can't even bring myself to tell Elliot. Instead, I'm just going to lie here and hope that eventually I will become so hot and flustered that I actually melt and never have to face anyone ever again.

But I will have to face people again. *How am I going to face people again? What am I going to do?* I reach into my bag for my phone. I squint at the screen, hardly daring to look, in case there are loads of mocking texts, but thankfully there are no new messages. I open the Internet browser. In the absence of being able to ask Elliot what I should do, I'm going to do the next best thing and ask Google.

How do you get over dire humiliation? I type into the search engine. Forty-four million results come up. OK, good, surely somewhere among all of them I will find my answer. I click on the first link. It sends me to a website called Positively Positive.

"Search for the lesson in your humiliation," the article advises. *"Things always seem better when we can attach a reason or meaning to them."* Hmm . . .

Lessons from what happened tonight:

Lesson 1: When going up onstage in front of three hundred people, always make sure that your shoelaces are tied.

Lesson 2: Untied shoelaces are a total health hazard—if tripped on, they can cause you to fall over so hard your skirt will actually fly up over your bum.

Lesson 3: If you are wearing a skirt short enough to fly up over your bum, should you trip on your shoelace on a stage in front of three hundred people, make sure you are wearing your least embarrassing underwear.

Lesson 4: Never, ever, under any circumstances, wear multicolored unicorn knickers.

Lesson 5: Never, ever, under any circumstances, wear multicolored unicorn knickers that are so old they've FADED and FRAYED AT THE EDGES—no matter how comfy they might be.

Lesson 6: If you are stupid enough to wear multicolored unicorn knickers that are so old they've faded and frayed at the edges and you end up flashing them to three hundred people, do not crawl off, I repeat—DO NOT CRAWL OFF— the stage with them still on display.

My life is over! And the Positively Positive website lied. Try-ing to find a reason for my humiliation has only made me feel a million times worse. I cringe as I run through the whole terrible saga again in my mind. My life is a disaster. I seriously ought to have one of those government health warnings tat-tooed on my forehead. The sad fact is the only place I feel happy and confident is on my blog.

Instinctively, I click through to the blog on my phone. I have twelve new comments on my post about outgrowing a friendship. As I scroll through them, I feel slightly calmer. Yet again, they are all so loving and kind.

I totally get what you're saying . . .

I've definitely grown out of friends before . . .

I'll be your friend . . .

You sound so lovely . . .

It's her loss not yours . . .

I know this sounds weird but I think of you as one of my closest friends . . .

My eyes fill with tears and I hug my knees to my chest. The fact is I'm totally honest on my blog, totally me—and my readers seem to really like me. So I can't be all bad, can I? And at least none of them have seen my underwear.

According to Elliot, there are currently over seven bil-lion people alive on the planet. Out of all those billions of people, only about three hundred have seen my unicorn knickers. That's the equivalent of less than one pebble on the whole of Brighton beach. OK, so a lot of those three hundred people are my fellow schoolmates but still—they're bound to forget about it soon. I wriggle down in the bed and close my eyes. *Billions of people have not seen your knickers*, my inner voice whispers gently, as if it's telling me a bedtime story. *Billions of people have not seen your knickers*.

I'm having this really cool dream about a gigantic advent calendar with hundreds of doors when suddenly my email notification pings. I fumble around in the dark to turn it off when there's another ping and another. I squint at my alarm clock. It's 1 a.m. Why am I getting so many emails at this time? As the phone goes off again and again, my first thought is that people are commenting on my blog but when I click into my inbox all I see are Facebook notifications.

Megan Barker has tagged you in a post, the first one says. The others are all telling me that various people have commented on that post—half of the cast of the play by the looks of things. I feel really sick as I click on the link and wait for the page to load. On the page is a video of the cast taking a bow. I break out in a cold sweat as I watch myself going onstage and then tripping over. The camera zooms in, right in, on my knickers, so close you can actually see a piece of frayed thread hanging down the inside of my thigh. I fling the phone onto the floor.

Oh my God.

I'd totally forgotten that the play was being filmed. This is awful. Worse than awful. My entire body is prickling with horror and embarrassment. What am I going to do? *Take a deep breath and keep calm*, I tell myself. I can delete the post—can't I?

I pick up my laptop and turn on my bedside lamp. My

phone goes off again. I swallow hard and log on to Facebook on my computer. The tiny red icon in the top right-hand corner informs me that I have twenty-two new notifications. Oh no!

Seventeen people have liked the video already. I make myself look at the comments. "*Whoops*," Megan has written in the original post. The other comments are mainly LOLs and red-faced emoticons. Then I see one from Bethany, who was the nurse in the play: "*Ew, that is so gross!*" Underneath it, Ollie has put "*I think it's kind of cute.*" I don't think I've ever felt so sick. I hover my cursor over the post and remove the tag. This instantly removes the video from my wall, but my news feed is still full of it as one by one, various cast members comment on the link and share it.

How could Megan do this to me? I would never, ever do something like this to her. I quickly fire her a private message. "Please can you take that video down?" I sit and stare at the screen waiting for a response, but nothing.

"Come on!" I mutter over and over again. But there's not a peep from Megan.

After about half an hour, my Facebook feed falls quiet. My school friends must have finally gone to sleep. I should try to get some sleep too. But how can I? In the morning everyone else is going to see the video. I feel as if I'm sitting on a ticking bomb, just waiting for it to go off.

I lie in bed for hours, checking and rechecking my phone. Refreshing and re-refreshing my Facebook page, in the hope that Megan has seen my message and taken down the video. At 5:30 a.m., when I'm starting to go a little demented from tiredness, I send her another message begging her to remove it. Then I lie back down and close my eyes. It will be OK, I tell myself. As soon as she wakes up and sees my messages she'll delete it.

I finally fall into a fitful sleep just as it's turning light outside. Then I hear Elliot knocking—and knocking and knocking—our secret code equivalent of dialing 999. I sit bolt upright, filled with dread. I knock back, telling him to come over. The text alert goes off on my phone. *Please, please let it be Megan*, I think, grabbing it. But it's from Elliot.

> OMG HONEY! DO NOT GO ONLINE UNTIL I GET THERE. I'M LEAVING RIGHT NOW

I hear his front door shut and the sound of his feet pounding up the path. I run downstairs to let him in.

"Have you just woken up?" Elliot says as soon as I open the door.

I nod.

"OK, I don't want you to panic but something terrible's happened," he says gravely.

"It's OK, I know," I say back.

"You do?" I can't help thinking Elliot looks the tiniest bit disappointed; he does love being the bearer of bad news.

"The video?" I say, leading him up the stairs.

Just as we're walking across the landing, my parents' bedroom door opens and Dad comes out. When he sees Elliot, he shakes his head and grins. "It's seven o'clock in the morning," he says.

"Actually it's one minute to, but thanks, Mr. P," Elliot says, looking at his watch.

Dad raises his eyebrows and sighs. "No, I wasn't giving you the time. I was trying to say that it's a bit early for a visit, isn't it?"

"It's never too early to give your best friend some moral support," Elliot says seriously.

Dad instantly looks at me, worried. "Is everything all right, love? You rushed up to your room last night like you needed to put out a fire."

"Yes, I'm fine," I say. "It's just a . . ."

"Homework crisis," Elliot finishes for me. "Those pesky French verbs."

"But Penny isn't doing French." Dad stares at me like he's trying to see inside my mind to work out what's really going on.

"No, but I am," Elliot says, quick as a flash. "That's why I need Penny's help."

"Oh." Dad frowns and scratches his head. He doesn't look convinced at all. "Well, when you've sorted your French crisis, come down and have some breakfast. I'm making eggs over easy," he says in an American accent, "and we need to talk about New York."

"Will do," I call over my shoulder as Elliot and I race up the second flight of stairs.

As soon as we're in my room, I shut the door tight.

"Why didn't you tell me?" Elliot says.

"I was too embarrassed." I sink down onto my bed. "And, anyway, it'll be OK. I've sent Megan a couple of messages asking her to delete the video so hopefully it'll be off Facebook as soon as she wakes up."

Elliot stares at me. "When did you last go on Facebook?"

"About five o'clock this morning." I get a sick sensation in the pit of my stomach. Why do I get the feeling Elliot knows something I don't? And how has he even seen the video? I untagged myself from the post, so it shouldn't have come up on his Facebook feed; he isn't friends with any of my schoolmates. I open up my laptop and refresh my Facebook page. "Oh no!"

Some kid from Year Nine has tagged me in a link to the video—the video that is now on YouTube. I've also been tagged in a link to the school "unofficial" Facebook group. The video is on there too.

"I'm so sorry, honey," Elliot says to me gravely. "But it looks like you're about to go viral."

Chapter Eleven

"Penny!" Mum exclaims as soon as I walk into the kitchen. "What's the matter?"

I sit down at the table and put my head in my hands. If I wasn't feeling so numb I would wail.

"She's about to go viral," Elliot says solemnly, sitting down next to me.

"She's got a virus?" Dad turns to face me. "I thought you looked a bit peaky earlier, love. Do you want a Lemsip?"

"No, she's about to go viral . . . you know, as in on the Internet," Elliot explains. "Like Rihanna did that time that naked video of her was posted on Twitter."

"There's a naked video of you on the Internet?" Dad sits down at the table opposite me. I've never seen him look so serious.

"No!" I say, shaking my head.

"Well, semi-naked," Elliot says thoughtfully.

"There's a semi-naked video of you on the Internet?" Dad stands up, and sits back down again. He looks at Mum.

Mum comes and sits beside me and takes hold of my

hand. "What's going on, darling?" And that's all it takes for me to go into a full-on meltdown.

"There's—a—video—of—me—in—my—unicorn—knickers!" I gasp between sobs.

"So, in some ways, it's actually worse than being naked," Elliot says.

"Unicorn knickers?" Dad looks completely bewildered. "What unicorn knickers? What video? Will someone please explain what's going on?"

"Penny fell over onstage last night when she was taking a photo and she flashed her knickers to the entire audience," Elliot explains.

"My worst knickers," I sob. "Well, actually, they were my favorite—that's why I wore them." I look up at Mum through tear-filled eyes. "They were so comfy. But not anymore. Now I just want to burn them."

"Want to burn what?" Tom says, trudging into the kitchen, his hair all messy from sleeping.

"Her unicorn knickers," Elliot says.

"OK, clearly I'm still asleep and dreaming," Tom says, slumping down in a chair.

"So you're not actually *naked* in this video?" Dad says.

"Yep, definitely still dreaming," Tom mutters, putting his head on the table and closing his eyes.

I shake my head.

"Well, that's OK then, isn't it?" Dad says, looking at me hopefully. "So what if they saw your knickers for a second? They'll have forgotten all about it by today."

"Please tell me I'm dreaming," Tom mutters, his eyes still closed.

"But they didn't just see them for a second," I wail. "It's on a video on the Internet, in close-up and slow motion. People will be able to watch it over and over again. And they're so faded and frayed!"

"What's so faded and frayed?" Dad says.

Elliot and I answer in unison: "Her unicorn knickers!" "My unicorn knickers!"

"Oh dear." Mum hugs me to her. "Haven't you had those knickers since you were twelve?"

"Mum!"

She gives me a bashful smile. "Sorry."

Tom looks up at us through sleepy eyes. "I'm not dreaming, am I?"

Elliot shakes his head. "Fraid not."

"OK." Dad places both his hands on the table. "Who posted the video online?"

"Megan," I say.

"Mega-nasty," Elliot mutters.

"Megan?" Mum looks really shocked.

"Yes, she put it on her Facebook page and now someone's put it on YouTube and someone else has posted it on the school Facebook page." I start to cry again as I think of the entire school watching action replays of my knickers.

Tom stares at me. "Are you serious?"

I nod.

"Right." Tom gets to his feet, suddenly looking wide awake.

"What are you doing?" Mum says, looking at him anxiously.

"I'm going to go up to school and find everyone who's

posted it online and I'm going to make them take it down."
I've never seen Tom look so mad.

Mum jumps to her feet and grabs hold of his arm. "You can't do that; you're not a student there anymore."

Tom frowns at her. "So what? Penny is and she's my sister. I'm not going to sit back and do nothing."

I smile up at him gratefully.

Dad shakes his head. "It's OK, son, I'll take care of it. The last thing we need is you getting into any trouble." He takes hold of my hand. "Don't worry, sweetheart. I'll go up to the school this morning and I'll get them to take it off their Facebook page."

I shake my head. "It's the unofficial Facebook page—the teachers don't have any control over it. And so many people have been sharing it; everyone's going to see it anyway."

I think of going into school and everyone looking at me and laughing at me and suddenly it's as if I'm being pulled underwater. I can't breathe, I can't swallow, and my entire body starts to do this weird shaking thing. I just can't cope with any more drama.

"Pen? Are you OK?" Elliot's voice sounds muffled and far away.

Everyone else's voices blend into one, kind of like a radio being tuned. "Penny?" "Pen?" "Sweetheart?" "Get her some water." "Oh my God, she's going to faint."

I feel someone holding my shoulders. Someone strong. Dad.

"Take a really slow, deep breath, honey." Mum.

"Here's some water." Tom.

I close my eyes and take a really slow deep breath. And

another. In my mind I picture the sea, crashing in and rolling out, crashing in and rolling out. And, slowly, my body stops shaking.

"Penny, what just happened?" Mum says. She's looking so concerned it makes me want to cry again. But I'm too scared to cry in case it brings the panic attack back, so I just keep focusing on my breathing.

"Are you OK?" Dad says. He's still holding my shoulders tightly. It feels nice. Like I'm anchored in place.

"Shall I tell them?" Elliot asks softly.

I nod. And as I keep on focusing on my breathing, Elliot explains about the panic attacks I've been getting since the car accident.

Mum and Dad both look ashen-faced.

"I'm sorry," is the first thing I'm able to say.

Dad looks at me and shakes his head. "What? Why are you sorry?"

"You should have told us," Mum says.

"I didn't want to worry you. And anyway, I thought it would get better, you know, once a bit of time had gone past."

"Shall I make some tea?" Tom asks, and we all stare at him in shock. Tom *never* offers to make tea. I smile at him and nod.

"OK, first things first," Dad says, putting on a business-like voice. "We're going to get you some help, to try to get these panic attacks under control."

"Yes, there are lots of things you can do," Mum adds. "I know some great breathing exercises from when I used to get stage fright."

"You used to get stage fright?" I ask in disbelief. It's hard to imagine my mega-confident mum being scared of anything.

Mum nods. "Oh yes—it was terrible. Sometimes I was actually physically sick before a show, but I managed to get it under control and you will too, honey."

"That's right," Dad says, smiling at me. "And I'm going to call the school and tell them you're off sick." He takes hold of my hand. "I think you should stay off till the new year—give this all a chance to blow over. There's only two days of term left."

I give him a weak smile. "Thanks, Dad."

"And thirdly," he says, glancing at Mum, "we want you to come with us to New York."

Elliot sighs.

I look at Dad, alarmed. "But I—"

"And we want Elliot to come too," Dad interrupts.

"Oh my God!" Elliot's mouth drops open so wide I can practically see his tonsils.

"We were planning on asking you both today anyway," Mum says with a smile. "But now that this has happened, it's even more reason for you to come."

"It'll only be for four days," Dad says. "We'll fly out on Thursday and come back Sunday, Christmas Eve." He looks at Tom and smiles. "So we'll still all be able to have Christmas Day together."

I look at Elliot. He's now grinning like he just won the lottery.

"I think it will do you a world of good to get away," Mum says. "It'll give you the chance to properly get over the accident—and this stupid video nonsense."

"Yes, by the time we get back, it will be Christmas and it will have all blown over," Dad says.

"He does have a point," Elliot says to me, right before his phone goes off. He looks at the screen and frowns before taking the call. "Hi, Dad . . . I'm next door. Where else would I be? . . . OK, OK, I'll be there in a minute." He ends the call, looking at us apologetically. "It was my dad, wondering if I'm going to school today. I'd better get going." He turns and grabs both my hands. "I know you were nervous about going on a plane, Pen, but we can all help you with that, can't we?" He looks at my parents and they start nodding like those toy dogs people put in the back windows of their cars.

"Of course we will, darling," Mum says with a smile.

"We'll all be there for you," Dad says.

Elliot's phone starts ringing again. "Hello, Mum . . . I just told Dad . . . I'm next door . . . I'll be back in two seconds." He puts his phone in his pocket and sighs. "I swear, my parents never talk to each other about anything!" He suddenly looks really worried. "Oh, I hope they let me come with you. What if they say no?"

"Don't worry, darling," Mum says. "I'll go round and have a word with them later. I'm sure they won't mind—especially as our clients will be paying for everything."

Elliot nods and grins. Then he turns and looks at me hopefully. "So, what do you reckon, Pen?"

I take a deep breath and smile. "I reckon we're going to New York!"

20 December

Facing Your Fears

Hey, guys!

Thanks again for all of your comments on my blog about friendship. I know it sounds weird as I haven't actually met any of you or anything but I really do think of you all as my friends——you're always so lovely and kind and your support means so much to me.

So, most of you will probably remember my recent post about the panic attacks I've been having since the car accident. Well, this week I had a bit of a Glass Slipper Moment.

A Glass Slipper Moment is the name Wiki and I give to things that happen that are really bad at first but that actually end up leading to something really good——like when Cinderella loses her glass slipper but it ends up reuniting her with Prince Charming.

91

Earlier this week, something really, truly, hideously horrible happened to me and it caused me to have another of my stupid panic attacks. But I think/hope it's all going to lead to something really good.

I'm going away somewhere this week and I'm going to have to go on a plane.

This is making me feel really anxious but I'm hoping that if I can do this— if I can face my fear—then it might make it go away for good.

When I was little I used to think that a witch lived under my mum and dad's bed.

Every time I had to go past their bedroom to get to my own room, I'd run as fast as I could, so that the witch didn't fly out on her broomstick and turn me into a toad.

Then one day my dad saw me racing along the landing looking all scared and he asked me what was up.

When I told him, he made me come into the bedroom with him and he shone a torch under the bed.

The only thing that was under there was an old shoe box.

Sometimes you have to face up to your fears to realize that they aren't actually real.

That you aren't actually going to die—or get turned into a toad.

I'm going to do that this week, when I get on a plane.

How about you?

Do you have any fears that you'd like to face up to?

Maybe we could do it together . . . ?

Why don't you post your fear and how you're going to face up to it this week in the comments below?

Good luck and I'll let you know how I get on in next week's blog.

Girl Online, going offline xxx

★ *Chapter Twelve* ★

"What you need," Elliot says to me as we take a seat in a café in the departure lounge, "is your own personal Sasha Fierce."

"My what?" My heart pounds like crazy as I look around the lounge. Very soon we're going to be called to board the plane. And then I'm going to have to get on the plane that's going to somehow stay miles up in the sky without crashing down. But what if it does come crashing down? What if—

"Sasha Fierce," Elliot says. "You know, Beyoncé's alter ego, her stage persona."

I frown at him. "What are you talking about?"

Elliot leans back in his chair and stretches out his long legs. He's wearing a vintage Harvard sweatshirt, pinstripe skinny trousers, and bright green chucks, which perfectly match his bright green glasses. How can he look so laid-back and cool when we're about to get on a giant metal tube and go shooting up into the sky?

"When Beyoncé first started out in the music business, she was really quiet and shy and she hated going onstage," Elliot says. "So she invented an alter ego called Sasha Fierce who

94

was brave and feisty and cool. Then, every time she went onstage she could pretend to be Sasha and it helped her act all confident and hair swishy."

"Hair swishy?"

"Yeah, you know . . ." Elliot swishes his head back and forth, causing his glasses to come flying off and land in my lap.

"Right," I say, handing his glasses back, "and how is this supposed to help me?"

"You need to invent your own version of Sasha Fierce and then pretend to be her when you get on the plane." Elliot strokes his chin the way he always does when he's deep in thought. "How about Sarah Savage?"

"No! That makes me sound like some kind of psycho!"

I look at my parents queuing up to buy coffee—and a calming camomile tea for me. Although my mouth is as dry as sandpaper, I don't want them to come back because then we'll have our drinks, and then we'll have to get ready to board the plane and—

"OK, how about Connie Confident?"

I look at Elliot and raise my eyebrows. "Seriously?"

Elliot sighs. "All right, you think of one then."

A woman walks toward us, wheeling a small, bright pink case. She's wearing tight grey jeans, pointy black boots, and a beautiful cape coat. She looks effortlessly cool and serene. Even her hair is immaculate—a sleek black bob, glowing with mahogany highlights. As she walks past me I see that she's wearing a necklace with the word STRONG on it. It's like one of those "signs from the universe" that Mum is always going on about.

"Strong," I whisper.

Elliot looks at me. "What?"

"The surname for my alter ego is Strong."

Elliot nods. "Ah, OK. Yes, that's good. How about the first name?"

I think for a moment. How do I want my alter ego to make me feel apart from strong? Calm, I guess. But Calm Strong is a rubbish name. As I think of feeling calm, the image of the sea pops into my head. "Ocean!" I blurt out.

Elliot nods. "Ocean Strong. Hmm, yep, that could work."

Ocean Strong. As I roll the name around in my head, I picture a comic-book superheroine wearing a skintight sea-green bodysuit and cape, with long auburn curly hair spilling over her shoulders. *I am Ocean Strong,* I tell myself, and, incredibly, it starts to work. My heart rate starts to slow back down to normal and my mouth doesn't feel quite so dry. *I am Ocean Strong.* I picture my alter ego surfing a huge wave, calmly surveying the horizon while adopting a superhero stance.

Just at that point Mum and Dad get back to the table with the drinks.

"Everything OK?" Mum says, looking at me.

"Yes," I reply, and I even manage a smile.

While Mum, Dad, and Elliot chat about New York and all the places they want to see, I focus on a breathing exercise Mum taught me and continue adding details to Ocean Strong in my mind. If Ocean Strong had to get on a plane she wouldn't bat an eyelid. She'd just stride on board, head held high, gaze fixed straight ahead. If Ocean Strong had been in a car accident, she wouldn't let it ruin the rest of her life; she'd be fearless and brave and keep on fighting evil-doers. I feel my phone vibrate in my pocket, breaking my daydream; it's a text from Megan.

> Hi, Penny! Kira told me you're going abroad for Christmas. Is it true? Can you get me some Chanel perfume in duty free? I'll give you the money when you get back. Thanks xoxo

This is the first time I've heard from Megan all week. Even though I haven't been to school since the play—she hasn't bothered asking if I'm OK. Even Ollie sent me a message on Facebook to see if I was all right. There's no apology about the video either, although she did take it down from her page.

I turn off my phone and put it in my bag. If Ocean Strong had an embarrassing video of her put online, what would she do? I picture my alter ego laughing it off before leaping on her surfboard and heading off in search of new adventure. And suddenly something weird happens—I start feeling really good about myself. Some rubbish things have happened to me recently but I haven't let them beat me. And not only have I not let them beat me but I'm going off to New York to have an adventure. I might be clumsy and panicky and make some terrible underwear choices but what I'm about to do is actually pretty cool. *I* am pretty cool, because I am Ocean Strong.

Chapter Thirteen

Thankfully, all four of us are seated together in the middle section of the plane and I'm sandwiched in between Elliot and Dad. This instantly makes me feel safe but as soon as the plane engines start firing up I feel that horrible tightness start gripping at my throat.

"So, tell me more about Ocean Strong," Elliot whispers in my ear.

"She's got a really cool surfboard," I say, gripping onto the armrests.

Elliot nods appreciatively. "That's nice. I think she needs some kind of catchphrase too."

The pilot's voice comes over the PA system. "Flight attendants, prepare for take-off." His voice is deep and clear, and reassuringly reminds me of Dad's.

"What do you mean?" I say to Elliot.

"Well, like Batman says, 'To the Batmobile, Robin,' and Judge Dredd says, 'I am the law.'"

"Oh. Right."

The engines are screaming now and the plane starts to move.

I close my eyes and rack my brains for an Ocean Strong catchphrase.

"And the Teenage Mutant Ninja Turtles had 'Cowabunga' and Lobo has 'Bite me, fanboy.'"

I open my eyes and glare at Elliot. "I am not having 'Bite me, fanboy' as my catchphrase!"

The plane starts hurtling down the runway. I get a flashback to our car screeching across the road in the rain and I hear Mum screaming. I turn to look at her but she's chatting and smiling to Dad.

"How about 'Here I come to save the day'?" Elliot asks.

"Whose catchphrase was that?"

"Mighty Mouse."

I laugh. "Ocean Strong can't have the same catchphrase as Mighty Mouse!"

"'My spider-sense is tingling'?" Elliot suggests with a grin.

Now I'm laughing and scared all at once. The plane is tilting up into the air and the ground is sliding away.

"You OK?" Elliot whispers, placing his hand over mine.

I nod and grit my teeth. "Please can you keep telling me catchphrases to take my mind off it?"

Elliot's eyes light up. "Of course!"

By the time the plane has stopped climbing, I know the catchphrases of every single superhero from Captain America to Wonder Woman to Wolverine.

"All right, Pen?" Dad says, looking at me anxiously.

I nod and smile, and think to myself that having Mum and

Dad and Elliot makes me the luckiest girl alive . . . as long as we make it through this flight alive.

Elliot turns out to be the best flight companion ever. He just talks and talks for the whole six hours. Even when we watch a movie together, he provides a hilarious running commentary all the way through. And at the odd moments where I feel myself starting to get anxious, like when the seat-belt sign pings on when we hit a spot of turbulence, I just focus on my breathing and conjure up the image of Ocean Strong in my head.

As the flight attendants prepare for landing, I feel a shiver of excitement mixed in with my fear. As the plane descends, the people in the window seats start peering out but I stay staring straight ahead at the back of the seat in front of me. *I am strong just like the ocean*, I say over and over in my head. And then suddenly there's a slight jolt and we're on the ground. I'm so happy and relieved I want to cry.

"We made it," I whisper to Elliot. "We're here."

As we get up to go, I glance out of the plane window and catch my breath. Everything looks so American—from the long-nosed silver trucks to the men working on the wheel of the plane next to ours, with their navy-blue baseball caps and cargo pants.

Elliot's grin is so wide it practically reaches his ears. "We're in New York," he whispers excitedly. "We're in New York!"

Even having to wait almost two hours to get through customs doesn't dampen our enthusiasm. As we join the queue for a taxi, Elliot and I keep grinning at each other and shaking our heads in disbelief.

"I can't believe we're really here," Elliot keeps saying again and again, clapping his hands together.

As I watch the bright yellow taxis speeding off with their passengers, I feel as if the plane has plonked us down right in the middle of a movie set. Everything looks so different—and yet so familiar. Poor Mum doesn't look very excited, though; pretty much as soon as we landed she had to start making calls to people about the wedding. Right now she's on the phone to Sadie Lee—the woman in charge of the catering. Apparently there's been some kind of problem getting the quail for the *Downton Abbey*–style menu.

"OK, well I suppose that will have to do," she says, pacing up and down beside us. "And don't forget the custard for the bread pudding."

Dad goes over and places a hand on Mum's shoulder. She leans into his shoulder. In all my fear and excitement, I'd kind of forgotten that Mum is actually here to work. I go over and join them for a group hug.

Finally, we reach the front of the queue.

"Where to?" the driver says, jumping out of the cab. He's dark and swarthy and wearing a black jumper, jeans, and a serious scowl.

"The Waldorf Astoria, please," Dad says, causing Elliot to have another clapping fit.

"This is the best day of my life, ever!" he cries.

The cabdriver looks at him like he's crazy, then he sees our huge pile of luggage—we needed two huge cases just for the bridal-party outfits. "Geez!" he says. "You guys sure you don't need a pickup truck?"

Mum smiles at him apologetically.

The cabdriver starts slinging the cases into the boot, muttering.

"Don't worry," Elliot says to me quietly. "New York cab-drivers have to be rude—it's their *thing*."

The cabbie straightens up and looks at Elliot. "What did you call me?"

Elliot practically jumps out of his skin. "Nothing. I was just saying, it's all part of your act, as a New York taxi driver."

"What's part of my act?"

"Being—er—being—rude." Elliot looks at the floor like he's hoping it will open up and swallow him whole.

"That's no act, son," the cabbie growls. "Now get in."

We all shuffle into the cab. I daren't look at Elliot in case I start to giggle. I'm so full of nervous energy and excitement I feel like I might explode. As the driver pulls out of the airport, I catch my breath. Everything is so huge—from the wide-open highway to the gigantic billboards lining the roadside.

"So, had any snow yet?" Dad says to the cabdriver, doing that typical British thing of, when in doubt, ask about the weather.

"Nope," the driver replies. "Where the hell d'you think you're going?" he yells out of the window as a truck cuts in front of him.

I clench my fists so tightly my nails cut into my palms. Instantly, Mum and Elliot, who are sitting on either side of me, place a hand on my knee. I close my eyes and think of Ocean Strong.

Once we get to the heart of New York my head feels like

it might actually burst from all the incredible sights it's taking in. I'd expected the skyscrapers but I hadn't expected them to be quite so *sky-scraping*. And I hadn't expected to see so many old buildings mixed in with the new. Every block we go past seems to have at least one old stone church nestled between the gleaming towers. And the people are even more fascinating. The sidewalks are crowded with businesspeople and Christmas shoppers. Just when I focus on one interesting-looking character, another one bursts into view. I watch as a beautiful woman in a charcoal-grey suit and bright blue trainers effortlessly weaves her way along the crowded pavement, suddenly disappearing into a juice bar. Then my eyes fall on a young Hispanic guy with purple hair coming out of a bookshop the size of an aircraft hangar and being swallowed up by the throng. There's a cop biting into a hot dog at a traffic crossing and a nun in a dark blue habit, gliding through the mayhem as calmly as if she's in a trance. Everywhere I look I see an epic photo opportunity. Even the noise seems bigger here, a chorus of sirens and car horns and shouting. Next to me, Elliot keeps squeezing my arm with excitement.

And then, finally, we get to Park Avenue. The road is so wide that the traffic lights are suspended over them on huge poles, swaying slightly in the wind. They're the same yellow as the taxis that seem to make up practically every other car. My eyes open wider and wider as I take in the palatial hotels lining the street. All I can think is, *I am going to take some amazing photos while I'm here.*

When we pull up outside our hotel, even Dad looks speechless. The grey stone front seems to stretch up for miles. Two huge Christmas trees twinkling with red and gold lights are standing on either side of the large revolving door, like guards on duty. As I step out of the taxi, I feel something cold on the end of my nose. I look up and see that it's starting to snow. Not heavily, just a few tiny flakes drifting down, as if they've sneaked out of a cloud to see what's going on.

"Good afternoon, ma'am!"

I look over and see a doorman dressed in the smartest uniform ever, smiling at me.

I smile back shyly. "Afternoon."

"Welcome to the Waldorf," he says, coming over to help us with our cases.

I look at the Christmas trees and the twinkling lights and the snowflakes shimmering in the air like powdered silver, and I don't feel like I'm in a movie anymore; I feel like I'm in a fairy tale. As we all follow the doorman into the hotel, I cross my fingers and hope it has a really happy ending.

Chapter Fourteen

Imagine the most incredible, beautiful, luxurious fairy-tale palace your brain is capable of conjuring. Then add more marble, more gold, more chandeliers, and more general shininess and sparkliness and then, maybe, you'll have something close to the Waldorf Astoria.

"Wow!" Elliot exclaims, as he gazes around the lobby.

"Beats the Hastings Travelodge, eh, kids?" Dad says with a wink.

I'm too stunned to even giggle.

Mum looks slightly terrified. "This is huge," she whispers to Dad. And I'm not sure if she's talking about the lobby, the hotel, or the wedding she's got to organize.

By the time we've been shown to our rooms, Elliot and I are doing a great impression of a pair of goldfishes—opening and closing our mouths but with no words coming out other than "Oh my God."

We've been put in two adjoining rooms right next door to Mum and Dad's.

"We need one of these back at home," Elliot calls over

to me from the adjoining door. "How cool would that be, if I could just pop over to see you without ever having to go outside?"

"It would be very cool," I say, perching on the edge of my bed. My room is like something out of a stately home. The furniture is all made from gleaming mahogany, the chairs and the desk and the bed all with ornately carved legs. The color scheme is burgundy and gold, which isn't something I would ever choose for my bedroom at home, but here it's perfect. I look over to the window. The velvet curtains go all the way from the ceiling to the floor and are tied back with wide sashes. "Oh my God, is that . . . ?" I jump off the bed and race over to the window.

Elliot follows me. "The Empire State Building," he gasps as we gaze out at the New York skyline.

We turn and look at each other for a second, then we both start jumping about like kids on Christmas morning.

For the rest of the afternoon, Mum and Dad are busy in meetings with Cindy, Jim, and the catering manager. Elliot and I are supposed to be napping off our jet lag before we go out for the evening but we're far too excited to sleep. Instead, we've built a nest of cushions and pillows on my bed and we're channel surfing our way through American TV.

Elliot is also looking up interesting facts about the Waldorf Astoria on his laptop. My laptop is still tucked away inside my suitcase. I've decided to leave it there for the rest of the trip. I've also turned off the Internet on my phone. I want it to truly feel as if there's an ocean between me and everyone from school and my Unicorn Knickers Shame.

"Oh my God, Pen, listen to this!" Elliot starts reading from his screen. "The Waldorf Astoria was created by two feuding cousins called Waldorf and Astor who each built rival hotels next to each other." He turns to me, laughing. "Then, when they made up, they built a corridor between them."

"Seriously?"

"Yep." Elliot continues reading. "Oh, but it's not this building. This one was built in 1931. The original hotel was knocked down to make space for the Empire State Building."

We both glance to the window and once again I get that pinch-me-I'm-dreaming feeling.

"You're not going to believe this," Elliot exclaims with a gasp. "This was the hotel where room service was first invented!"

"You're kidding?"

"Nope. And—and"—Elliot can barely contain his excitement—"there was a secret underground train platform."

"What?"

"It was for VIPs who wanted to arrive here in secret, like the president." Elliot looks at me, his eyes wide as saucers. "Oh, Pen, I love this place."

In the end we order some room service because, as Elliot said, "It would be rude not to, given that they invented it." We order a Waldorf salad because it was also invented here and a huge margherita pizza. I'm just starting to feel really sleepy when Mum and Dad get back. Dad is looking his usual laid-back self but Mum is looking super-stressy.

"There's so much to do!" she wails, plonking herself down on my bed. "I knew we should have come sooner."

"It'll be fine," Dad says, giving her a reassuring smile.

"We've got all day tomorrow to sort everything out. And Sadie Lee is a star."

Mum nods. "Yes, she's amazing. Her bread pudding tastes divine." Mum turns to me. "Cindy and Jim were wondering if you could take some behind-the-scenes photos for them. They've got a professional photographer booked for the wedding day, but they were saying how nice it would be if they could have some pictures of us setting things up and putting the *Downton Abbey* touches to everything. And they've asked if you'd take some fun shots on the day too—the little things the professional photographer won't see."

"Seriously?" I feel an excited fluttering in my stomach. "But why me?"

"I showed them some of the pictures you've taken at other weddings and they were very impressed."

Dad starts nodding and grinning proudly. "They really were."

"So they should be," Elliot says. "Penny's an awesome photographer."

I feel all smiley inside. "Wow. When do I start?"

"Tomorrow, while I'm setting everything up," Mum says.

"Don't worry, Elliot," Dad says. "While the girls are busy we can do a bit of sightseeing. How do you fancy a tour of the museums?"

Elliot looks up at Dad and to my surprise I see that his eyes are gleaming with tears. "That would be epic," he says quietly. "Seriously, you guys are the best. Thank you so much for bringing me here."

"Oh, honey," Mum says, laughing. "You're very welcome."

And we all smother Elliot in a hug.

Chapter Fifteen

The next morning, I'm woken by a knocking sound.

"Pen, are you awake?"

My first thought is, how am I able to hear Elliot's voice so clearly through my bedroom wall? Then I open my eyes and catch a glimpse of crisp white bed linen and plush burgundy carpet and it all comes flooding back. I'm in the Waldorf Astoria. I'm in New York. I survived the flight!

"Yes," I say, shuffling up to a seated position.

Elliot comes bounding through our adjoining door. "I've been awake for ages," he says. "I'm too excited to sleep."

I look at the clock and see that I've slept for ten whole hours. This is an incredible achievement after the nights of fitful sleep back home.

Elliot plonks himself down on the end of my bed and opens his laptop. "OK, I know you didn't want to go online while we're over here but there's something you need to see."

I instantly feel sick. "No, please, Elliot, I don't want to see anything to do with the stupid video. I just want to forget about it."

Elliot shakes his head and smiles. "It's not the video; it's your blog."

I stare at him. "What do you mean?"

"I mean that you, my dear, have gone viral again—but this time in a very good way."

"What?" I crawl up the bed toward him and turn the laptop around so that it's facing me. I see my post about facing my fears.

"Scroll down," Elliot says.

I scroll down. There are 327 comments.

"What the . . . ?" I stare at the screen blankly. I've never had this many comments. Ever.

"They've all been posting about their fears," Elliot says, "and how they're going to face them. They've been sharing it too. Look how many followers you've got."

I look at the followers bar on the right-hand side of the screen. "Ten thousand?"

Elliot nods. "Ten thousand, seven hundred, and fifteen, to be precise."

I sit back, stunned. "Oh wow."

"You should read them, Pen, some of them are so moving. There's one girl who says she's going to stand up to the bully in her class and there's another who's going to confront her fear of dentists. And, oh my God, you have to read this one." Elliot starts scrolling through the comments. "Look." He turns the screen back to face me.

Hi Girl Online, my fear is a bit different to the others on here and, to be honest, I've never told anyone about it before. But if you've got the courage to face your fear after your car accident, then I feel like I ought to face up to my own fear too.

My fear is my mum. Well, not exactly my mum herself . . . I'm afraid of her drinking. Ever since she lost her job she's been drinking more and more and I hate what it does to her. It makes her really angry and moody and she always shouts at me. But that's not what I'm most afraid of. I'm most afraid that she doesn't love me anymore. That probably sounds really dumb but she seems so different——like she doesn't care anymore, about anything or anyone, even me. But your blog post has inspired me to do something. Today, I'm going to tell my auntie how I'm feeling. I know she won't be able to fix anything but she might be able to give me some advice, and just telling someone might help me to feel a bit better. Thank you so much for being so brave and for inspiring us to be brave too. Lots of love, Pegasus Girl xxx

I look at Elliot, my eyes filling with tears. "Oh my God."

Elliot nods. "I know and look at this." He scrolls right down to the bottom of the comments.

Hi again. Just wanted to let you know that I told my auntie and she was so lovely. She came over to see my mum and my auntie has asked us to both come and stay with her for a while. My mum didn't get angry with me at all——she was really sad and she said how sorry she was and that she was going to get help. Thanks so much, Girl Online, you're so right: sometimes you have to face up to your fears to realize that they aren't actually real. Lots of love, Pegasus Girl xxx

Tears spill down onto my face. I wipe them away and stare at Elliot. "I can't believe that—that something I wrote . . ."

"I know." Elliot puts his arm around my shoulders. "I'm so proud of you, Ocean Strong."

I snuggle into him. "Thanks, Elliot."

He shakes his head and frowns at me. "Thanks, *Waldorf Wild*."

I raise my eyebrows.

"It's my new Sasha Fierce name."

Nothing beats Dad's "Saturday Breakfast," but breakfast at the Waldorf definitely comes a very close second. After we've all feasted on crispy bacon, blueberry pancakes, and maple syrup *all on the same plate* (which might sound weird but actually works), Mum and I go up to the suite where the wedding's going to be held while Dad and Elliot head out to do some sightseeing. Although I'm really flattered and excited to be asked to take some photos for Cindy and Jim, I can't help feeling a little wistful. I hope I get the chance to go out later; I'm itching to see some more of New York.

As soon as we enter the wedding suite, I look at Mum and gasp. "Oh, Mum—it's perfect."

She nods and smiles. "I know."

With the portraits on the walls and plush carpets and antique furniture, it looks just like the set from *Downton Abbey*.

Mum puts her To Have and to Hold planner down on a small table by the door and I instinctively turn my camera on. She's put the planner right next to a beautiful antique table lamp, which seems to perfectly sum up the theme of the wedding. I zoom in close enough to pick up the lettering on the planner and take the picture.

"So, this is the room where they're going to get married," Mum says, gesturing at the rows of gilt-edged chairs that have been arranged in front of a grand fireplace. "Then after the ceremony the guests will be brought through to the dining room for the wedding breakfast."

"Why's it called a wedding *breakfast*?" I ask as I follow Mum toward a pair of huge doors on the other side of the room.

"I'm not exactly sure," Mum says. "Maybe because it's the first meal the couple have as husband and wife?"

I make a mental note to ask Elliot; he's bound to know. "Oh wow!" The double doors open onto an even grander room, which is full of round tables. Huge old-fashioned chandeliers are suspended from the ceiling, with lights that look just like candles. Each table has a beautiful centerpiece woven from holly and white rosebuds. And at the far end of the room the long head table is trimmed with a border of sepia Union Jack bunting. It all looks really beautiful—and really British.

"Oh, Mum, it looks amazing!"

She looks at me hopefully. "Do you think so?"

"Absolutely."

"Hello! Hello! Well, this must be Miss Penny."

I turn to see a woman coming through a small door at the end of the room. She's wearing a polo neck and smart trousers and has her long grey hair tied up into a bun. She's clearly in her sixties, and she's striking-looking, with really high cheekbones and eyes as brown as conkers. Her lipstick is a beautiful shade of dark red against her porcelain skin.

"Hi, Sadie Lee," Mum says. "Yes, this is Penny."

"It is so lovely to meet you," Sadie Lee says, giving me a twinkly-eyed smile. "I've heard so much about you."

Before I can reply, she's giving me a hug. She smells lovely—a really comforting mixture of soap and cinnamon.

"How did y'all sleep?" Sadie Lee asks in a husky Southern drawl, looking from Mum to me.

"Great," I say.

But Mum shakes her head. "I'm afraid I was too nervous to get much sleep."

Sadie Lee looks at her and smiles. "Honey, there's no need to be nervous. You're doing a wonderful job. Or as they'd say in *Downton Abbey*—it's going to be simply splendid." Sadie Lee throws back her head and laughs a really warm, throaty laugh.

There are some people you officially fall in love with within seconds of meeting them. Sadie Lee is definitely one of those people.

"Penny's going to be taking some behind-the-scenes photos for the Bradys," Mum explains.

"What a great idea." Sadie Lee smiles at me. "Well, you know, I'm about to start doing some baking for the reception buffet so y'all would be very welcome to come and take a few pictures in the kitchen if you'd like?"

"That would be perfect," Mum says. She looks at me. "Will you be OK, Pen? I just need to go and check that the waiting staff's costumes all fit, OK?"

"Of course."

As Mum heads off, I follow Sadie Lee into the kitchen. After the olde worlde vibe of the other rooms, it's really weird to see the sleek stainless-steel counters and huge industrial-sized ovens.

"We're doing most of the cooking tomorrow," Sadie Lee explains. "But I thought I'd get the cakes for the reception buffet done today. I'm making a traditional British afternoon tea."

"Don't you have any staff to help you?" I say, looking around the empty kitchen.

She shakes her head. "Uh-uh, not today. But tomorrow I'll have a whole team of chefs."

I take a few pictures of Sadie Lee baking and a close-up of her flour-splattered cookbook. Then I decide to go and take some pictures of the dining room. But I leave the kitchen through the wrong door and come out into another huge room. This one has a long polished wooden dance floor running down the center of it, with small round tables lining either side. I'm about to leave when I hear the gentle strum of a guitar coming from the far end of the room. It's so dark I can only just make out the silhouette of someone seated on the stage.

I go and investigate, creeping down one of the carpeted areas at the side of the dance floor. As I get closer to the stage, the sound of the guitar gets louder and I can hear someone singing. They're singing so quietly I can't quite make out the words, but whatever it is sounds beautiful and really, really sad. I tiptoe a bit closer until I see the figure of a boy sitting cross-legged on the stage, playing the guitar with his back to me. He's surrounded by musical equipment—a drum kit, a keyboard, and a microphone stand. There's something so magical about the image that I can't resist turning on my camera and sneaking a tiny bit closer. I focus and take the shot, but—to my horror—I forget to turn the flash off and the stage is flooded with light.

"Whoa!" The mystery singing person leaps to his feet and spins around, putting his hands over his face. "How did you get in?" he yells in a really strong New York accent. "Who sent you here?"

"I'm sorry—I couldn't resist—you looked so—" Thankfully, I manage to stop myself from committing an Act of Gross Embarrassment and change tack. "I'm taking some photos for the wedding that's happening here tomorrow. How did *you* get in? Are you the wedding singer?"

"Am I the wedding singer?" He peers at me from between his fingers. There's a tattoo of a bar of music notes on his wrist.

"Yes. Are you practicing?" I walk a bit closer to the stage and he actually takes a step back, like he's scared of me. "I wouldn't do that song tomorrow, if I were you."

He stands motionless, with his hands still half covering his face. "Why not?"

"Well, it's not very wedding-y. I mean, it was beautiful—what I heard of it—but it sounded so sad and I don't think that's the right kind of vibe for a wedding, you know? You need to be thinking more along the lines of the theme from *Dirty Dancing*. That always goes down really well at weddings. Did you guys get *Dirty Dancing* over here?"

He lowers his hands and stares at me, like he's trying to work out if I'm an alien from another planet. And now that I can see him properly, I'm so stunned I wouldn't be surprised if I had a thought bubble bursting from my head saying, *WOW!* He's what Elliot would call Rock-God–tastic: all messy dark hair, chiseled cheekbones, faded jeans, and scuffed-up boots.

"Yeah, we got *Dirty Dancing* over here," he says, but his

voice is a lot softer now, almost like he's trying not to laugh. "It was actually made in America."

"Ah, yes, of course it was." That familiar sinking feeling returns. Even when I'm in New York, I'm a liability. I'm now an *international* embarrassment waiting to happen. But then a strange feeling comes over me—a strong, determined feeling. I am *not* going to make a fool of myself on this trip. Even if it means not talking to anyone other than Elliot and Mum and Dad. Even if it means not talking to someone totally Rock-God–tastic—someone totally Rock-God–tastic from New York.

"Well, sorry to bother you, and good luck tomorrow," I say, my cheeks burning, and I turn to go.

Chapter Sixteen

"I'm not the wedding singer," he says, before I've even taken a step.

I stop in my tracks. "You're not?"

"No."

I turn and look at him. He's grinning at me now—a really cute lopsided grin, featuring several dimples. "So what are you doing here then?"

"I like breaking into hotels and playing really sad songs in their wedding suites," he says, grinning even more.

"Interesting career choice," I say.

"It is," he says, nodding. "But the pay's lousy."

What if he's a crazy person? my inner voice whispers. *A New York crazy person. What if he's broken into the hotel suite? What if I have to make a citizen's arrest? Do they even have citizen's arrests over here? Aaargh! What am I going to do?*

He doesn't look like a crazy person, though. Now that he's smiling, he looks like a very nice person, but still . . .

"Why the frown?" he says.

"I was just thinking."

"What?"

"You're not—crazy—are you?"

He laughs really loud. "No. Well, yes, but only in a good way. I've found that life's a whole lot better if you get a little crazy sometimes."

I nod. That definitely makes sense to me.

"What's your name?" he asks, picking up the guitar and placing it back on its stand.

"Penny."

"Penny." It sounds really good said in his voice. "I'm Noah. And I'm guessing from the accent that you're British, right?"

"Yes."

"Sweet. And you're a photographer?"

"Yes—well—an amateur photographer, but one day I hope to be professional. My mum's doing the styling for the wedding here, that's why they've asked me to take some behind-the-scenes pictures. So, why are you here really?"

"Really?" He tilts his head to one side, still grinning.

I nod.

"My grandma's working on the wedding too."

"Your grandma?"

"Yes, Sadie Lee. She's doing the catering."

"Oh, yes, I've met her." I breathe a sigh of relief. *He's not a crazy person. I've met his grandma. I love his grandma. I won't have to make a citizen's arrest.*

"I gave her a lift here this morning and she said I could hang out for a bit if I stayed out of everyone's way," Noah continues. "So I came through here and saw the guitar and I couldn't resist playing it."

"Are you a musician then?"

He gives me a funny little smile. "No, not really—it's just something I do in my spare time. Are you hungry?"

"What? Oh, yes, a bit."

He jumps down from the stage. The closer he gets, the cuter he gets. His eyes are as dark brown as Sadie Lee's and just like hers they seem to twinkle when he smiles. It makes me feel all strange and light, like I'm made of feathers and could drift away at any minute.

"Let's go get some food from Sadie Lee. But first"—he stares right at me—"can you please say 'tomato'?"

"What?"

"'Tomato.' Please, can you say it for me?"

I grin and shake my head; he is definitely crazy, but good crazy. "OK then, tomato."

"Ha!" He claps his hands together with glee. "*Tom-ah-to*," he mimics. "I love the way you Brits say that. Come on." And with that, he strides off in the direction of the kitchen.

The kitchen now smells amazing, with one counter lined with trays of tiny jam tarts and fairy cakes ready to go into the oven and one lined with trays that have just come out. Sadie Lee is over by the huge sink, rinsing out a mixing bowl.

"Hey, G-ma," Noah calls out to her. "You got any food that needs testing? Me and Penny here are starving."

"Noah!" Sadie Lee exclaims joyfully, as if she hasn't seen him for years. "Penny!" she cries, when she sees me. "You guys have met."

"Yep, Penny caught me pretending to be the wedding singer."

Sadie Lee looks really confused. "Pretending to be the wedding singer but—"

"Never mind—you had to be there, I guess," Noah says, cutting her off, and then he looks at me and winks before turning back to Sadie Lee. "So whatcha got cooking?" He looks at the tray of freshly baked jam tarts hungrily.

"Oh, no you don't," Sadie Lee says, flicking at him with a tea towel. "These are for the wedding."

"What, all of them?"

"Yes, all of them. But if you guys want—"

Just at that moment, Mum bursts into the kitchen. "There's been a disaster!" she cries, causing Noah and Sadie Lee to look instantly alarmed. But I know better; I've seen Mum react like this when she's burned a slice of toast.

"What's up?" I say.

"The tiara has broken," she says, glancing questioningly at Noah, then back at me. "It's snapped right in half and Cindy is adamant that she has to have an authentic Edwardian tiara. I don't know what to do! I've left messages at a couple of vintage stores but—" Mum's phone starts ringing and she slams it to her ear. "Hello? Oh yes, thank you for calling back. I'm looking for a vintage Edwardian tiara—it's for a wedding tomorrow so it's kind of an emergency."

We all watch in silence.

"You do? How much is it? And what kind of condition is it in? Oh, that's brilliant. Thank you. Yes. This afternoon. Thank you, bye." Mum sighs with relief. "OK," she says to us, "there's a store in Brooklyn that has one." Then Mum's smile curves down into a frown. "But how am I going to get to Brooklyn when I've still got the dress fittings for the flower girls? And I've got to check the cake. And meet with Cindy and Jim?" She throws her hands up into the air.

"It's OK," Sadie Lee says, her Southern drawl instantly calm and soothing. "Noah can go pick it up for you."

"Sure," Noah says, nodding.

"Noah's my grandson," Sadie Lee explains.

"Ah, I see. I'm so sorry," Mum says, holding her hand out to Noah. "I didn't even introduce myself."

"No problem," Noah says, shaking her hand. "What's the address for the store?"

As Mum writes it down for him, Noah turns to me. "Want to come with me, Penny, and see some of the Brooklyn sights?"

My heart does a little cartwheel of excitement. I look at Mum. "Would that be OK, Mum? It would be nice to get out for a bit."

Mum barely glances at me; she's distracted by a message on her phone. "Sure, sure."

I go over and take hold of her hands. "It's all going to be OK," I tell her quietly.

She smiles at me gratefully. "Thanks, darling. I'll call the store back and pay for the tiara on my credit card so they don't sell it to anyone else before you get there. Here, take this—it's cold outside." She slips off her jacket and hands it to me, then she looks at Sadie Lee and Noah. "Thanks, guys."

"No problem," Noah says. He turns to me and grins. "Come on then, my lady," he says in a hilarious British accent. "Your carriage awaits."

Chapter Seventeen

We're just by the service lifts when Noah stops in his tracks. "Sorry, I forgot I need to tell Sadie Lee something. Be right back."

As I watch him race back into the kitchen, my brain starts doing that thing where it automatically composes a Facebook update: *Penny Porter is about to go out to Brooklyn with a super-cute New Yorker who looks like he just strolled off the pages of* Rolling Stone *magazine.* I shake my head and laugh. This kind of thing just doesn't happen to me. I'm the kind of girl who falls into holes and tells boys she has fleas and shows the entire universe her worst knickers—in close-up. Maybe this whole thing is a dream. Maybe I'm actually still asleep in Brighton. Maybe it's still the night after the play. Maybe I—

"All righty, let's go." Noah comes bursting out of the kitchen with a grin on his face. He holds something out to me. In his hand are two of Sadie Lee's fairy cakes. "She'll never know they're missing," he says with a grin. "We can be their official food testers. They don't want anyone dropping dead from cake poisoning at the wedding, do they?"

I shake my head. "No, definitely not." I take a bite of the cake, and it's so light and fluffy it practically dissolves on my tongue. "Oh wow!"

Noah nods. "I know. Sadie Lee makes the best cakes in all of New York—if not the world." He calls the lift. "So, what's the most fun thing that's ever happened to you?"

I look at him blankly. "Pardon?"

He laughs. "Oh man, your accent is so cute." The lift arrives and we get in—which is super bad timing as now we're in a really small well-lit space together and there's no way I can hide my blushing cheeks.

"What's the most fun thing that's ever happened to you?" Noah repeats. He takes a woolly hat from his back pocket and pulls it down tight over his head.

"What, ever?"

"Yes."

My mind goes completely blank. As the lift starts zooming down through the floors, it's like a clock counting down: 20, 19, 18 . . . What *is* the most fun thing that's ever happened to me? 17, 16, 15 . . . And then an answer comes to me and I'm so desperate to say something that I blurt it out without thinking: "Magical Mystery Day!"

"Say what?" Noah looks at me.

Oh crap. Now my face actually feels as if it's on fire. "Magical Mystery Day," I mutter, staring intently at the lift display: 10, 9, 8 . . .

"What's Magical Mystery Day?"

5, 4, 3 . . .

"It's a day my parents invented when my brother and I were little. We had it once a year."

The lift arrives in the basement and the door opens. But Noah doesn't move.

"And what happened on Magical Mystery Day?" he asks.

I dare myself to glance at him. To my surprise, he looks genuinely interested. "Well, it would always be on a week-day and we'd be given the day off school. My dad would have made a huge Magical Mystery cake, which we'd eat for breakfast, lunch, and dinner. That was one of the rules—on Magical Mystery Day you had to have cake with every meal. And the other rule was that we had to go on a Magical Mystery Tour."

Noah grins. "Like the Beatles' song?"

I nod. "Yes. Mum and Dad would take out a map and one of us would have to close our eyes and point at a random place and then we'd go off and have an adventure there."

The lift doors close again. Noah quickly presses the button to open them.

"Magical Mystery Day sounds awesome," he says wistfully.

We step out of the lift into a huge underground car park.

"It was," I say, relieved that he doesn't seem put off by my bonkers family tradition. "I used to love the way it was our secret. How everyone else would be at school or work and we'd be feasting on cake and out having an adventure. And I loved the way we never knew when it was going to happen either. Our parents would just spring it on us."

"Like a surprise Christmas Day?" Noah says.

I look at him and grin. "Yes, exactly."

He nods and even in the dim lighting of the car park I can tell he's impressed.

"You mustn't tell anyone I told you, though," I add. "We

were always sworn to absolute secrecy because my parents would have to tell the school that we were off sick."

Noah nods. "The first rule of Magical Mystery Day is: you do not talk about Magical Mystery Day," he says in a deadly serious voice.

"Precisely."

Noah grins. "So, do you guys still do it?"

I shake my head and laugh. "No, we haven't done it for ages. I suppose we grew out of it."

Noah frowns. "How can you outgrow Magical Mystery Day? How can you outgrow cake and adventure?"

I laugh. "Good point."

Noah takes his car keys from his jeans pocket and presses the key tag. A shiny black Chevy truck just ahead of us beeps and the lights flash on and off.

"How old are you?" Noah asks.

"Fifteen—nearly sixteen." Instantly my inner voice starts having a freak-out. *Why did you say "nearly sixteen"? It's going to look like you like him. It's going to—*

"Right, and I'm eighteen," Noah says. "We are definitely not too old for cake and adventure."

We get to the truck and I instantly go to the passenger side. Noah follows me. "What say we make today Magical Mystery Day?" he whispers conspiratorially.

I stare at him. "Seriously?"

He nods and looks around from side to side as if to check that no one's listening. "We've already had some cake, now I can take you on a Magical Mystery Tour of Brooklyn."

I cannot stop grinning now. "That would be brilliant!"

"Awwwwwesome," he corrects in a really strong New

York accent. "You're in the Big Apple now, you have to say, 'That would be awwwwwesome.'"

"That would be awwwwwesome," I say, opening the truck door.

Noah frowns at me. "Oh, are you driving?"

"What? No. Why do you say—oh . . ." I glance inside the truck and see that everything is back to front and I've actually opened the driver's door. But miraculously I don't melt with embarrassment. "Sorry, I forgot you drive on the wrong side of the road here." I slip past Noah to the other side of the truck.

"Hey, we aren't the ones who drive on the wrong side," he calls across the truck to me. "We drive on the right side— literally."

I go to get in the truck and see a battered notepad on the passenger seat. I pick it up and sit down. It feels so weird sitting on this side with no steering wheel in front of me.

"Oh, hey, I'll take that," Noah says, taking the notepad from me as he gets into the driver's seat. He shoves the pad into the glove compartment. I wonder what secrets the pad contains. Maybe Noah's a budding writer. Maybe he's a poet. He kind of looks like a poet with his messy hair and big dark eyes. I glance around the truck, once again getting the strange sensation that I'm in some kind of weird parallel universe. The dashboard is covered with CD cases and guitar picks and there's a knotted string of black beads hanging from the rearview mirror. Even Noah's truck is Rock-God–tastic.

"Most of the world drives on the right-hand side of the road," Noah says, putting the key in the ignition. "It's pretty much only you Brits who drive on the left."

"Just because most of the world does something, it doesn't make it right," I say, putting on my seat belt. "What about war and making kids take science at school and . . . cherry-flavored Coke? Wrong, wrong, wrong."

"Cherry-flavored Coke?" Noah looks at me and raises his eyebrows.

"Extra-wrong!" I say, pulling a fake grimace. "It tastes like medicine."

It's only when Noah pulls out onto Park Avenue that it dawns on me that I've actually got into a car without feeling any kind of panic. It turns out that chiseled cheekbones and twinkly, dimply smiles are an even better distraction than superhero alter egos and breathing techniques. But as soon as we approach the first huge junction, I start feeling jittery. It was OK yesterday in the taxi because I was sandwiched in the back between Elliot and Mum but being in the front—in what should be the driving seat—is making me feel really vulnerable and exposed.

"So, are you in college?" I ask, gripping onto the edge of my seat.

Noah shakes his head. "Nah, I'm taking a break from studying for a while."

"What, like a gap year?"

"Kinda. So, Miss Penny, if you were a musical instrument, what would it be?"

I'm starting to realize that Noah isn't a fan of the standard question. "A musical instrument?"

"Uh-huh."

A taxi goes zooming past us on the inside lane, causing my heart to skip a beat. I close my eyes and try to pretend that we aren't in a car, on a road, potentially about to die. "A cello," I say, simply because the cello is my favorite instrument.

"Figures," Noah says.

I open my eyes just enough to give him a sideways glance. "Why?"

"Because cellos are beautiful and mysterious." Then the weirdest thing happens—Noah's face actually goes bright red. "Anyways, aren't you gonna ask me what instrument I'd be?" he says, looking cool again. I feel all weird inside. Like something important just happened but I'm not quite sure what.

"If you were a musical instrument, what would it be?" I ask.

"Today, I reckon I'd be a trumpet."

"Today?"

"Yes. I go through different instrument phases. Yesterday was definitely a bass-drum day but today I'm feeling way more trumpet."

"I see," I say, not really seeing at all. "So, why a trumpet?"

"Because trumpets always sound so happy. Listen." He presses play on the stereo. The air is filled with the sound of a trumpet playing. Although I don't recognize the piece of music, I've heard enough of my dad's CD collection to know that it's jazz. And Noah's right; the trumpet does sound really cheerful, tootling away. He turns down the volume and looks at me. "We're gonna be crossing the Brooklyn Bridge soon. Have you seen the bridge yet?"

I shake my head. "No, we only got here yesterday. I haven't really seen anywhere yet."

"You haven't?" Noah looks at me. I shake my head again.

"Well, it's a good thing this is Magical Mystery Day then, isn't it?"

I'm just about to reply when a car comes shooting around the corner straight toward me. "Oh no!" I cry, throwing my hands up in fear.

Noah laughs. "It's OK. They're allowed to drive on that side. We drive on the *right* side, remember."

My body is frozen to my seat but my mind is spiraling back to that freezing wet night, the car spinning, Mum screaming, the whole world turning upside down. *Stay calm*, my inner voice urges. *Don't freak out. Think of Ocean Strong.* But my calm voice is fading away and now all I can hear is the screeching of brakes and my voice yelling for Mum and Dad. I bite down on my bottom lip to stop myself from crying. But it's no good; it's like I'm haunted by the accident. I just can't get it out of my head. A raw heat whooshes through my body like a forest fire. I can't swallow, I can't breathe. I need to get out of the car. I feel like I'm going to die.

"I guess it must seem kind of scary, everything being the opposite way around," Noah continues. His voice sounds faint and muffled beneath the ringing in my ears.

I shut my eyes tight and cling onto the seat. I feel tears trickling down my burning face and I want to wail with despair. Why won't this stop? Why does this keep happening? Why can't I get over the accident?

⋆⋅*Chapter Eighteen*⋆

"Hey? Are you OK?" Noah's voice is suddenly louder.

I try to nod my head but my entire body feels paralyzed. I feel the car turning and then coming to a stop. I cautiously open my eyes. We've pulled into a side street, lined with towering buildings. Noah is staring at me; he looks really worried.

"I'm s-sorry," I stammer, my teeth starting to chatter. I've literally gone from baking hot to freezing cold in a couple of seconds.

Noah leans into the back of the truck and fetches a tartan blanket. "Here," he says, placing it on my lap.

I pull the blanket up to my shoulders and hug it around me tightly. "Thank you."

"What just happened?" His voice is so soft and so concerned that it takes everything I've got not to dissolve into tears.

"I'm sorry," I say again. It's all I seem able to say.

Noah pushes his hair back from his face and looks at me intently. "Quit saying that. There's nothing to be sorry for. What happened?"

My body is still shivering violently. I feel crushed by disappointment. I can't believe that after getting through the flight OK, this has happened again. Is this how my life is going to be from now on? Plagued by stupid panic attacks?

Noah opens the glove compartment and starts rummaging around. He pulls out a chocolate bar. "You need some sugar," he says, opening the wrapper and handing it to me.

I make myself take a bite of the chocolate. Noah's right: as it melts on my tongue I do start to feel a tiny bit better. "I'm—"

"If you say 'sorry' one more time I'm going to have to play you Sadie Lee's favorite country ballad," Noah says, "and you wouldn't want that, trust me. It's called 'You Flushed My Sorry Heart Down the Toilet of Despair.'"

I give him a weak smile. "OK, I'm not sorry."

"Good. Now what just happened?"

"I—I was in a car accident a while ago and ever since I've been getting these stupid panic-attack things. I'm so sor—"

"Don't say it!"

I glance at Noah. He's still looking super-concerned.

"That sucks," he says. "You should have said something—before we got in the car."

"I know, but, to be honest, I forgot. I was having such a good time . . ."

"Really?"

I look at Noah and nod. He smiles a little. Then his face goes serious again. "So what do you want to do? Should we leave the car someplace and get the subway? Do you want me to take you back to the hotel?"

"No." Even though I'm still numb from the panic attack,

there's one thing I know for sure—I do not want my adventure with Noah to end.

We sit in silence for a moment—well, New York silence, which means there's still a load of sirens and horns and yelling going on in the background. But weirdly it doesn't feel awkward. Even though I've had a meltdown in front of a boy I really like within an hour of meeting him, it doesn't feel like the times with Ollie in the café or on the beach. For some really bizarre reason, I don't feel eaten up with embarrassment. There's something about Noah that makes me feel safe to be myself.

"I've got an idea," Noah says, finally breaking the silence.

I look at him hopefully.

"How about I carry on driving, but this time I take it real slow and I tell you everything I'm going to do? So if there's a turn coming up, I'll warn you there's a turn coming up, and if I see anything ahead that could panic you, I'll let you know."

I nod. "OK."

"It won't last forever, you know."

"What?"

"Feeling like this. Trust me. You know the saying 'Time's a great healer'?"

I nod.

Noah swivels right around in his seat so that he's fully facing me. "I hated that phrase the first time someone told me it. I thought it was just something people said to try to make you feel better. But it's true. Time is a great healer. You will get better."

There's something about the certainty in his voice and the

way he's looking at me that makes me believe him without a shadow of a doubt. "Thank you," I whisper.

"You're welcome." He turns the key in the ignition. "All righty, shall we do this?"

"Yes," I say, trying to inject as much confidence into my voice as possible.

And so we make our way very slowly through Manhattan, with Noah giving a running commentary like an alternative tour guide, except instead of pointing out the landmarks, he tells me when he's going to "hang a left" or that we're "approaching an intersection."

By the time we get to the Brooklyn Bridge, I feel like I've managed to push a lid down on my jitters, the way you sit on a bulging suitcase to get it shut. And I'm so glad because the bridge is amazing. There are huge Gothic-style archways at either end, like the entrance to an old castle, and the whole thing is encased in steel girders so it's kind of like driving through a long cage—which is great because it makes me feel way safer. The view is breathtaking.

"You OK?" Noah says as we get about halfway across.

I nod, my eyes fixed on the skyline. Whereas the buildings in Manhattan are mainly gleaming mirrored glass or white stone, the Brooklyn skyline is made up of browns and reds, and it looks beautiful against the clear blue sky—like autumn leaves.

"Welcome to my hometown," Noah says as we approach the final archway on the bridge.

I turn to look at him. "Do you live here?"

"Sure do. So, what do you think?"

"I love it. It reminds me of autumn." *Why did you say that? Why can't you just speak normally?* my inner voice instantly yells.

"The colors?" Noah says.

"Yes." I breathe a sigh of relief that he understands what I was trying to say.

"I get that. Your hair reminds me of autumn too."

I look at him questioningly.

"Autumn has all the best colors."

I look away but my mouth won't stop curling into a grin.

As we drive off the bridge, Noah carries on his running commentary of turns and intersections until we get to a way quieter, residential area where the streets are narrower and lined with trees. I begin to properly relax again.

"Thank you," I say, staring out of my side window at the row of tall brownstone houses. "I feel so much better now."

Noah grins at me. "No problem. Let's go get the tiara and then we can get on with the rest of the Mystery Tour."

"Good plan."

Noah turns the corner into a small street lined with quirky-looking cafés and stores. It's like an American version of the Lanes. He pulls into a parking spot and turns to me and smiles. "You sure you're OK?"

I nod. "Yes, definitely."

He reaches over to the backseat for a scuffed leather biker's jacket and puts it on. Then he looks up and down the street, like he's checking for something, before he gets out of the truck, and I follow. It feels good to be outside on solid ground. I take a deep breath of the crisp cold air.

"The store's just up here," Noah says, pointing ahead of us.

As we walk past a secondhand bookshop, the door opens and a girl comes out. She looks at Noah and smiles like she knows him, but he just keeps on marching ahead.

"I think we just went past someone you know," I say, running to keep up with him.

"What?" Noah looks distracted.

"That girl, back there." I turn and look back to see the girl still standing outside the bookshop, staring after us.

"No, I don't think so." He pulls up the collar on his jacket against the cold. "Here we are." We're standing by a store called Lost in Time. The window is crammed full of antique treasures. Noah opens the door and bustles me in. It's like walking into an Aladdin's cave. Everywhere I look I see something that immediately makes me want to take its picture—an old sewing machine, a gramophone, rails of vintage clothes. Elliot would love it here. I feel a wistful pang and wonder how Elliot is doing with Dad. I cannot wait to see him again and tell him all about Noah.

As I follow Noah through the store, I see a beautiful china doll dressed in a dark blue velvet dress with a lace collar that's yellowing from age. Her hair is long and silky and the exact same shade of auburn as mine. She even has some freckles painted onto her nose. The doll is sitting on top of a pile of old books and her head has flopped to one side, making her look really sad. I instantly reach for my camera and take a shot. As the flash goes off, Noah jumps and spins around to look at me.

He instantly relaxes.

"She looks so sad," I say. "I wonder how she ended up here.

I bet she misses her owner." I pick up the doll and straighten out her dress. "I hate the thought of abandoned toys. When I was younger, I wanted to start a toy orphanage. But then it got a bit out of control because every time we went to a school fair or walked past a charity shop I'd want to rescue every toy in there." *Stop rambling*, my inner voice snips. I put the doll back on the pile of books.

"I know exactly what you mean," Noah says.

I look at him hopefully. "You do?"

"Uh-huh. Only with me it's musical instruments. I can't stand it if I see an old guitar abandoned in a thrift store. Instruments were made to be played."

I nod. "Just like toys were made to be played *with*."

"Exactly."

We look at each other and smile and I feel a strange sensation inside of me, like on some invisible level, part of me and part of Noah just slotted together.

We both walk over to the counter at the far end of the shop. An old man with an epic curly white mustache is sitting behind the counter, reading a book. "Yes," he says without even looking up.

"We've come to collect a tiara," Noah says, looking at the scrap of paper Mum gave him, "for a wedding."

"Have you now?" The man slowly puts his book down and peers at us over the top of his glasses.

Noah and I glance at each other and I have to fight the urge to giggle.

"Aren't you all a little too young to be thinking about getting hitched?" The man continues staring at us.

"It's not for *our* wedding," Noah says.

"No—we're not getting married!" I exclaim, a little too forcefully.

Noah frowns at me. "Are you saying you wouldn't marry me?"

"No—I—yes—I . . ." My face starts working its way through the crimson spectrum.

"And after we've been together for a whole"—Noah pauses to look at his watch— "a whole one hour, fifty-seven minutes."

"I'm sorry," I say, playing along with the joke. "I know it's been ages, but I'm just not ready for that kind of a commitment."

Noah looks at the man and sighs. "My heart is broken—broken!"

The man raises his white eyebrows and looks at us. Then he shakes his head and gets up and disappears off into the back of the shop.

Noah and I glance at each other.

"Where's he gone?" I say.

Noah shrugs. "Your cruelty must have really gotten to him. He's probably out back sobbing his heart out. He's probably—"

"Here you are." The man comes back into the shop carrying a flat square box. He puts the box on the counter and takes off the lid. Inside, on a bed of pale pink satin, is a beautiful tiara made of creamy teardrop pearls—it's even better than the original one. I breathe a huge sigh of relief on Mum and Cindy's behalf.

"It's perfect," I say.

Noah nods in agreement.

"I think my mum already paid for it on her credit card," I say to the shop owner.

"She sure did." He puts the lid back on the box and puts the box in a small paper bag.

"Thank you," Noah and I say in unison.

"Welcome," the man grunts, going back to his book.

"Have a nice day," Noah says in a fake cheery voice.

The man doesn't say a word.

"Wow, he was friendly," I whisper sarcastically, as we head to the door.

"That's New York charm for you," Noah whispers back.

I go to open the door and I feel him reach around from behind me to open it for me.

"Don't worry, we're not all like that," he says.

And I don't know why, but there's something about the way he says it that sends a shiver of excitement shimmying up my spine.

★ Chapter Nineteen ★

Stepping out into the icy air helps my pulse return to somewhere close to normal. The sky is now filling with banks of white clouds and people are hurrying by with their heads down against the chill breeze.

"You hungry?" Noah asks.

I nod. Now I come to think of it, I'm absolutely starving.

"OK, I know this great place we can go to that has food and adventure all rolled into one." He looks at me and grins and I get that shivery feeling again.

"Food *and* adventure," I say, trying to joke my way back to un-shivery normality.

"Uh-huh. This place was made for Magical Mystery Day."

"Well then, we must go there immediately."

As we head back to the truck, I see the girl from the bookstore. She's standing outside a café now, chatting on her phone. When she sees us, she starts really staring at Noah again.

"There's that girl, the one I thought knew you," I say.

Noah casts a brief look at the girl and pulls his hat down. "Never seen her before," he mutters, quickening his pace.

As we pass the girl, I glance at her.

"It is," she says animatedly into her phone but still staring at Noah. Then I realize what's going on. He's so striking-looking that this kind of thing must happen all the time. He's literally a girl-gaze magnet. I feel a sudden pang of sorrow. What am I doing having fluttery feelings for someone like Noah? For all I know, he might have a girlfriend. He *must* have a girlfriend. How could the owner of those cheekbones and that smile not have a girlfriend?

"Why the sad face?" Noah asks as we get into the truck.

"I'm not sad," I say as breezily as I can, gazing out of the window. The girl is walking toward us now, still holding her phone.

"OK, let's go," Noah says, quickly pulling out onto the road.

I instinctively grip onto the seat. Thankfully, a call from Mum provides a welcome distraction.

"Did you get it?" she says without even saying hello.

"Yes and it's lovely," I tell her. "Even better than the original."

I can actually hear her sigh of relief.

"Noah and I were just going to get some lunch," I say, praying that she won't need me to come back to help her with anything.

"What's that? Oh, could you hang on a second, darling?"

"Sure."

I hear the shriek of children's laughter. "No dancing on the tables, please," Mum says in a shrill voice. "Sorry, Penny, it's the flower girls—they're very *full of life*. What were you saying?"

"Would it be OK for me to go and get some lunch with Noah?"

"No!" Mum yells. "Do not get chocolate all over your dress! Oh, Penny, I swear, if their mothers don't come back soon I am going to go insane. Yes, of course you can go for lunch, darling. Your dad just texted and he and Elliot have gone off to see a movie in Times Square, so take your time. Have some fun," she says wistfully. The shrieking in the background reaches fever pitch.

"Thanks, Mum. Love you."

"Love you too, sweetheart. No! Do not eat the flowers!"

We're driving through a more industrial area now. Every so often I catch glimpses of the river between the buildings.

"All OK back at the ranch?" Noah asks.

"Yeah. I think my mum might be about to have a nervous breakdown but she said I can stay out as long as I like."

"Awesome." Noah glances at me. "I mean, awesome that you can stay out, not awesome that she's having a nervous breakdown. But don't worry—it's impossible to have a nervous breakdown with Sadie Lee around. She's like a walking, talking, baking, comfort blanket."

I laugh. "Sounds like the perfect grandma."

"Oh, she is." There's something about the serious way Noah says this that makes me instantly look at him, but his face is expressionless and fixed on the road. "So, up at that turn I'm going to hang a left," he says, "and then we're pretty much there."

"Oh." We're surrounded by grim-looking warehouse buildings now, and there are hardly any people around. I can't see anywhere that looks remotely like a hotbed of food and adventure, but maybe once we get around the corner we'll emerge into the heart of a quirky little neighborhood, crammed full of vintage stores and cafés.

Instead, when we get around the corner, we emerge into an industrial wasteland full of garbage Dumpsters and tumbleweed. OK, there isn't actually any tumbleweed, but there should be—it's totally a tumbleweed kind of place.

Noah pulls up outside a warehouse building that looks long abandoned. The walls are crumbling and covered in faded graffiti like old tattoos. Most of the windows are boarded up with sheets of corrugated iron and the few that aren't are lined with heavy metal bars. Even the trees that are dotted about look derelict, leafless, and spindly against the beige brickwork.

"I know it looks kind of sketchy," Noah says in what has to be the understatement of the year, "but once you get inside it's a whole other story."

"We're going inside—there?" I stare at the building. The only time I've seen anything like this before has been in the scariest scenes of really scary movies—usually involving crazed psychos armed with guns. Or, one time, an actual chain saw.

Noah laughs. "You're gonna love it, seriously."

I turn to stare at him. Maybe he really is crazy, and not in a good way. "But w-what—is it?" I stammer.

"I'm taking you to a secret café—for artists," he says.

I admit it; now I'm interested. "Really?"

"Yep. No one knows it's here. They never advertise it. It's strictly invitation-only."

"So how do you know it's here?" Although the idea of an invitation-only, secret café for artists intrigues me, I'm still not fully convinced.

"My dad used to have a studio here," Noah says, taking the keys from the ignition. "The whole building's full of artists' studios. It began in the seventies when the building was empty and a whole bunch of artists started squatting in it. Then, in the nineties, when the authorities wanted to bull-doze it, the artistic community got together to protest and the mayor granted the building a special status."

"Wow."

Noah nods. "This is the real New York," he says wistfully. "Places like this. It's also my favorite place in the world," he says.

I immediately get that fluttery feeling again at the thought of him bringing me to his favorite place in the world.

"And, hey, it seemed like the perfect place for Magical Mystery Day—it's top secret and it has cake."

"It's perfect," I say, and Noah starts to grin.

We get out of the truck and the icy wind is so biting it makes me shiver.

"You cold?" Noah asks.

I nod. "A bit."

He takes off his scarf. "Here." I stand dead still as he puts the scarf around my neck. He's so close to me I daren't lift my gaze from the floor. Then I do look up, and for a split second we're staring into each other's eyes. And *click*—I feel another part of me slotting into place with him.

"Come on." He places his hand gently in the small of my

back and guides me over to a gap in the metal fence surrounding the building.

We scramble down a steep bank covered in weeds and stubbly grass, and over to a large metal door. There's an old keypad next to the door. Noah presses some of the numbers and there's a clicking sound. He pulls the door open and ushers me in. We're standing in a concrete corridor lit by harsh flickering fluorescent strip lights. The one appealing thing is the graffiti on the walls. This graffiti isn't like the faded tags on the outside. These are proper works of art, whole murals stretching all the way along the corridor.

A door in the wall opens and a woman comes out. She's wearing a long tie-dyed dress and her hair is pulled back into hundreds of beaded braids. It's so nice to see someone so bright and colorful and friendly-looking that I'm instantly reassured.

"Noah," the woman cries as soon as she sees him.

"Hey, Dorothy, how's it going?"

"Great. I just found out I've got two pieces accepted for an exhibition downtown."

"That's awesome." Noah gives the woman a hug. Then he turns back to me. "This is my friend Penny. She's come all the way from the UK. I wanted to bring her someplace special for lunch."

Dorothy gives me a warm smile. "Well, you came to the right place. Welcome to New York, honey."

"Thank you."

"OK, I'll catch you guys later—gotta go have a meeting with the gallery. Well done, Noah. I'm so proud of you."

Dorothy gives him another hug and starts heading off along the corridor.

Noah looks really embarrassed as he turns to me. "Come on, let's go eat."

I follow him to a door at the end of the corridor that opens onto a stairwell.

"The café's down in the basement," he explains, holding the door open for me.

"Why was Dorothy proud of you?" I ask as we head down the concrete steps.

"Oh, she was just messing," Noah says.

"What do you mean?"

"I think it was because I was with you."

I look at him blankly.

"Because you're a girl," he says, the tips of his cheeks beginning to flush. "She's always on me that I should have a girlfriend—not that you're my girlfriend," he adds hastily, his cheeks blushing even redder.

"No," I say, and we look at each other for a split second.

He shrugs, and then we carry on walking.

But I can't help feel a glow spread all the way up from my toes. Because even though he's Rock-God–tastic, and even though he lives in a whole other country, on a whole other continent, and even though I'll be going back home in two days' time and will probably never see him again, part of me wants to jump up and down for joy. He doesn't have a girlfriend.

Chapter Twenty

Once we get to the bottom of the stairwell, Noah leads me over to a door.

"It's going to be really dark at first," he says. "Is that all right?"

I nod, but I must look apprehensive, as he instantly takes hold of my hand.

"Don't worry," he says. "It has to be dark to get the full effect."

"OK," I say, not having a clue what he's on about, but it really is OK—anything would be OK right now—his hand holding mine feels so warm and so strong.

"Ready?" he says.

"Yes."

I hear him flick a switch and suddenly we're standing in a beautiful underwater world. At least it feels as if we are. The whole corridor has been painted to look like a seascape. The black walls glimmer with luminous pictures of fish and shells and emerald-green strands of seaweed.

"It's done in a special paint," Noah explains, "so that the

ultraviolet lights in the ceiling make it glow." He looks at me hopefully. "Do you like it?"

"I love it," I say, slowly turning around to take it all in. Every fish, every shell, every tiny detail is a work of art in itself. It's incredible.

"How does it make you feel?" Noah asks quietly.

I turn to look at him. "How does it make me feel?"

He nods. "Yes. My dad used to say that you should always ask yourself how art makes you feel."

I look back at the glimmering walls. "It makes me feel calm and peaceful. And it makes me feel as if I'm in a magical world—as if I'm a mermaid." There's something about the darkness that makes me feel safe to say exactly what I'm thinking rather than try to censor myself for the sake of being cool.

"You look like a mermaid," Noah says.

"Really?"

"Yes, with all that long, curly hair."

I smile. For years, I've felt insecure about my hair—that it's too red, too long, too curly. But now I'm starting to think for the first time that it might not be "too" anything at all.

"I'm kind of glad you don't have the scaly tail, though," Noah says, squeezing my hand.

Oh yes—did I mention he's still holding my hand?

The fluttering feeling returns to the pit of my stomach, as if it's full of fairies all flapping their wings in excitement. "Yes, I'm glad about that too," I say softly.

"Come here—I want to show you something." Noah leads me along the painted seabed, past the picture of a treasure chest overflowing with gold and an old anchor with the name *Titanic* carved on it. "See that starfish?" Noah points to a bright turquoise starfish with a smiley face.

"Yes."

"I painted that."

"What? Really? Did you do all of this?" I stare at him in amazement.

He shakes his head. "No, my dad did. But he let me paint the starfish. I was only about ten at the time."

"That must have been so cool."

"It was. He didn't let me see any of it in the ultraviolet light till he'd finished the whole thing. You know how I brought you down here in the dark?"

I nod.

"That was exactly what he did to me. I'll never forget it." Noah is smiling, but somehow he also looks sad.

"I bet. Well, I'll never forget it either," I say.

He stares at me for a moment and I feel as if he's about to tell me something, but then he lets go of my hand. "Come on, let's go get some lunch."

I follow him along the magical seabed wondering what just happened. At the very end of the corridor there's a picture of an octopus—its tentacles glowing in every color of the rainbow. As we get closer, I can hear the muffled sound of voices and the clinking of cutlery.

Noah turns to me and grins. "Are you ready?"

"Yes."

He reaches out for what looks like the octopus's nose protruding from its face and turns it. A hidden door swings open. The octopus's nose turns out to be the handle.

Noah beckons me to follow him. By this point I'm not

sure what to expect. I feel just like Alice in Wonderland when she fell down the rabbit hole. It wouldn't have surprised me at all to see a mad hatter's tea party on the other side of the door.

"Oh wow!" As I follow Noah into the café, my eyes widen to take it all in. The room is dark and full of mismatching retro chairs, clustered around chunky wooden tables. Candles flicker at the center of each table, wax spilling down the sides of their wine-bottle holders. Apart from a few lamps dotted about the place, this is the only light. The walls are painted deep red and full of framed photos and paintings. It doesn't just look amazing, it smells amazing too—a rich mixture of tomatoes and herbs and freshly baked bread.

"Do you like pasta?" Noah asks.

I nod, too busy drinking in the surroundings to say anything.

"Cool. They do the best pasta here—the chef's Italian. He's the real deal. Let's grab this table." Noah leads me over to a table tucked into an alcove. We sit down on a squishy leather sofa, smiling at one another.

"Happy Magical Mystery Day," Noah says.

"This has been the best Magical Mystery Day ever," I say.

"Well, it's not over yet." Noah grabs the small menu card from the table and moves nearer so that we can both look at it. Once again, I'm conscious of how close we are and I'm so distracted by this fact that all the lettering on the menu blurs into one.

"The lasagna here is incredible," Noah says.

I look up at him and the thought bubble above my head becomes filled with the words "KISS ME." For a split second, as he looks into my eyes and moves his head the tiniest bit closer to mine, I wonder if he's thinking exactly the same thing. But then a guy comes bounding over to our table and the moment is lost.

"Noah, my man!" the guy says. He's tall and thin and wearing low-slung jeans and a skater T-shirt. "Long time, no see. How you been?"

"Oh, you know—busy," Noah replies.

The guy smiles. "I bet."

"Penny, this is Antonio. Antonio, Penny—she's come all the way from the UK to eat here today so you don't wanna disappoint her."

"For real?" The guy looks at me and I nod. "Well then, you guys have got to try my new meatballs." He perches on the edge of our table and leans in close. "The sun-dried tomato sauce is a top-secret recipe handed down from my grandma's grandma. You won't get anything like it outside of Italy."

"All righty, that's sold me." Noah turns to me. "What do you think, Penny?"

"Sounds great."

Antonio looks at Noah and grins. "Man, that accent is cute."

Noah nods and I blush.

Once Antonio has taken our order and disappeared off into the kitchen, I take another look around the café. There are only a handful of other diners—all hipsters, in skinny jeans and faded T-shirts, hunched over laptops or huddled in conversation. It's the most laid-back restaurant I think I've ever seen.

"This place is so cool," I say, speaking my thoughts out loud.

"I knew you'd like it," Noah says.

"Oh yeah? How come?"

"Because I like it."

I raise an eyebrow at him.

"We have a lot in common, you and I."

"We do?"

"Oh yes." Then, just when I feel like something special's about to happen, like he's about to tell me something important, he shifts away from me on the sofa. "Just gotta use the restroom. Be right back."

As I watch Noah walk away, I take a moment to process everything that's happened. It's weird because although on paper there's no way a knicker-flashing, international disaster zone like me should be in this place, with this person, there's something about the way Noah and I fit together that makes it seem like the most natural thing in the world. I decide there and then not to worry anymore about what things look like "on paper." I watch as a girl walks over to an old jukebox in the corner and puts some money in. The song "What a Wonderful World" comes on and I feel so happy it's like every cell in my body has turned into a shooting star. This is Dad's happy song—the one he always plays when we're celebrating something. It seems so perfect—*this* seems so perfect—that my eyes fill with happy tears.

"Penny for your thoughts," Noah says, when he gets back to the table.

"They're worth way more than a penny," I say with a grin.

"Oh, really?" Noah slides back onto the sofa, right up close to me. "How much more?"

"Way out of your price range, I'm afraid."

"Is that so?"

"Yep."

Noah grins at me. "I'd tell you my thoughts if you gave me a penny."

"Really?" I fumble in my bag for my purse and hand him a penny. "Go on then."

"I was thinking, I'm so glad I gave Sadie Lee a lift to work this morning. And I'm so glad I hung around to play that guitar."

My heart starts beating really fast. "Yeah?"

"Yep. That sure was a nice guitar."

"Oh."

He gives me a knowing smile, then looks away.

Chapter Twenty-One

"Your turn," Noah says, handing me back the penny.

"What?"

"Your turn. A penny for your thoughts."

"But I told you—they're worth way more than a penny."

"Oh no." Noah frowns at me and shakes his head. "Once a person's told you their thoughts you have to tell them yours—for the exact same price. That's the rules."

"There are rules?" I pull a fake disgruntled face but my head is filling with nervous chatter. How can I tell him I was thinking "KISS ME"? He'll think I'm a lunatic. I need to make up something else. But I don't exactly have the greatest track record when it comes to thinking up clever things to say to boys on the spot. I make a mental note not to mention anything to do with fleas.

"Go on," Noah says, nodding at the penny in my hand.

My mind goes completely blank. All I can think of is the truth. "I was thinking about how perfect today is." *Oh my God, could you be any more intense?* my inner voice starts yelling.

"You were?" I feel Noah move back toward me.

I nod, still unable to look at him, just in case I've read things all wrong.

"I think—" Noah begins.

"Yo! Meatballs!"

We both jump at the sound of Antonio's voice. He plonks two steaming dishes down on the table. In any other circumstances they would look incredible, but right now I hate those meatballs with their stupid secret sauce and their jaunty sprigs of basil. Why couldn't he have brought them over one minute later? Why couldn't I have heard what Noah was going to say? To make matters even worse, Antonio then hangs around for about FIVE WHOLE MINUTES telling us all about his grandma's grandma and how she grew the most amazing "*to-may-toes*" and how people would come from all over Naples just to try a mouthful of her special sauce. By the time he eventually goes back to the kitchen, the moment has well and truly been lost. I try to wrap some spaghetti around my fork but just as I put it in my mouth, half of it unravels. Of course, it's at exactly this moment that Noah looks at me.

"How's your meatballs?" he asks.

"Mmm, good," I mumble, trying—and failing—to style out the fact that I have about six inches of spaghetti dangling from my mouth like a family of worms. As soon as Noah looks back down at his own dish, I try sucking the spaghetti up through my teeth. Just at that moment, the song playing on the jukebox finishes and the silence is filled with a horrible slurping noise. *My* horrible slurping noise, as the spaghetti shoots up into my mouth, splattering my face with tomato sauce.

Noah looks at me. But instead of mocking me or looking ashamed to be sitting at the same table as me, he loads his own fork with spaghetti and sucks it up into his mouth. A blob of sauce splats onto the middle of his forehead. We both look at each other and crack up laughing, and in that moment I don't just think Noah is drop-dead gorgeous and Rock-God–tastic— I really, really *like* him too, and that feels way more important.

"Here," he says, picking up his napkin. "Let me get that." And he moves closer and gently wipes the tomato sauce from under my eye. And from over my eye. And from my forehead. And from my chin. And from my upper lip. And my lower lip. And . . .

"Seriously?" I say, staring at him. "Did I really get sauce all over my face?"

He shakes his head. "No. I just like dabbing girls' faces with napkins. It's a fetish of mine. Don't worry—my shrink says it's harmless."

Laughing, I pick up my own napkin and wipe the sauce from his forehead.

"Aha, you have the same fetish," Noah says, laughing. "I told you we had lots in common."

We both put our napkins down and carry on eating. Sheer joy has now set up camp in my entire body. Even my toes are tingling.

"So, is your dad still an artist?" I say, determined to find out as much as I can about Noah.

When he doesn't instantly reply, I look up at him. He's stopped eating and is staring down at his plate. "No, no he's not. My dad . . . he's dead. Both my parents are."

I put down my knife and fork, feeling terrible. "I'm so sorry. I didn't realize."

"I know. It's cool." But Noah looks really sad and I want

to kick myself for asking the question. "They died four years ago. So, you know, I'm OK to talk about it."

"Oh." At first I feel completely stuck for something to say—I can't even begin to imagine what it must be like to lose one of my parents, let alone both. Just the thought of it makes me shiver. "So, do you live with Sadie Lee then?"

Noah nods. "Yes, me and my little sister, Bella."

"You have a sister?"

"Uh-huh." Noah's expression immediately softens.

"How old is she?"

"Four—almost five."

"Four? But . . ."

"She was just a baby when they died."

"Oh—that's so sad!"

Noah nods. "I know. But Sadie Lee's a great mom to her and I try to be the world's best big brother." He pushes his plate away and looks at me really intently. "They were killed in a skiing accident—an avalanche. After it happened, it was like I saw the world in a whole new light. Have you ever been asleep and having a really awesome dream and then suddenly it turns into a nightmare?"

I nod—most of my dreams have turned out like that lately.

"Well, that's how my life felt back then. Like, before the accident, everything was safe and fun and nice, and then, after, everything was terrifying. That's why I totally get how you were feeling in the truck. Your accident's made you see how fragile life can be."

"Yes!"

Noah shifts in closer to me. "OK, I'm gonna tell you something pretty embarrassing but, what the hell, I've seen you splatter your face with Antonio's grandma's grandma's tomato sauce." He starts fiddling with the edge of his napkin. "I got real jittery after Mum and Dad died. I was so scared something was going to happen to Bella or Sadie Lee, I'd have to keep checking in with them when I wasn't with them, to make sure they were OK. It got to be a real pain. I could never fully relax when we weren't together."

"Do you still get like that?"

"No, thank God. Sadie Lee figured out something was wrong and she arranged for me to go see a counselor."

"And that helped you get over it?"

Noah nods. "Yeah—that and writing."

I think back to the battered notepad in the truck. "What kind of writing?"

"Just my thoughts, my fears—that kind of thing. There's something so good about just getting it all down on a page."

I'm reminded of how my recent blog posts made me feel and nod.

"You know when I said to you in the truck that time's a great healer?"

"Yes."

"I remember Sadie Lee saying that to me after my parents died and at the time it made me really mad, but it's true. It is." He takes hold of my hand and smiles at me. "You will get over the accident. You won't feel anxious forever. Do you wanna know something my counselor told me that really helped?"

"Yes. Please."

"Don't fight it."

"What do you mean?"

"When you get panicky, don't fight it. That makes it a million times worse. Just say to yourself, 'OK, I'm feeling anxious right now, but that's all right.'"

"And that works?"

"It did for me. My counselor got me to visualize my fear inside my body. She got me to give it a color and a shape and then she'd say, 'Just sit with it and watch what happens.'"

"And what did happen?"

"It would fade away."

"Wow."

We both sit in silence for a moment.

"Well, this wasn't exactly how I'd intended our lunch to go," Noah says, looking apologetic. "Sorry."

"Don't be silly; it's been great. This has really helped—so much. You have no idea. I'd been getting so scared that I was going crazy."

Noah nods. "You're not crazy—not at all—well, only in a very good way."

I smile at him. "Ditto."

My phone starts ringing inside my bag. I want to ignore it. I want to stay sealed in my little bubble with Noah, but I can't.

"Sorry, I'd better take that. Mum might be having an emergency."

Noah nods. "Sure."

But I see from the caller ID that it's Elliot. Feeling a pang of guilt, I send the call to voicemail. I'll explain it all to him later—I'm sure he'll understand. I put my phone back in my bag. "It's OK. It was only Elliot."

"Who's Elliot?"

"My best friend. He's over here with us. He's out sightseeing with my dad."

Noah nods. "Are you sure you don't need to call him back?"

"No, it's fine. I'll see him later."

Noah grins at me. "Cool."

"Yo! Yo! Yo! How were the meatballs?"

Seriously?! Antonio bounds over to our table with a massive grin on his face. I now want to drown him in his grandma's grandma's sauce.

"They were awesome," Noah says.

"Yes, they were great," I say through gritted teeth.

"Awesome!" Antonio sits down on the edge of our table and I want to groan out loud. "So, Noah, you've been busy, my man!"

"Uh-huh." Noah pulls his wallet out of his pocket. "Sorry, dude, we've gotta go. I've got to get Penny back."

Antonio starts clearing up our dishes as Noah takes a load of dollar bills from his wallet. "OK, well, you come by again soon, you hear? It's good seeing you here again."

Noah nods and gets up from the table. As I follow him, I feel a bittersweet mix of relief and disappointment. I'm sad at having to leave this magical place but glad it will mean getting Noah back to myself again.

We say goodbye to Antonio and go back into the underwater corridor. This time, Noah doesn't put the light on immediately.

"I sure am glad I got to go on a Magical Mystery Tour with you, Penny," he says so quietly I can barely hear him.

"I'm glad too," I whisper back.

Then, as he reaches past me to turn the light on, his hand brushes against mine. And although it's the slightest of touches, like throwing a pebble into a pond, the tingling it causes ripples throughout my entire body.

Chapter Twenty-Two

When we step out into the cold daylight, it's like being woken suddenly from a deep sleep. I squint and rub my eyes at the pale winter light. I look at Noah and he looks at me. Everything feels different. Like we went into the old warehouse two completely separate people and came out with an invisible bond between us. He smiles at me.

"Do you wanna go someplace else?"

Just as I nod, his phone starts to ring. He takes it from his pocket. "It's Sadie Lee," he says to me before taking the call. "Hey, G-ma! Yes, all good. Why, what's up? Ah, OK. No problem, see you soon." He ends the call and sighs.

"Is everything OK?" I ask with a definite sinking feeling.

"Yeah. But they want us to come back. Your mum wants to see the tiara and Sadie Lee needs me to take her to go pick up Bella from nursery." He scuffs his foot on the floor. "Can I see you again before you go home? How long are you here for?"

"Just till Sunday." I feel full of dread. Tomorrow I'll be busy all day and night with the wedding, and our flight leaves early on Sunday morning. I won't have time to see him again.

"When on Sunday?"

"First thing in the morning." I look down at the ground.

"No way! So this is it?"

I nod. But my head is full of angry questions. How can this be it? How have I met someone so funny and kind and right for me and only be able to spend a day with him? This is so unfair.

"Well then, I'm gonna have to look into coming over to the UK for my next vacation," Noah says with a grin.

It takes every muscle in my face to smile back at him. We trudge over to the truck and get in.

All the way back to the hotel I feel numb with sorrow and disappointment. On the surface, everything is OK. Noah does his running commentary of driving directions and we exchange small talk, but all I can think is, this is so unfair.

By the time we're back in the underground car park at the hotel, I feel as if I'm going to burst into tears.

"Do you know what an inciting incident is?" Noah says as he turns off the engine.

I shake my head.

"It's the point at the start of a movie where something happens to the hero that changes their life forever. You've seen *Harry Potter*, right?"

I nod.

"Well, the inciting incident in that movie is when Hagrid tells Harry Potter he'll be a great wizard someday and gives him the invite to Hogwarts."

"Oh, right."

Noah looks down in his lap, like he's embarrassed. "I think that's what you might be to me."

"What? A wizard?"

"No! My inciting incident."

I glance at him. In the half-light of the car park, his cheekbones look even more chiseled than ever. "What do you mean?" I ask, hardly daring to believe what I think he means.

"I mean, I think this might be the start of something."

We sit in silence.

"I think you might be my inciting incident too," I say with a small smile.

When we get back up to the wedding suite, I'm amazed Mum and Sadie Lee can't immediately tell something's happened. I feel so excited and alive; I'm surprised I'm not glowing like one of the fish in the underwater mural. But they're both too busy putting the finishing touches on the wedding cake—a fondant husband and wife, dressed in twenties-style clothes.

"Elliot and Dad are back," Mum says. "They're up in their rooms."

"OK." I look at Noah and he looks at me and it feels as if an electrical current is passing between us.

"Are you ready to take me to fetch Bella?" Sadie Lee asks Noah. I feel a pang of sorrow at the thought of him leaving, but it's softened by another thought: we are each other's inciting incidents. This means I have to see him again.

"OK then," Noah says, giving me a knowing smile. "It sure has been fun hanging out with you."

"You too." I instantly feel my face blush.

He brings his arms up as if he's going to hug me, but for some completely ridiculous reason, known only to the God of Awkward Moments, I go to fist-bump him. I've never fist-bumped anyone in my life.

"Oh!" Noah sees my raised fist and quickly meets it with one of his own. Then he grips my hand in his and pulls me in for a gangsta-style shoulder-bump. "I'll call you later," he whispers in my ear.

I nod, hoping he won't notice my burning face.

And then he and Sadie Lee are gone. Before I have time to show the tiara to Mum, her phone rings.

"Hi, Cindy," she says, raising her eyebrows to me.

"Here's the tiara," I mouth, placing the box down on the kitchen counter. "I'm going up to my room."

Mum nods and I walk back out through the wedding suite. By the time I get to the elevator, I have a text from Noah.

> Thank you for an awesome day. Speak to you later. N

I quickly start texting him back.

> Thank YOU xxx

I look at the text and frown. Three kisses is way too many. Especially when he didn't send me any. I delete the kisses. Now the text looks really blunt and unfriendly. I add a smiley-faced emoticon. But it looks too immature. Maybe if

I did a winky face . . . ? No, no, that looks way too suggestive. I delete the winky face and add a P for Penny. Now it looks like I'm copying exactly what he did. I need to show that I have some kind of originality and flair. Three lifts come and go, but I'm still standing there, typing and deleting, typing and deleting. How can I create an original and mature impression without seeming too keen or too formal? In the end, I go with: "Thank YOU, Penny" and I add a thumbs-up emoticon. Which seemed like a great idea until the moment I pressed send.

As soon as I get to my room, I go straight over to the adjoining door.

"Elliot, are you in there?"

I open the door. Elliot is lying facedown on his bed, fast asleep. I carefully shut the door and go over to my own bed. Then I lie down and stare up at the ceiling. I want to savor this feeling for as long as I can. I close my eyes and hug one of my pillows to me as I replay every moment of the day in my head. *Thank you, thank you, thank you*, I whisper to the God of Inciting Incidents.

Then, when I realize I'm far too excited to fall asleep, I go over to my suitcase and pull out my laptop. Carefully avoiding my email and social networks, I go straight to my blog and sign in. There are now over four hundreds comments on my post about facing fear. I "like" them all and reply to the girl who'd been scared of her mum's drinking. Then I open up a new post and start to type.

22 December

From Fear to Fairy Tale

Hey, guys!

Wow, you are all so amazing. I've just been reading your comments on my last post and they're making me cry——but in a really good way.

I used to feel so alone before I started this blog. I used to feel like no one really understood me (apart from Wiki, of course). But reading your comments has made me realize that actually hundreds——and maybe even thousands (!)——of you totally get me.

And that makes me feel so happy.

And un-alone *(is "un-alone" a word . . . ?!)*.

And that, actually, even though I sometimes feel as if I'm the only person who struggles with this thing called "life," I'm not.

166

Thank you for being so honest about your fears——and so brave in facing them.

And please keep posting your updates because I'm sure they'll help every-one reading this to face their own fears too.

But, guys . . . something has happened to me since I faced my fear and got on a plane.

Something truly amazing.

And I want to share it with you because the Glass Slipper Moment I was telling you about has actually come true.

Not in the way I thought it would——never in my wildest dreams would I have imagined things turning out the way they have!

Because what happened next has made me wonder if maybe when you confront your worst fear, you enter some kind of magical parallel universe where all kinds of things are possible——because I've met a boy.

A boy that I really like.

And I think he really likes me!

And for all the new followers of this blog *(thank you, by the way!!)* you might want to check out my previous posts <u>Disastrous and Dateless</u> and <u>Pothole of Doom</u> to see that this kind of thing doesn't happen to me. Ever!

I'm the kind of girl who falls into holes and starts jibbering like a nervous wreck in front of boys. They never like me——not *like* like me.

They only ever want to be my friend. Or give me Chinese burns. Or make fun of me.

But this morning I met a boy who seems to *like* like me *(I'm going to call him Brooklyn Boy)*. And it feels amazing because I haven't had to pretend to be something I'm not. I haven't had to try to be cool. I've totally been myself——and he still likes me.

Earlier today I was in a car with Brooklyn Boy and I started getting anxious again——in front of him.

But he didn't think I was a freak. In fact, he was really lovely and he gave me some really cool advice that I want to share with you.

First of all, he told me that time is a great healer and that nothing lasts forever, not even the very worst things. And he should know because he lost two of the people closest to him a few years ago.

He also told me that when he lost those people, it made him get really anxious about losing the other people he loved. In the end he went to see a counselor who gave him an exercise to do whenever he started getting fearful.

Basically, it's that whenever you get fearful or anxious you shouldn't fight it. You should just . . . watch it in your body.

So, if your fear is making you feel all tense in your head, or sick in your stomach, or tight in your chest, you have to picture it as an actual shape and give it a color. And then just think to yourself that it's OK to feel anxious and just allow it to be and it will start to fade away.

I haven't tried it myself yet but Brooklyn Boy says it really helped him.

So, for all of you who posted about feeling anxious about different things, why don't you try it yourself next time you feel that way? And I will too and then we can report back here on the blog.

I don't know what the future is going to hold for me and Brooklyn Boy——
I'm only here for another day——boo! ☹

But I feel like something really special has happened between us.

And so I can't believe that this is it. That I'll never see him again.

Charming didn't give up on Cinderella, did he? He kept on searching and searching until he was reunited with her and her slipper.

Because when you find someone who really likes you for you, and you really like them for them, you have to do all you can to not lose them.

I love you guys so much and I'm so grateful for all of your support.

Keep posting about facing your fears——and keep believing in fairy tales.

Girl Online, going offline xxx

Chapter Twenty-Three

"What, in the name of Godzilla, have you been up to?"

I open my eyes to see Elliot staring down at me through a pair of glasses with stars-and-stripes frames.

"What time is it?" I mumble, looking over to the window. It's now dark outside and the New York skyline is twinkling away like the window of a jeweler's shop. I must have slept away the whole rest of the afternoon.

"Time you told me what the hell you've been up to." Elliot plonks himself down on my bed. "*Who* is Brooklyn Boy?"

"Oh." I look at my laptop on the pillow next to me and everything comes back. Elliot must have read my blog post.

"I met him earlier. His grandma is doing the catering for the wedding."

"What, and now you're in love?"

"No, I . . ."

Elliot takes his phone from his pocket and starts reading from it. "'Because when you find someone who really likes you for you, and you really like them for them, you have to do all you can not to lose them.'"

I cringe. It feels so over-the-top now that Elliot's reading it in his most sarcastic voice. It also feels kind of unreal now that I've had a sleep, like maybe I dreamed the whole thing.

"Have you been drinking?" Elliot looks at me over the top of his glasses like a very stern doctor.

"No!"

"Brainwashed by a crazed cult?"

"No!"

"Then how can you be in love with this guy if you only just met him?"

"I'm not in love with him." Disappointment starts seeping through my body like an icy fog. "We spent most of the day together and we really connected." Oh God, now I sound like a gushing Hollywood actress being interviewed on *Oprah*.

Elliot frowns so hard I think his glasses might fall off. "You really connected?"

"Yes. We have a lot in common."

"So, how old is he?"

"Eighteen."

"Where does he go to college?"

"He doesn't."

"Oh, so what does he do?"

"Nothing. I don't know. I think he's on a gap year." I'm beginning to feel like I'm being cross-examined by one of Elliot's lawyer parents.

"Right, so you've met your soul mate but you didn't actually find out what he does."

"I was only with him for a few hours."

Elliot gives me a knowing smile. He's starting to really

wind me up now—why's he being so mean? And to think I'd been looking forward to telling him all about Noah.

"We didn't really bother with small talk," I continue.

"Oh, really. So do your parents know about this?"

"No! There's nothing to know." I look at Elliot in alarm—he'd better not tell them.

"How can you say there's nothing to know when you've put it all over the Internet?"

I sit up straight in bed and glare at him. "I haven't put it all over the Internet. I blogged about it, that's all. I thought it might help people facing their fears. He gave me some really good advice."

Elliot glares back at me. "What about how I helped you on the plane? Why didn't you blog about that?"

Suddenly, the truth dawns on me. Elliot's jealous because he didn't get a mention. "Oh, Elliot, I'm always blogging about you. What about the time you helped me pick a dress for the school prom? And the day you told me top-ten ways to style out a fall. I blogged about them, didn't I?"

But Elliot just stares sulkily at the bed. "I can't believe you blogged about him before telling me," he mutters. "If I'd met someone who liked me for me, I'd have totally told you first."

Now I feel really bad. I lean forward and touch him on the arm. "I did try to tell you. I've been dying to talk to you about it all day, but when I got back up here you were asleep."

Elliot looks at me. "You could have woken me. And you could have returned my call earlier."

"I'm sorry." I feel heavy with disappointment now. "There's no point getting all moody about it—I'll probably never see him again."

There's a long, awkward silence and then Elliot places his hand over mine. "I'm sorry. It was just that when I got your blog update it made me feel a bit weird—a bit left out."

"I could never leave you out of anything. You're my best friend." I pull Elliot into a hug.

Although Elliot and I have patched things up, I can't help but feel slightly dejected. I so wanted to be able to talk through everything with him, to relive my magical day all over again, but how can I if it's going to make him upset? Before either of us can say anything, there's a knock on the door.

"Hey, daughter of mine," Dad yells in a fake American accent even worse than Ollie's. "D'ya wanna go eat?"

Dinner should have been really fun. We ended up going to Chinatown, to this restaurant called The Cheery Chopsticks, where the waiting staff were like pantomime actors. Everything they did was a grand performance, from the way they helped us off with our coats to the way they delivered the food to our table. But I couldn't relax. Although Elliot was pretty much back to his normal self and Mum finally seemed relaxed about the wedding and actually looking forward to the big day, all I could think was, I shouldn't have blogged about Noah. Elliot's reaction had totally unnerved me. He's never been negative about a blog I've posted in the whole time I've been writing Girl Online. Maybe it was really over-the-top and silly to write what I did. Maybe I read way too much into what happened with Noah. Maybe I just imagined the connection between us.

By the time we get back to the hotel, I'm determined to delete the post as soon as I get to my room. With every step we take along the plushly carpeted corridor, all I can think is, *Delete, delete, delete.*

"What's that outside your room, Pen?" Mum says.

Delete, delete, delete. "What?"

"Did you order some room service?" Dad asks.

"Pretty weird room service," Elliot mutters.

I look up and see a brown cardboard box on the floor by my door.

"Uh-oh! You don't think it's a bomb, do you?" Elliot says, looking at us all with wide eyes.

I frown at him. "Why would someone put a bomb outside my room?"

Elliot shrugs. "I don't know. They might not be targeting you directly. They might have just chosen a room at random."

I shake my head. Even though I am one of the unluckiest, most accident-prone people on the planet, I really think having my hotel room randomly bombed would be a step too far.

"It's not a bomb," Dad says. "It's probably been left there by accident. We can call down to Reception and see if they know anything about it. Oh . . ."

I watch as Dad picks up the box. "What is it?"

"It is for you—look."

Instantly, my heart begins to pound. Could it be from Noah? Who else knows I'm here?

I go over to Dad and take the box from him. The handwritten label on the top says, *To Penny, Happy You-Know-What Day! N*

"Who's it from?" Dad says, looking suspicious.

"Noah," I mutter, my cheeks immediately flushing red.

"Who?" Dad says.

"Noah," I repeat.

"Yes, I got that, but Noah who?"

"He's Sadie Lee's grandson," Mum explains. "Penny went with him to get the replacement tiara today."

"So, what's in the box?" Dad asks, raising his eyebrows.

"I don't know," I reply. They all stare at me, waiting for me to open it.

"I'm going to go to bed," I say. "I'm feeling really tired."

Dad looks at Mum and raises his eyebrows again. She smiles at him and shakes her head as if to say, it's OK. I breathe a sigh of relief.

"See you guys in the morning," I say, quickly getting my key card from my bag.

"Yes, bright and early," Mum says.

"But—" Elliot begins.

"Night!" I say, and I slip through my door and shut it behind me before any of them can say another word.

My heart's still pounding: what could it be? I check my phone to see if Noah's texted but there's nothing. I open the top of the box and peer inside. I see a load of silky auburn hair and I gasp—the doll!

I also notice an envelope taped to the inside of the lid. I open it and pull out a note.

Dear Penny,

So, I went back to the store and just as I was walking past the doll she told me that it is her greatest dream to be adopted by a kindhearted British girl with really cute hair and freckles just like hers. It was such a heartfelt plea that I just couldn't resist—even though it meant having to talk to the Store Owner from Unfriendly Hell twice in one day. This time he said to me, "Son, don't you think you're a little too old to be playing with dolls?" I told him I hoped that one day I'd be just the right age for something—marriage, dolls, whatever. He wasn't amused.

I've also enclosed a piece of Sadie Lee's famous devil's food cake (just to make sure you stick to the Magical Mystery rules and have cake with every meal).

N

I pull out the doll and a huge slab of cake wrapped in silver foil. I sit the doll on my pillow. She already looks so much happier, gazing at me through her glassy green eyes. Then I get that fluttery feeling again and all of the stress of the evening begins to fade. Noah really is lovely and he really does like me. I hadn't imagined our connection after all.

★ ·*Chapter Twenty-Four*· ★

I'm just about to text Noah when I hear a gentle tapping on the adjoining door.

"Pen, can I come in?" I hear Elliot call.

"Of course," I reply.

The door opens and Elliot pads over to me. He's wearing his pajamas, a backward Yankees cap, and no glasses, which makes his face look even thinner.

"Hi," he says, scanning the bed, obviously looking to see what was in the box. His gaze falls on the doll. "No way!" he exclaims. "Is that what he sent you?"

I nod and, even though I'm trying to play it cool, my mouth involuntarily curls into a grin.

"She's beautiful!" Elliot sits down on the bed and picks up the doll.

"I know. We saw her in the vintage store earlier—when we went to pick up the tiara. I told him how abandoned toys always make me sad. He sent a note saying she wanted me to adopt her." My face flushes with embarrassment and I wait for Elliot to make some kind of mocking comment, but he doesn't. He just keeps on smiling at the doll and smoothing down her hair.

"Look at the dress. It must be Victorian. Do you know how much it cost?"

I shake my head.

"It won't have been cheap. This is no Barbie, my dear."

"I know."

"Oh my God! Did he send you that cake too?" Elliot's eyes go even wider as he spots the devil's food cake.

"Yes. His grandma made it. She's an amazing cook."

Elliot puts the doll back on the pillow and smiles at me. "OK, OK, I'm starting to see why it was love at first sight. Go on then."

"What?"

"Tell me all about it."

So we get under the duvet, and I tell him all about my magical day with Noah. When I get to the bit about his hand brushing mine, Elliot actually starts waving his hands up and down in excitement. I decide against telling him about the inciting incident, though—I want to keep that just between me and Noah.

"Holy swoon-gate!" Elliot exclaims when I finally get to the end of my tale. "If that's what Brooklyn boys are like I'm emigrating as soon as possible!"

I laugh and break off a piece of Sadie Lee's cake and pop it into my mouth. It's so soft it feels like velvet on my tongue.

"I'm sorry I was such a grump earlier," Elliot says. "I totally get why you were so excited now."

As soon as he says this, I think of my blog post. In all of

the excitement of the special delivery from Noah, I completely forgot to delete it.

"That's OK," I say. "I should have told you before I blogged about it."

We look at each other and grin and I'm filled with a wave of relief that everything is back to normal between us.

"OK, I'm going to let you get some sleep," Elliot says, getting up from the bed. "You've got a big day ahead."

"I'm really sorry. I've hardly got to hang out with you."

"That's OK. I've been having a great time with your dad and tomorrow we're going to the Statue of Liberty *and* on a ghost tour."

"A ghost tour?"

"Yep. It's going to be epic—it even includes a visit to the hidden tomb of twenty thousand yellow-fever victims."

I start to laugh. "Cool . . . I think."

As soon as Elliot's gone back to his room, I pick up my phone and a blanket from the bed and go over to the armchair by the window. Once again, the view takes my breath away. And once again I get that can-this-really-be-happening-to-me feeling. I wrap the blanket around me and snuggle into the chair. Then I click on Noah's number and press call. With every long purr of the American ring tone, my nervousness ramps up a notch. Thankfully, he answers it after just three.

"Hey," he says softly.

"Hey. Thank you so much for the doll." I feel awkward all of a sudden, too formal, too polite.

"You're very welcome. So, tell me, Miss Penny, are you by a window right now?"

"Yes! Right by one."

"Have you seen the moon?"

"No, hang on." I open my window and peer out. A huge, perfectly round moon is suspended right over the Empire State Building. But it's not the size or shape that takes my breath away, it's the color. It's glowing bright amber. "Oh my God, it looks amazing! Why's it so orange?"

"Well, I thought it might have been spray-painted by aliens or something but, according to Sadie Lee, it's something to do with pollution in the atmosphere."

"Oh. I think I prefer the alien theory."

"Me too. So listen. Given that you appear to have done something very strange to me—"

"What do you mean?"

"Well, I don't exactly make a habit of buying china dolls, you know?"

I laugh.

"I think it only right and fair that you see me one more time before you go," he continues.

"I'd love to—but when?"

"How about I swing by after the reception? Sadie Lee says it'll all be over by midnight. I have something really cool planned."

I instantly think of my parents. Somehow I hardly see them letting me head off into New York at midnight with a boy I've only just met.

"And don't worry—we won't be leaving the hotel," Noah says, as if reading my mind.

"I'd love to." I say it so quickly the words practically blur into one. I wrap the blanket more tightly around me and imagine that I'm in Noah's arms.

"So, I'll see you tomorrow then," Noah says softly.

"Yes. See you tomorrow."

"Goodnight, Penny."

"Goodnight, Noah."

I put down my phone and take a deep breath. Then I look out onto the New York skyline and gaze up at the incredible moon. I feel so different—and it's not just about meeting Noah or being in New York. It's that for the first time ever I feel as if my life is my own—that I'm in charge of my own destiny. I'm no longer just reacting to what everyone else does or says. With Noah as my inciting incident, I'm finally writing my own script.

Chapter Twenty-Five

When I wake up the next day, I have that Christmas-morning feeling. Like I know before I've even opened my eyes that something really lovely is going to happen before I've remembered what it is. And then, in seconds, it all comes flooding back. Noah—I'm going to see Noah. I open my eyes and see the doll staring right at me. She's fallen over in the night and is now lying facing me on the pillow.

"Good morning!" I say to her, because I'm so overexcited I'll even talk to a doll. "Did you sleep well?"

I imagine the doll saying, *"No actually, I slept terribly because my eyes are glued open. How would you sleep if your eyes were glued open?"*

OK, I need to get up.

I have a shower, then I sit cross-legged on my bed with a towel around my wet hair and open my laptop. I feel really nervous as I wait for my blog to load. What if my readers thought my last post was stupid and over-the-top? What if I've got some negative comments?

But I needn't have worried—the comments are all even

lovelier than ever, most of them containing little red heart emoticons and demands for more details about Brooklyn Boy.

I'm just about to see if Elliot is awake when I get a text message. *Please, please, please be from Noah*, I silently plead. As I pick up my phone, I notice the doll gazing at me from where I've sat her up on the pillow. "*Oh, purlease*," I imagine her saying. I take a deep breath and try to be cool, but as soon as I see that the text is from Noah, the fluttering begins.

> I dreamed that I was taking you all around New York and every place we visited turned into cake. What could this mean?! N

I quickly text back.

> That you've been struck by the Curse of Magical Mystery Day . . . ? Sounds amazing, though. Imagine if the Empire State Building turned into cake!

> Have you looked outside yet?

No, why? Has the moon turned green?

I go over to the window and pull back the curtain. Feathery flakes of snow are tumbling from the sky. The buildings down below look as if they've been sprinkled in icing sugar.

Oh wow——it looks so beautiful!

Yep——now it feels like Christmas! Have a great day and see you at midnight!

You too!

Even though I think it's going to be the slowest, dullest day in history because I'm so excited to see Noah, the wedding is actually really good fun. As the guests start to arrive, the suite becomes more and more like *Downton Abbey*. The men look so handsome in their black and grey dress suits with their hair all slicked back. And the women look stunning. Every twenties-style dress is a work of art, made from satin and lace and the most intricate beading, all in the most beautiful muted shades like lavender, emerald, and plum. Even the children are in costume, looking just like china dolls in their ruffles and buttoned-up boots. I can't help feeling a bit wistful as I look down at my own servant's costume—a plain, starchy black A-line dress with an even starchier white apron over the top of it.

While the professional photographer takes some posed shots of the groomsmen and the guests, I sneak around with my much smaller camera, taking impromptu shots. I get a few lovely close-ups of the detail on some of the dresses and a super-cute shot of two of the flower girls whispering in each other's ear. Then, just as someone announces the bride's arrival and the guests all rush to their seats, I take a really romantic picture of Jim at the top of the aisle, looking so nervous and hopeful and handsome as he waits for Cindy to appear.

In the end, they decide not to put on British accents to read their vows, which I'm really glad about. The vows are so beautifully written and heartfelt. They've added in all these really fun, personal details like Cindy promising not to moan about Jim watching baseball and Jim promising to learn to love reality TV. By the time the ceremony's over, I'm a gooey emotional wreck.

As the guests all start tucking into the wedding breakfast, Mum pulls me over to one side. Her eyes are bright and sparkly and she's grinning from ear to ear.

"Pen, you'll never guess what! I've been asked if I'll theme a party. Here in New York."

"What? When?"

"Next week." Mum looks over at the head table. "You know the maid of honor—the big lady with all the hair?"

"Yes."

"Well, it's her thirtieth birthday on the day before New Year's Eve and she's asked if I'll help her organize a mods-and-rockers theme for it."

"Wow! But—but we're flying home tomorrow. How are you going to do it?" I get a horrible sinking feeling at the prospect of Mum staying here and us all having Christmas at home without her.

"She's said she'll pay for us to all stay on longer—to have Christmas and New Year in New York. And they'll pay for us to rearrange our flights too. These people are seriously rich, Pen, money's no object to them."

I stay rooted to the spot as I try to process the news. "We're going to stay here for Christmas?"

Mum nods. "Yes. I've called your dad and he's fine about it."

As soon as I start feeling excited, my brain instantly starts searching for reasons why this can't possibly happen—why it has to be too good to be true. "But what about Tom? And what about Elliot?"

"Elliot can stay too," Mum says with a smile. "Well, hopefully he can; I'll need to call his parents. And Tom will be fine. He texted me this morning asking if he can spend Christmas with Melanie and her family."

I'm now so excited I feel like dancing the conga all the way through the dining room. I don't, though, because there are way too many trip hazards.

I'll be spending Christmas and New Year in New York. I'll be able to see Noah. My life cannot possibly get any better.

"And Sadie Lee has invited us to spend Christmas with her, at her home in Brooklyn," Mum says, instantly proving me wrong. My life can and did just get a trillion times better.

Elliot and Dad join us for the evening reception. Elliot looks amazing in a vintage suit and cravat. I look down at my servant's attire and sigh. It's hardly what I'd have chosen to see Noah in—I feel so dowdy, but at least I look in character. We all gather around as Cindy and Jim start their first dance together as husband and wife. Cindy has changed into a stunning twenties flapper dress. It's made of shimmering silver-blue satin, which changes color in the twinkling lights like a moonstone. As I watch the band play the opening chords of "Unchained Melody," my skin tingles as I think back to yesterday, when I first spotted Noah sitting on that same stage in the dark. It's only three hours till midnight now. As I glance at the ornate clock on the wall, I feel even more like Cinderella—only in my case I'm looking forward to midnight, rather than dreading it.

"Penny, why haven't you gotten changed?" Mum whispers in my ear.

I turn to face her. "What do you mean? Into what?"

Mum frowns. "I thought I told you about the dress. Didn't I tell you abut the dress?"

I look at her blankly.

"Oh my goodness! I must have been so busy I completely forgot." Mum grabs my arm.

"Downstairs, in my room, there's a dress for you."

"What kind of dress?"

Mum smiles. "You'll see."

"But don't I have to stay in theme?"

"You will be." Mum's smile gets increasingly mysterious and she passes me her key card.

"OK then."

I turn to go—and quickly snap a picture of one of the flower girls crawling under a table, clutching a chicken leg.

As soon as I walk into Mum and Dad's room, I start to laugh. Dad's side of the room is practically empty, apart from a copy of a sports biography on his bedside table and his suitcase placed neatly against the wall. Mum's side looks like a tornado has hit it—a clothes and cosmetics tornado. I pick my way through the chaos and go over to the bed.

There, laid out on top of the covers, is a beautiful flapper dress. It's made from emerald-green silk, with a beautiful fringe of silver beads around the bottom. There's a matching beaded headband lying on the bed next to it and a pair of black Mary Jane shoes. I can't believe that's really for me, but there's a note on the hanger marked: FOR PENNY.

I'm so excited I can barely breathe. But then, of course, my good old inner voice starts going to town. *What if it doesn't fit you? What if it looks stupid on you?* However, as I pick up the dress, I can't imagine it looking stupid on anyone. I wriggle out of my starchy servant's outfit and pull the dress over my head. The material feels so soft it gives me goose bumps as it brushes against my skin. I actually gasp out loud when I see my reflection in the full-length mirror. The dress fits me perfectly and makes me look so grown-up and so—well, so *interesting*, like an old movie star. I put on the shoes and then look at my hair. I'd tied it up in a bun for my servant look but it's not really working with the dress.

I shake it loose and grab a brush from Mum's dressing table. Once I've got it under control, I plait both sides and pull them up into a milkmaid braid. Then I place the headband on top. Finally, I sit down at Mum's dressing table and put on some liquid eyeliner and some more mascara. A quick dusting of powder and a squirt of perfume and I'm finished. I go over to the full-length mirror for a final check.

I suddenly get a flashback to the day I was getting ready to go and meet Ollie, and how nervous and unsure I'd felt. Now I look at myself and I can't stop grinning. It's hard to believe that was only a week ago—it feels like a whole lifetime. And I feel like a whole new person. I put on the shoes, pick up my bag, and head for the door.

Chapter Twenty-Six

When I get back to the wedding suite, I find Mum and Dad and Elliot sitting at a table in the corner of the reception room.

"Darling!" Mum says.

Dad gapes at me. "You look . . ."

"Flapper-tastic!" Elliot exclaims.

"Thank you!" I do a twirl and the beaded fringe at the bottom of the dress fans out around me. Then I sit down with them. "Thanks so much, Mum."

"My little girl's growing up," Dad says wistfully.

"Dad!" I say, blushing with embarrassment.

"OK, I need to try calling my parents again," Elliot says. "Keep everything crossed that they say I can stay for Christmas."

Mum and I immediately cross our fingers. Dad crosses his eyes.

"So, Sadie Lee tells me that Noah's coming by to see you later," Mum says as soon as Elliot's left.

I nod.

"Hmm, I think I'd better meet this Noah," Dad says.

"You will," Mum replies. "We're going to be spending Christmas with him."

Just hearing her say this makes a heavenly chorus ring out in my head. Then I realize it's the text notification on my phone. The text is from Noah.

> So, any chance you can escape from the party early? I don't normally like long goodbyes but this time I'll make an exception. (I told you you're making me act all weird!) N

> How early?

> Now early?

> Are you here?!!

Yes——in the service car park. Just say the word and I'll come meet you in the kitchen . . .

Mum and Dad are getting up to dance.

"That was Noah," I say. "He's here already. Would it be OK if I go and see him in the kitchen?"

"Of course," Mum says.

"Bring him through here," Dad says over his shoulder as he leads Mum to the dance floor. "I'm sure Cindy and Jim won't mind."

I slip off into the kitchen and find Sadie Lee wiping down one of the huge stainless-steel counters. I've barely seen her all day as she's been holed up out here overseeing all of the meals.

"Hello," I say.

"Hello, sweet girl." Sadie Lee turns to me with a beaming smile. Her face is slightly flushed and a few strands of grey hair have made their way out of her bun but apart from that she still looks effortlessly chic. She looks me up and down. "Why, don't you just look adorable!"

"Thank you, it's my evening attire."

"It's beautiful, that's what it is. Let me get a look." Sadie comes over to take a closer look at the beading on my dress. "You look just like a picture I have at home of my grandmother. She was one of the original flapper girls. Oh my! Noah's eyes are going to pop right on out of his head when he sees you."

At the mention of his name, I instantly blush and feel super-self-conscious. "He just texted me to say he was here——in the car park."

Sadie Lee nods and gives a knowing grin. "I know. He's on his way up."

"Thank you for inviting us to spend Christmas with you."

"Oh, honey, you are so welcome. I love having a full house at Christmas. It will be just like—" She breaks off and I guess she must be thinking about Noah's parents.

"I was so sorry to hear about—about the accident," I say quietly, hoping that it isn't too forward of me.

She gives me a sad smile. "Noah told you?"

I nod.

"He's very taken with you, you know."

I smile back at her. "I—I really like him too."

Sadie Lee comes closer, and her voice takes on a more urgent tone. "I'm so glad he's met someone he can talk to. He's under—"

"Hey, what's up? Oh my!" I turn to see Noah staring at me, his eyes wide.

"What did I tell you!" Sadie Lee nudges me. "Popping right out of his head."

"You look—majestic!" Noah says, still standing rooted to the spot over by the door.

"Thank you," I say shyly. "So do you."

Noah's wearing black skinny jeans and a scuffed leather biker jacket, over a pale grey hoodie. His hair looks shinier and softer than yesterday, like it's freshly washed, and his eyes look even chocolatier than I remember them. As he starts to smile, the dimples return on either side of his mouth. He looks so cute I can't decide whether I want to hug him or take a picture of him.

"Do you have it?" he says, glancing quickly at Sadie Lee before returning his gaze to me.

"Sure do," she says, bringing a wicker picnic hamper out from under the counter.

"I was wondering," Noah says to me in a fake posh voice, "if you would like to accompany me on a picnic."

"A picnic?"

"Uh-huh—but not just any old picnic," he says with a twinkle in his eye.

"Oh no?" I say, playing along.

"No. I'm talking about a moonlit picnic."

Instantly my heart sinks—there's no way Mum and Dad will let me leave the hotel.

"On a secret roof terrace," Noah continues. "Right behind this very kitchen."

"Really?"

"Really."

Sadie Lee starts to chuckle.

"I would be honored," I say. I look at Sadie Lee. "Please could you tell my parents where I've gone? They're through in the reception, probably embarrassing themselves on the dance floor."

"Sure thing, honey." She looks at Noah, concerned. "But isn't she going to freeze out there, in that dress?"

He shakes his head. "Don't worry, G-ma, I've got it covered."

"Now why doesn't that surprise me?" Sadie Lee says with a chuckle. "OK, y'all have fun—and don't go keeping her out there too long. We don't want her folks thinking she's been abducted."

Sadie Lee heads off into the reception room, leaving Noah and me alone.

"So," he says, bringing the hamper over to me.

"So." I feel so self-conscious I have to look at the floor.

"If you could invite any fictional character to a picnic, who would it be?"

I instantly smile. Noah's random questions are definitely great icebreakers. "Augustus Waters from *The Fault in Our Stars*," I say. "So I could bring him back to life."

"Great answer," Noah says. "I'd bring that sappy guy from *Twilight*—so I could kill him."

I laugh and look up at Noah, and the second our eyes meet I feel a kind of jolt inside. It's so powerful it almost takes my breath away.

He smiles and looks away. "It's good to see you again."

"You're welcome," I say. I don't know why I say it—well, I do: it's because I'm an International Embarrassment Waiting to Happen, cursed by the God of Awkward Moments.

"I'm welcome?"

"No."

"I'm not welcome?" Noah tilts his head to one side and grins at me.

"Yes, you are—it's just—I—I didn't mean to say that. I don't know what . . ." I turn away slightly, so he doesn't get third-degree burns from the heat coming from my face. "I meant to say, thank you."

"*You're welcome!*" Noah says loudly, and we both crack up laughing. "Come on," he says, guiding me toward a door that I'd assumed was to a cupboard. The door actually leads to a narrow passageway, which leads to a fire exit. "Sadie Lee told me about this place," he explains. "It's where the kitchen staff come for a smoke." He gives me a bashful grin. "Which makes it sound like the least glamorous picnic venue ever but don't worry—we'll make it cool. And, much as I hate to see you covering up that dress, I'd hate for you to get pneumonia out there." He pulls a fleecy hoodie from his bag.

It's so huge on me it almost comes down to my knees.

"Hmm." Noah frowns. "How come it looks a whole lot better on you than it does on me?"

And, just like that, he ignites my confidence and it starts to grow.

Noah opens the fire exit and we step outside onto an expanse of flat concrete rooftop surrounded by high metal railings. He takes me over to an alcove in the wall, where he lays out the tartan blanket from his truck.

"After you, ma'am," he says, gesturing to me to sit down.

Noah sits down across from me and opens the hamper. He takes out a flask and a couple of cups. Then two plates and some really fancy cutlery and various parcels wrapped in tinfoil. I watch, my mouth watering, as he unwraps the parcels to reveal a selection of beautiful handmade canapés and chocolate-covered strawberries and fairy cakes. Then finally he pulls out two candles and a book of matches. "This must be Sadie Lee's idea," he says with a grin. "That woman's such a romantic."

He lights the candles and we sit there for a moment, grinning at each other, then looking away.

"I was hoping it would be a clear night," Noah says, staring up at the dark sky. "I was hoping we'd be able to see the moon again."

"It doesn't matter. This is perfect."

Way down below us I can hear the noise of New York but we're so far up that the sirens and horns could almost be as soft as birdsong.

"I was thinking," Noah says, unscrewing the flask. Steam spirals up from it into the cold air. "Maybe we could write each other once you get back home—and Skype—and instant message?" He looks at me and sighs. "Look, Penny, I wish you weren't going tomorrow."

I instantly grin. Sadie Lee obviously hasn't told him that we're staying. I wonder if she deliberately left it for me to tell him.

"There's no need to look so happy about it," Noah says, shaking his head.

"I'm not," I say, my grin getting even wider.

"Really? You could have fooled me!"

"I'm not happy because I'm leaving—I'm happy because I'm *not* leaving. Not tomorrow, anyway. My mum's been asked to organize a party, here in New York, the day before New Year's Eve. We're staying here till the new year!"

Noah's mouth drops open. "You're kidding?"

"Nope."

He beckons to me across the picnic blanket. "Come here."

I get onto my knees and shuffle toward him. As soon as I'm close enough, he grabs one of my hands. I feel giddy with anticipation.

"And do you want to know the best bit?" I say.

"That isn't the best bit?"

I shake my head. "No, the best bit is Sadie Lee's invited us to spend Christmas with you!"

Noah starts to laugh. "Yep, that's definitely the best bit." Then his expression goes all serious. He looks at me and I feel a weird tugging in the pit of my stomach. "So . . ." he says.

"So . . ." I echo back, my heart pounding.

He's so close I can see a tiny fleck of ink on the side of his face. His hand closes tighter around mine and this automatically pulls me even closer, until our faces are just centimeters apart. *He's going to kiss me! Is he going to kiss me? What should I do?* I close my eyes to try to block out any panicky thoughts. And then I feel his lips on mine—as light as a feather—and I feel myself kissing him back. Somehow, miraculously, I seem to know what to do. And then he lets go of my hand and I feel his strong arms wrapping around me, pulling me even closer. As the kiss gets more intense, I feel as if I'm melting into him.

And then my phone starts to ring. I let it go to voicemail while Noah hugs me tight.

"See, I told you—you are my inciting incident," he says softly.

I nod and we break apart, although I notice we're still sitting with our legs touching. "I'd better just check my phone," I say, worried that Dad might be having a freak-out that I've gone off with Noah.

But the missed call is from Elliot. I go to my voicemail to retrieve his message.

"Penny! Where are you? Your mum says you've sneaked off somewhere with Prince Charming. Can you please, please come back ASAP? Bring him too; I'm sure the Bradys won't mind. There's been a catastrophe. My stupid parents won't let me stay on—they're making me fly home for Christmas—alone—can you believe it?!" There's a short silence, during which my heart starts to sink. "Unless of course . . . Penny, would you come home with me?"

Chapter Twenty-Seven

I guess my shock and horror must be obvious, because as soon as I put my phone back in my bag I see Noah staring at me, worried.

"What's up?" he says. "You look as if someone just told you Santa doesn't exist—he does, by the way, that's just a vicious rumor made up by adults to spoil our fun."

I laugh but it comes out really forced. "It's my friend Elliot," I say. "He's got to go home tomorrow. His parents won't let him stay on. They want him home for Christmas."

Noah sighs. "That sucks."

We both sit back down and Noah picks up the flask. "Sweet tea?"

I nod, even though I don't really know what "sweet tea" is. All I can think of is Elliot's question—will I go home with him? I feel totally torn. Much as I hate the thought of Elliot having to fly home on his own, I hate the thought of leaving Mum and Dad and Noah even more.

Noah passes me a cup and I take a sip. It's not like any

kind of tea I've had before. It's citrusy and sweet, kind of like hot lemonade.

"This is lovely," I say.

"Another of Sadie Lee's specialties," Noah replies. "In South Carolina, where she's from, they drink it all the time in the summer, with ice. This is her New York winter version."

I take another sip and try to get back into the picnic vibe, but it's no good. I can't stop thinking about Elliot. I look at Noah. "Would it be OK if we went inside to the party? Elliot sounded really stressed. He said he needs to talk to me."

A flicker of disappointment crosses Noah's face and I feel really bad. But I can't leave Elliot waiting, especially after he got so upset with me yesterday.

Noah nods. "Sure. Tell you what—you go see him. I'll head off home."

"No! I mean, can't you come with me? I don't want you to go."

Noah laughs. "I can't gate-crash someone's wedding. And, anyways, I'll be seeing you tomorrow."

"Yes, but I'm sure the Bradys won't mind. They're a lovely couple. I can tell them you're Sadie Lee's grandson. I can say you're my plus one."

Noah raises his eyebrows and gives me a cheeky grin. "Your plus one, huh?"

"Yes. Please come with me."

Noah shakes his head. "Listen. When I came here tonight, I thought it was to say goodbye. Now you're gonna be here for another week, so it's all good. I don't mind waiting till tomorrow. You go spend some time with your friend. He doesn't need me getting in the way."

"You wouldn't be getting in the way, you—"

Noah puts his finger to my lips. "Shhh."

"But the picnic . . ."

"We can have picnics every day when you're staying at mine." He grins at me. "Go see your friend."

I sigh. "OK."

"But first . . ."

Noah pulls me toward him and kisses me again, cupping my head with his hand and stroking my hair.

"Whoa!" he says, when we finally come up for air.

"Great kiss!" I say, because of course I can't possibly do something momentous like properly kiss a boy without saying something embarrassing.

"Yes," Noah says with an amused twinkle in his eye. "Great *kisser.*"

I laugh and look away. And even though my face is flushed, I don't really care. That's the difference with Noah—I can be an International Embarrassment Waiting to Happen, but it doesn't matter because he doesn't care.

"Come on," he says. "Let's get you back inside."

When I get back to the party, my lips are still tingling from our kisses. But the second I spot Elliot the tingle starts to fade and my heart sinks. He's sitting at the table on his own, looking utterly dejected.

"Where have you been?" he asks as soon as I sit down.

"Sorry, Noah wanted to go for a picnic and—"

"A picnic?"

"Yes, but don't worry I—"

"So where is he now?" Elliot interrupts, looking toward the door.

"He's gone home."

"What? Why? He didn't have to do that. I told you to bring him here."

"He didn't want to gate-crash the wedding."

"But they wouldn't have minded—he's the caterer's grandson."

"I know but . . . anyway, what happened? What did your parents say?"

"They freaked." Elliot looks down at the table and starts picking at the tablecloth. "They said that there was no way I could stay here for Christmas, that that wasn't what they agreed to—like this is some legal case they're working on. They'd rather I fly home on my own than stay here with you guys because they want a family Christmas. But"—Elliot pauses as if for dramatic effect—"they did say that if you came home with me you'd be welcome to spend Christmas at ours."

"Oh—I—"

"Aha, the wanderer has returned!" Dad cries as he plonks down into the seat next to me. He's red-faced and out of breath. Clearly some serious dad-dancing has been going on in my absence.

Mum sits down next to him. She's not looking quite so ruffled, but then, she's still a great dancer from her theater days. "Penny, where's Noah?"

"He's gone back home," I say.

Mum frowns. "Already? Why didn't you ask him to join us? I'm sure the Bradys wouldn't have minded—he is Sadie Lee's grandson after all."

Geez, if I hear that one more time! "It's OK. I needed to see Elliot—about his parents."

"Ah yes." Dad shakes his head, looking at Elliot. "It's such a shame. Christmas won't be the same without you."

Elliot nods and sighs, then he turns to me. "So, what do you think, Pen?"

"I don't know." I gaze at the crowded dance floor, as if searching for inspiration. How can I possibly get out of this without hurting Elliot's feelings?

"What does she think about what?" Dad asks.

"My parents have said that Penny is welcome to spend Christmas with us, if she comes home with me tomorrow." Elliot looks at Dad hopefully.

I look at Mum and she raises her eyebrows. I focus really hard and try to send her a psychic daughter-mother message to beg her not to let me go.

"Oh, I don't know . . ." Mum begins.

"I know one of my parents' Christmas-ready meals on a tray won't be the same as one of your dad's epic feasts," Elliot says, turning to me, "but then you won't be having one of your dad's epic feasts this year anyway, will you? You'll be having a hotel Christmas dinner."

"But—" I begin.

"We won't be spending Christmas at the hotel," Mum says gently. "We're going to be staying at Sadie Lee's."

Elliot's eyes widen. "Sadie Lee's?"

"Yes," Mum replies, "the woman who did the catering

for the wedding. She's invited us to spend Christmas at her house."

"Oh. I see," Elliot says flatly.

"And we really want Penny with us," Dad says softly.

"Yes, it'll be bad enough having Christmas without Tom," Mum adds.

I feel a surge of relief. Now I don't have to tell Elliot I don't want to go home with him; I can blame my parents.

"That's OK, I understand," Elliot says quietly.

"We'll only be staying a week," I say.

"Eight days," Elliot says quickly.

"OK, eight days. I can Skype with you."

"Are you sure you won't be too busy?" Elliot mutters.

"Hey, it's our song!" Dad cries as "When a Man Loves a Woman" starts playing. He leaps to his feet and holds out his hand to Mum. "Madam, would you do me the honor?"

"Why, I would be delighted," Mum cries, taking his hand.

As I watch them head back to the dance floor, I smile. It's weird because recently their public displays of affection had been making me feel really wistful, like they were members of an exclusive Couples Club I'd never be able to join. But now watching them reminds me of Noah and it makes me feel all warm inside.

"I suppose I'd better go and start packing," Elliot says, breaking my trance.

"I'll help you," I say, desperate to say something, *anything*, to make Elliot feel better. "We could have a midnight feast if you like? I have a parcel of picnic food."

"I have no appetite," Elliot says.

"Not even for chocolate-covered strawberries?"

"He brought you chocolate-covered strawberries?"

I nod nervously, unsure of what kind of response this will get given the mood Elliot's in.

"Seriously, does this guy have any flaws?"

"I'm sure he has tons," I say, although I'm not sure of that at all.

"Hmm. All right, come on then."

It's not until we've gotten Elliot's case packed that his mood finally starts to lift.

"I'm sorry," he says, flopping down on his bed. "I was just so disappointed not to be spending Christmas with you guys. But I suppose it's for the best that I've got to go home; I'd only be a big fat gooseberry if I stayed."

"No you wouldn't." I sit down on the bed next to him. "Look, the fact is, Noah and I live about ten thousand miles apart—"

"Four thousand, actually."

"OK, four thousand, but that's still more than an entire ocean, so it's not like this is going to affect our friendship at all. It's just—just . . ."

"A holiday romance?" Elliot offers hopefully.

"Yes, a holiday romance."

But as Elliot grins and nods, an unsettling thought occurs to me. This is the first time I've ever lied to him in all our years of friendship.

Chapter Twenty-Eight

I once read a magazine article that said every dream has a hidden meaning. Like if you dream that you're running up a hill but you never get to the top, it means that you're stuck in some area of your life, and if you dream that your teeth are falling out it means that you're feeling really insecure—or did that one mean that you're pregnant . . . ? I can't remember. Anyway, there are people, kind of like dream doctors, who will analyze your dream and tell you what the secret meaning is. As I wake up on Christmas Eve, I wonder what on earth a dream doctor would make of mine last night. Basically, I was trapped on a train with Megan and Ollie and every time we went through a station the train announcer would read out an embarrassing fact about me. So instead of saying, "Ladies and gentlemen, we will shortly be arriving at . . ." he said things like, "Ladies and gentlemen, did you know that Penny Porter once flashed her knickers to the entire world?" And all the time Megan and Ollie just sat across the table from me, laughing their heads off. And every time I tried to get up to leave, they made me sit down. And then the chair I was sitting on turned into a cake and I ended up getting chocolate icing all over my bum.

I sit up and turn on my bedside lamp. I hate dreams. I hate the way you can forget all about the things and people that have hurt you, but then a dream brings them flooding back. I pick up the china doll from the pillow next to me and hug her. It feels so weird to be thinking of Megan and Ollie again.

I get the sudden urge to check Facebook and YouTube to see if people are still talking about the video. Then thankfully I have a reality check. Why would I do that to myself? Especially as I've done so well since I got here, putting all of that to the back of my mind. I look around my room and feel a pang of sorrow. It's my last morning in the Waldorf Astoria. It probably sounds weird to say this but I feel so attached to this room. This was where my life became like a fairy tale. This was where I finally realized that I can actually control what happens to me. I decide to take some photos of it so that I can treasure the memories forever.

First, I take a picture of my unmade bed, with my doll sitting perched on top of a pile of pillows. Then I take a picture of the whole room from various different angles. Then finally I take some shots of the view from the window and one of the chair with the blanket draped over it, to remind me of the night I spoke to Noah on the phone and the moon turned orange. By the time I've finished, I feel way better. It's as if looking at the room through my camera has, literally, helped me to refocus. Megan and Ollie, the play . . . everything that happened is in the past. I need to keep focused on the present, and that means New York and Noah.

As my excitement starts to build, I feel the urge to dance. I grab the remote and turn on the TV. MTV is playing nonstop Christmas tunes. I start dancing around the room to "Santa Claus Is Coming to Town." I dance and dance until I've shaken off the horrible residue from my dream. Then I collapse down onto my bed and grin at my doll.

"Happy Christmas," I whisper to her breathlessly.

Thankfully, Elliot is back to his usual cheery self this morning.

"I've come up with a plan," he whispers to me over the breakfast table, "a plan so dastardly that it would make the Riddler blush."

"What is it?" I whisper back, pouring some maple syrup on my pancakes.

"It's called Ten Ways to Ruin My Evil Parents' Christmas," he says with a glint in his eye. "By the time I've finished, they're going to wish I was still here with you guys."

I start to laugh. "What are you going to do?"

"Number one: tell them that I've decided to drop out of school and join a hippie commune. Number two: tell them that from now on I will only be answering to my new hippie name, Rain Water."

By the time Elliot gets to number ten in his evil plan ("Tell them that I've got an American Hell's Angel boyfriend called Hank"), we are both cracking up laughing. Mum and Dad, who've been busy talking about the plans for the party, are now staring at us.

"What's so funny?" Dad says with a grin.

"I'm not sure I want to know," Mum says.

"Trust me, you don't," I say, grinning at Elliot.

After breakfast, we leave our luggage with the hotel reception and take Elliot to the airport.

As the cab pulls into the terminal, I look at Elliot anxiously. "Will you be OK, flying on your own?"

He nods and grins. "Actually, I'm kind of looking forward to it. I think it will give me a real air of mystery. I can just imagine all the other passengers thinking to themselves, who is this young man, traveling alone? What could his story be?"

I laugh and shake my head. "Yeah, well, you've certainly dressed for the part." Elliot is wearing his favorite vintage suit, a dark grey pinstripe, with polished brogues and a pocket watch on a chain—and his New York Yankees cap. Somehow, he manages to make this look totally cool.

Elliot gives me a hug. "I'm gonna miss you, Pen-face."

"I'm gonna miss you too."

"Enjoy your holiday romance."

"Yeah, whatever."

"No, seriously." Elliot pulls back and looks at me. "You deserve to have some fun after everything you've been through lately."

I feel myself start to well up. "Thank you."

"And I'm going to be demanding *all* of the deets as soon as you get back."

I laugh and nod. "OK."

And then Elliot's flight is called. I watch him striding through the gate with a weird mixture of sadness at him leaving, and excitement at what is to come.

"You OK?" Dad says, hugging me to him.

I nod.

"I just got a text from Sadie Lee," Mum says. "She says to

tell you both that she's just baked us a batch of brownies and we're welcome to get there as soon as we like."

I feel my own phone vibrate and my heart leaps at the sight of a new message from Noah.

> Morning! Tell me, how good are your tree-decorating skills? N

Grinning, I quickly reply.

> World-class. I'm actually Champion Bauble Hanger in my home town—three years running ☺

> Only three? Shame! I guess that'll have to do. Hurry up and get here, Inciting Incident, Bella and I need your help

At first my mind goes blank when I see the name Bella, but then I remember—Noah has a sister.

In the taxi on the way to the airport, I'd been so focused on keeping Elliot's spirits up, I hadn't gotten anxious at all, but going back to the hotel to pick up our luggage is a different story. By the time we pull into the Waldorf, I want to leap from the cab and walk all the way to Brooklyn. As I go into the hotel for one final look around the grand lobby, I tell myself to get a grip. "You can do this," I tell myself. "You're Ocean Strong." But my superhero name doesn't seem to have the same effect without Elliot here. I think of him sitting on his own on the plane and I feel a hollow ache. Then I remember the exercise Noah told me about.

"Ready, Pen?" Dad says, as he and a bellboy come over with our luggage piled up on a trolley.

I nod. "Yes."

As soon as I get back in the cab, I try to picture where in my body I feel the most anxious. As usual, it's the tightness in my throat. I close my eyes and try to picture it as a color and shape. I see a red fist clutching at my neck. At first it makes me feel even worse and I want to open my eyes but I force myself to take a deep breath and just allow it to be there. Nothing happens. The tension in my throat is still there; it hasn't gotten any better—but it hasn't gotten any worse either. I take another deep breath. *It's OK*, I say to the image of the red fist. *I don't mind you being there*. I take another breath. In the background, I can hear Mum and Dad chatting to the taxi driver but I'm so focused that I don't hear what they're saying. I try to picture the fist of tension again and this time it's more pink than red. It's a little bit smaller too. *It's OK*, I say to it again. The rest of my body starts to relax. Now it just feels as if there's a knot in my throat rather than a huge fist. I take another breath and it's much easier this time. *It's OK*, I keep saying over and over again inside my head. *It's OK*. As

I keep focusing on the image of the knot, it fades until it's snowy-white and then it completely disappears.

"Penny, look at the bridge," Mum says, nudging me.

I open my eyes and see that we're on the Brooklyn Bridge already, about to go under the first arch. On the other side of the river, the Brooklyn skyline stands solid and brown against the pale sky. My panic has passed, like a cloud skimming across the sun.

Once we get to Brooklyn, the cab pulls into a residential side street lined with trees. The houses are all four stories high and made of brownstone. We stop outside a house halfway down. A flight of steep stone steps leads up to a bright red door. A Christmas wreath made of holly and mistletoe hangs in the center of the door, and a miniature stone Santa is standing at the top of the steps, grinning down at us.

"Oh, it looks so lovely," Mum says, speaking my thoughts aloud.

But as I get out of the cab, my head fills with fearful thoughts. *What if you and Noah don't get along? What if it's really awkward spending Christmas together?* However, before I can torture myself any more, the door of the house opens and a little girl comes flying out. Her shiny dark brown hair is so curly it falls around her face in perfect ringlets. She looks at us shyly through huge brown eyes.

"Have you come for Christmas?" she says in the cutest New York accent ever.

"We certainly have," Dad says.

Sadie Lee comes out onto the steps. She's wearing a flour-dusted floral apron over her dress. "Hello!" she cries. "Welcome! Welcome!"

Noah steps out after her and we instantly make eye contact. "Hey," he says softly.

"Hey," I say back. Then I start busying myself with my suitcase to try to hide my embarrassment.

"Let me get that," Noah says, bounding down the steps. When he gets to Dad, he stops. "Hi, I'm Noah," he says, holding his hand out.

"Pleased to meet you, Noah," Dad says, shaking his hand. "I'm Rob."

I give a sigh of relief—so far, so good.

"Are you Penny?" Bella says to me as I come up the steps after Noah.

"Yes, I am. And you must be Bella."

She nods and grins shyly before turning to Noah. "You were right, Noah."

"Shhh," Noah says instantly.

"Right about what?" I say.

"She looks just like a mermaid," Bella says.

"Man! I thought you said you could keep a secret!" Noah says, winking at me.

Noah's house is straight from a cozy feel-good American movie. The hallway is the size of a living room. A beautiful grandfather clock stands in the corner next to a wide staircase. Noah and Sadie Lee lead us through an archway on the left, into a huge but really homey kitchen. I breathe in the rich smell of chocolate brownies.

"So, you guys will be sleeping in the spare room," Sadie Lee says to Mum and Dad. "And, Penny, you can go in with Bella."

"You have to have the top bunk," Bella says to me gravely. "I don't like the top bunk cos I'm scared I might fall out."

"The top bunk would be great," I say, smiling down at her. She takes hold of my hand. "Do you want to come see?"

"Yes please." I look at Noah and he grins at me.

"OK, but don't be long. We have a tree to decorate, remember?"

"Oh yes!" Bella squeals, and she starts tugging me by the hand. "Come on, let's go."

Bella's room is on the second floor of the house. She leads me across the landing to a door with a handmade sign stuck to it, saying: ALIENS KEEP OUT! (AND PIGS.)

"Noah made that for me," Bella explains. "I don't like aliens—or pigs—so that'll stop them coming in."

"Good idea," I say, trying really hard not to smile.

Bella's bedroom is possibly the greatest kid's bedroom I have ever seen. The main wall is covered with a mural of famous fairy-tale characters, from Snow White and her dwarfs to Dumbo the elephant and Little Red Riding Hood.

"My daddy made that for me when I was born," Bella says, noticing me staring at it. "But now my daddy's in heaven."

"I'm really sorry about that," I say, crouching down in front of her.

"My mom is too," Bella says matter-of-factly. "I think she might be an angel."

"I'm sure she is," I reply.

"This is my bed," Bella says, turning and pointing at a set of bunk beds next to the opposite wall. The bottom bunk has a curtain going all the way around it.

"Cool bed," I say, really meaning it. "I love the curtain."

"Me too," Bella says. "Sometimes I pretend it's a tent. I like your voice."

"Thank you."

"You sound just like Princess Kate. I love Princess Kate."

I take my case over to a space in the corner of the room and open it to get out a sweatshirt.

"Is that your doll?" Bella says, looking at the china doll lying in between my clothes.

"Yes, it is."

"Cooool!" Bella runs over to her bed and dives through the curtains. She reappears clutching a beautiful rag doll. "This is Rosie," she says, holding the doll up to mine. "Can they be friends?"

"Of course they can." I pull the sweatshirt over my head.

"Hello, I'm Rosie," says Bella, putting on a high-pitched doll voice. "What's your doll's name?" she says, turning to me.

"Oh. She hasn't got a name."

"She hasn't got a name?" Bella looks at me wide-eyed, like I've committed the worst crime known to doll-kind.

"Why don't you give her one?" I say, trying to redeem myself.

"OK then." Bella frowns for a moment, then she picks up my doll. "I'm Princess Autumn," she says in a grand voice. "Autumn's Noah's name for you," she whispers to me. "Only I'm not supposed to tell you. Do you love Noah?" She tilts her head to one side.

"Oh, well, we've only just met each other so—"

"I think he loves you," Bella interrupts. "He was writing a song about you last night. He never writes a song about any other girls. Grandma said he was acting all love-struck. 'Love-struck' means being hit in your heart by the emotion of love. That's what Grandma told me."

This time, I can't prevent myself from laughing. And the more I laugh, the harder it gets to stop. I feel giddy with happiness. Noah has a pet name for me. He was writing a song about me! Sadie Lee called him love-struck!

Now Bella's giggling too—so hard it's making her ringlets bounce.

"All right, what's going on in here?"

We both jump at the sound of Noah's voice—and carry on laughing.

"Don't tell him," Bella whispers through her giggles.

"I won't," I whisper back.

"Are you guys gonna help me decorate this tree or what?"

"Yes, yes, yes!" Bella cries, and she runs from the room.

"Well, you two sure seem to have bonded," Noah says, looking at me quizzically.

I nod and go over to join him.

"I'm so glad you're here," he says.

"Me too," I reply, and for a second I think he's about to kiss me. But then Bella races back across the landing and grabs us both by the hand.

"Come on, slow coaches!"

And as Noah grins at me and shrugs apologetically, I feel hit in my heart by an emotion very close to love.

Chapter Twenty-Nine

The Christmas tree is as tall as the living room and almost as wide as the bay window it's stood in. Its needles are thick and glossy and fill the room with a delicious piney scent. Mum and Dad head out for some emergency Christmas shopping, so Noah, Bella, and I set about decorating the tree from a battered old trunk full of the most beautiful glass baubles and ornaments I've ever seen.

It turns out that pretty much every decoration has its own story. As we hang them on the tree, Sadie Lee sits beside us in a rocking chair and recounts each tale. "My mamma bought me that Santa the year I turned sweet sixteen. That snowman belonged to your granddaddy—he called it Stanley. The reindeer was given to me at a church party back in Charlston."

Finally, all of the baubles are on the tree.

"Don't forget these," Sadie Lee says, handing Bella a box.

"Candy canes!" Bella exclaims.

The box is full of green, red, and white striped canes. They're shiny and bright and smell of peppermint. Carefully, we start hooking them over the branches of the tree.

"Yum!" Bella says, popping one in her mouth.

"Hey, Miss Piggy!" Noah says with a grin.

"I couldn't help it," Bella says. "It fell into my mouth."

We all start to laugh and Noah offers me a candy cane. It tastes just like a stick of Brighton rock.

"Is it time for the angel?" Bella asks Sadie Lee.

"It sure is, honey."

Noah takes a parcel wrapped in red tissue paper out of the trunk. Very carefully, he unwraps it to reveal a beautiful angel with wavy blond hair and a long ivory silk dress. Two wings made from golden gossamer fan out from her back. Noah climbs onto a chair and gently places the angel on top of the tree. Bella starts clapping her hands in excitement.

"Can I turn on the lights, Grandma, please?"

"Of course you can, honey."

We all wait as Bella scrambles around the back of the tree. "Merry Christmas!" she cries, and the tree comes alive with golden twinkly lights. It's so beautiful, I can't even speak.

"Merry Christmas," Noah whispers in my ear, putting his arm around my waist.

I snuggle into him, glowing with the thought that this is going to be the best Christmas ever.

It isn't till the afternoon that it dawns on me that I also don't have a single Christmas present for anyone. Noah doesn't seem all that keen on going shopping so I head out to the local parade of stores with Sadie Lee. I buy a pumpkin-scented candle and some fizzy bath goodies for Mum, an American cookbook for Dad, a book about princesses for Bella, and a beautifully carved set of wooden mixing spoons for Sadie Lee—when she's not looking. I decide to try a music shop for Noah's gift, but as soon as I get inside it dawns on me that I don't even know what kind of music he likes. And *then* it dawns on me how little I still know about him and I have a moment of panic. How can I feel so strongly about someone I've only just met? It doesn't make sense. I look at Sadie Lee sheepishly.

"What kind of music does Noah like?"

She instantly laughs. "That boy likes just about every kind of music. I'm not kidding—he could make a tune from the whistle of a train! But if you had to pin it down, I would go for something old—on vinyl. He loves vinyl."

I head off to the back of the store, where there are racks and racks of records. As I flick through them, I smile as I breathe in the smell. It's almost as good as the smell of books. Almost, but not quite. In the end I pick a record by someone called Big Bill Broonzy, just because I love the name. I take the record over to the counter to pay.

"Awesome choice, ma'am," the guy behind the counter says with a wide grin.

"Thank you," I say, feeling very proud that I've actually gone into a vintage record store in Brooklyn and made an "awesome choice"—even if it is entirely by accident.

The man's smile grows even broader. "Cute accent. Where are you all from?"

"England."

"No way!" He grabs my hand and shakes it enthusiastically. "Well, that just made my day."

I look at his greying dreadlocks and the silver skull on the chain around his neck. He looks so interesting.

"Would you . . . ? Could I . . . ? Would it be OK if I took a picture of you?"

He instantly grins. "Why, yes, of course, ma'am. How do you want me?" He starts puffing out his chest.

"Just as you were, looking at the record would be great," I say.

The man re-creates the pose and I take the shot. "Thank you."

"No problem." He hands me a business card from a pile on the counter. "And when you get back to England you can tell people you met Slim Daniels."

"I will," I say, glowing with newfound confidence. I'm no longer a stupid schoolgirl who always makes mistakes, I'm the kind of person who makes awesome choices in Brooklyn record stores and takes photos of people with names like Slim Daniels. Nothing—not even when I take a step backward and almost knock over a display stand—can ruin my happiness.

When Sadie Lee and I get back home, Mum is playing an elaborate game of princesses with Bella in the living room, and Dad and Noah are in the kitchen, preparing some veggies for tomorrow's Christmas dinner. They're laughing their heads off as we come in. This is good—very good.

"I thought I'd make us something light for dinner tonight," Sadie Lee says, putting on her apron. "Don't want to overdo it before the feast tomorrow."

"Good plan," Dad says. "Just let me know if I can help with anything."

"That would be lovely," Sadie Lee says. "I was thinking of making a chicken Caesar salad."

"That happens to be one of my specialities," Dad says proudly.

"It is," I say. "Can't wait."

"Oh no," Sadie Lee says, turning to me. "I'm afraid you won't be eating with us."

"That's right," Noah says.

"What?" I look from Sadie Lee to Dad to Noah. They're all grinning at me like they're in on a private joke. "Why won't I be eating with you?"

"We don't want you ruining your appetite before the big day," Noah says.

"We thought it would be best if you went on a fast for the next twenty-four hours," Dad says.

"What?!"

Noah starts laughing his head off. "Don't look so stressed. You won't be having dinner because we are going to be having Picnic Round Two."

"Is it all ready?" Sadie Lee asks him.

Noah nods and takes hold of my hand. "So, if you'd like to come with me, ma'am, I shall accompany you to your picnic blanket."

I look at them all and laugh. "Oh my God, that was so mean!"

I follow Noah out into the hallway and down a flight of stairs into the basement of the house.

The basement is like our living room back at home, with a really relaxed and laid-back vibe. There are two squishy sofas covered with cushions and throws and a huge flat-screen TV on the wall. Two brightly colored lava lamps are bubbling away on side tables, casting the room in an orangey glow. The basement's way bigger than our living room, though, stretching back the entire length of the house. At the very far end, I can just make out a pool table. The tartan blanket is laid out in front of the sofas, covered in plates of the most amazing picnic food.

"This looks fantastic!" I say, turning to Noah.

"Well, I figured after yesterday I needed to pull out all the stops," he says with a grin.

We both sit down on either side of the blanket.

"So, did your friend get back OK?" Noah asks.

I suddenly realize that I haven't bothered to check my phone since I got here. Elliot should have landed by now. I think of my phone upstairs in my bag and I contemplate going to get it, but I really don't want to disrupt the picnic for a second time, especially when Noah's gone to so much trouble.

"Yes, I think so."

"Good." Noah glances up at the TV before looking back at me. "I was wondering . . ."

"Yes?"

"It's just that when my parents were alive we had this tradition on Christmas Eve and I'd really like to do it again—with you."

"Of course. What is it?"

"We'd always watch the movie *It's a Wonderful Life* together."

As *It's a Wonderful Life* is one of my favorite movies of all time, this is a total no-brainer. "I'd love to!"

So Noah puts the movie on and we sit on the floor, leaning against the sofa, with the picnic spread out before us.

I've always loved black-and-white movies. Just like

black-and-white photos they seem so atmospheric, and much more dramatic. Noah shuffles up right next to me until our shoulders are touching. I don't think it would be possible to feel any more content.

And it stays like this right until the bit toward the end of the movie when James Stewart is on the bridge calling out to his guardian angel that he doesn't want to die; that he wants to live again and see his wife and kids. Suddenly I feel Noah pull away from me. I turn to look at him. In the flickering light of the TV screen, I see that his cheek is wet—as if he's shed a tear.

"Noah? Are you OK?"

He quickly wipes his face with the back of his hand. "Yeah, of course. I guess I must have got something in my eye."

I sit frozen, unsure of what to do or say. Then it hits me: how much this film must mean to Noah.

I crawl around so that I'm facing him. "Is it . . . are you thinking about your parents?"

Noah is motionless for a second, but then he nods, looking down into his lap. "Geez, way to impress a girl, Noah," he mutters, "start crying all over them."

I'm not sure what to do. Then his eyes flick up and he gives me a half smile. But almost as soon as our eyes meet, he looks away again, embarrassed. I want to give him a hug but I don't know if that's what he would want.

"It's OK, honestly," I say, gently placing my hands on his arms.

"I thought I'd be all right," Noah says, his head still down. "I thought it would be nice, watching it again . . ."

"Is this the first time you've watched it, since . . . ?"

He nods. I want to comfort him but I can't find the right words. What he's been through is so horrible—so huge—it feels as if all the words in the world wouldn't be able to make it any better.

Noah sighs. "It was a really dumb idea."

"No, it wasn't. I think it was a lovely idea."

"You do? Why?"

"Because it's a way of remembering your parents and—and keeping them alive."

Up on the screen James Stewart is now racing through the snow, yelling "Merry Christmas" to everyone and everything.

"My mom would always start crying like a baby at this bit," Noah says with a sad little laugh, "and Dad would always kiss her tears away."

Without thinking, I kneel forward and start kissing Noah's face. His tears taste salty on my lips.

"It's OK," I whisper as I hold him tight. "It's OK."

⋆⋆ Chapter Thirty ⋆

"Penny! Penny! He came!"

At the sound of Bella's voice I sit bolt upright in bed and rub my eyes, trying to see in the pitch-blackness. Suddenly, the thin beam from a flashlight shines in my face, causing me to blink.

"He came!" Bella says again. The torch beam swings away to reveal her little face peering at me from the top of the ladder at the end of my bed.

"Who came?"

"Santa, of course."

"Oh." I lie back down and grin up at the ceiling.

"Wake up!" Bella says. "We have to see what he's brought us."

"OK. Just coming."

I reach under my pillow for my phone to see what time it is. Five thirty! I also see that I have a new text message and breathe a sigh of relief. By the time I got to my phone last night, Elliot had texted me three times about his flight home and how much he hated his parents. I'd felt really bad about replying so late. But when I open my texts folder I see that it's from Ollie.

Happy Christmas, Penny! Hope you're having a great time in New York. Looking forward to seeing you when you get back. Ollie xx

What? Why is Ollie texting me? And why is he looking forward to seeing me? Then I remember the photo shoot on the beach. He probably just wants me to take some more profile pics for him. Whatever. I put my phone back under my pillow.

"Come on, lazy bones!" Bella calls from the lower bunk and I feel her prodding my mattress.

"OK, OK."

I clamber down the ladder and peep through the curtain into Bella's bed. She's sitting cross-legged, shining her torch on two stockings laid out in front of her. As soon as I see the mysterious lumps and bumps inside the stockings, I get that old familiar excited feeling. I guess you never truly grow out of Father Christmas.

"I didn't think I was going to get anything this year," Bella says to me, as I get into the end of her bunk.

"What? Why not?"

"Because I did something really bad at school," she whispers, "and I thought Santa might have seen but I guess he didn't."

"Ah. Well, I'm sure Santa doesn't mind if you're bad once in a while. It's very hard to be good all of the time."

'Tell me about it!" Bella says with a dramatic sigh—making me want to adopt her right there and then.

After emptying our stockings—mine was full of brightly colored candy, sweetly scented bath bombs, and a beautiful glass angel—I manage to persuade Bella that we should go back to bed. And somehow she agrees. But as I lie in the dark, my mind becomes way too busy to sleep. I'm unsettled by the text from Ollie, and worried that Elliot hasn't texted me back—it's already midday in the UK, so it's really weird that he hasn't sent me a message wishing me a happy Christmas. I hope he isn't annoyed at me for taking so long to reply to him.

Noah kept apologizing for getting upset about his parents last night. In the end I had to remind him that I'd ended up blubbing all over him within an hour of us meeting so it just meant we were even. But, actually, it feels like so much more than that. When you cry in front of someone, when you show them your most vulnerable side, it shows that you really trust them. It's so strange because, even though I still don't really know very much about Noah, on some deeper level it feels like I've known him forever. Is this what it means when people talk about meeting their soul mate?

I get the sudden urge to write a blog post. Creeping down from my bunk, I go over to my suitcase and take out my laptop. Bella is curled up on her bed fast asleep, hugging the new teddy that Santa brought her. I gently pull her cover over her, then take my laptop back up to my bunk and log on to my blog.

25 December

Do You Believe in Soul Mates?

Hey, guys!

Happy Christmas!

I hope wherever you are, and whoever you're with, you're having a great one.

Loads of you have asked me to write more about Brooklyn Boy and I could really do with your advice, so here goes.

I've always thought that the idea of soul mates—the idea that there's someone out there especially for you—sounds so cool and romantic, but I've never imagined it happening to me.

Like, I could imagine that somewhere in the 7 billion people on the planet there may be a boy who's just right for me, but knowing my luck he'd be living in the middle of the Amazon rain forest or a desert in Ethiopia and our paths would never meet.

But then I met Brooklyn Boy.

And the weirdest thing has happened.

Even though I've only known him for a few days, in many ways, in *important* ways, it feels as if I've known him forever.

So, I still don't know who his favorite band is, or his favorite flavor ice cream, but I do know that I can tell him anything.

And I know that I can cry in front of him and show him my weak side and I know that he won't judge me at all.

And I know that he can cry in front of me and show me his weak side and I won't judge him either—it just makes me like him even more.

It's so hard to try to describe how I'm feeling. The best way to put it is that when I'm with him I feel like I've met my matching person.

Like Cinderella and Prince Charming.

Or Barbie and Ken. *(Hmm, not sure that's such a great example but you know what I mean.)*

Can any of you relate to what I'm saying?

Have any of you felt this way before?

Do you think he might be my soul mate?

Could I really have been lucky enough to meet the one for me? And not have to go trekking through a rain forest or desert to find him!

Please let me know your thoughts in the comments below.

Lots of love,

Girl Online, going offline xxx

PS: If you haven't already worked it out, I'm still here—in New York! We've been able to stay until New Year's Day. And we're staying in Brooklyn Boy's house!! Fairy tales really can happen ☺

Chapter Thirty-One

After posting my blog, I'm just starting to drift off to sleep when I'm woken by a text alert. My first thought, as I fumble for my phone, is Elliot. But the text's from Noah.

Did Santa come . . . ?

Oh yes, Bella and I were up at 5:30 emptying our stockings! ☺

Man! I can't believe you opened them without me! Meet me in the kitchen

Evidence that Noah is my soul mate

1. I am able to cry in front of him.
2. He is able to cry in front of me.
3. Every time I see him it feels as if another part of us is slotting into place
4. It's like we're a "matching pair." (Kind of like curtains but way more romantic!)
5. When he asks me to meet him in the kitchen first thing in the morning, I don't panic about what I look like with zero makeup and bed-hair. I just pull on my snow leopard onesie and head straight down there.

In the kitchen, Sadie Lee and Dad are combining cooking forces and it smells amazing. Noah is seated at the round pine table in the corner, wearing a baseball top and sweatpants. As soon as he sees me, he gives me an extra-dimply grin and pulls back the chair next to him.

"Merry Christmas, Penny!" he says as I sit down. "Cute outfit."

"Thank you. I thought snow leopard would be a good Christmas Day look." I laugh. "Merry Christmas."

"Penny!" Dad and Sadie Lee chorus, turning from the huge stove to greet me. "Merry Christmas!"

If today were a Christmas movie, then this morning would be the bit where it cuts to a soft-focus montage of super-happy scenes, while "Jingle Bells" plays in the background. All of us laughing and joking and comparing stocking gifts around the breakfast table. Noah and I building a "snow princess" for Bella in the back garden. Dad joining us for a snowball fight. Mum and I helping Sadie Lee peel about a million Brussels sprouts. The only thing that stops it from being totally perfect is that I still haven't heard anything from Elliot. When I tried calling him earlier, it went straight to voicemail and I've sent him four texts. It's now two o'clock in the afternoon New York time, which means it's evening in London. Why has he gone all day without wishing me a merry Christmas?

As Noah and I set the dining-room table for dinner, I check my phone for the umpteenth time.

"Is everything all right?" Noah says.

"Yes. I'm just a little bit worried because I haven't heard from Elliot today." I put my phone back in my pocket and carry on laying napkins at each place setting.

"Maybe he's just enjoying his Christmas?"

I laugh. "Not with his parents. Elliot always says that his mum and dad think 'fun' is a four-letter word."

Noah places a pair of Santa-shaped salt and pepper pots in the center of the table. "I'm sure he'll text soon."

It suddenly dawns on me that ever since I've been here I've never seen Noah on his mobile phone. "How come you're never on your phone?" I ask, instantly squirming for being too nosy.

"I'm on a detox over Christmas," Noah says with a grin.

I look at him questioningly.

"An Internet and cell-phone detox. You should try it some time. It's liberating."

I frown. Much as my experience with the Unicorn Pants from Hell video was unpleasant and hurtful, I can't imagine life without the Internet or my phone.

"Go on, I dare you," Noah says. "Step away from the cell phone."

I laugh. "OK, but if I start twitching or having any kind of weird withdrawal symptoms I'm getting it straight back."

"Sure." Noah's face goes all serious for a moment. "Sometimes I really hate the Internet, you know?"

I stop laying out napkins and look at him. "Why?"

He sighs. "It's not—"

"Are you guys finished?" Mum comes into the room, holding a glass of wine. Her hair is hanging loose around her shoulders and her face is glowing. It's lovely seeing her looking so relaxed.

"Pretty much," Noah says.

"Make way, make way, incoming turkey," Dad calls, walking into the room carrying a humongous roast turkey on a silver platter.

I turn my phone off and sit down at the table.

The Christmas dinner is so delicious we decide to start a charity collection for every time someone says, "Mmmm!" Kind of like a food version of a swear box. By the time we've finished dessert—all four of them—we've collected twenty-seven dollars.

"Gift time! Gift time!" Bella shrieks, leaping from the table.

The rest of us all look at each other and raise our eyebrows.

"I actually don't think I can move," Noah says, slumped back in his chair. "It feels like I have a food boulder in my stomach."

"Me too," Dad says. He looks at Mum. "You might have to give me a piggyback, sweetheart."

Mum laughs. "No chance!"

In the end, we all somehow manage to stumble and stagger through to the living room, where Bella is already sorting the gifts under the trees into piles.

"I have a lot more gifts than you," she says to me solemnly, "but that's OK because I'm a child and they said on the news the other day that Christmas is for children, didn't they, Grandma?"

Sadie Lee laughs. "Yes, they did, honey."

"And if I get anything that I don't really like, I'll give it to you, 'kay?" Bella takes my hand and holds it tightly.

"That's so sweet of you," I tell her solemnly, "but it's OK—I really don't mind."

Bella grins and bounds back to her pile of gifts.

Noah and I are the last people to exchange gifts. As I watch him unwrap the record, I'm hit by a wave of doubt. What if he hates it? What if it's totally the wrong thing? What if Slim Daniels was wrong and it's not an "awesome choice" at all? But from the way Noah is grinning as he takes the record out of its paper, I think I chose well.

"How did you know?" Noah looks at me, wide-eyed. "I love this guy's music—I've wanted this album for years." He looks at Sadie Lee questioningly.

"I didn't tell her," Sadie Lee says with a smile.

Noah and I look at each other and I mentally add "knowing exactly what to get him for Christmas" to my list of soul mate evidence.

After Noah slipped the record out to sniff it, he hands me a gift that has the same amount of tape as paper. "Sorry about all the tape," he mumbles. "Gift wrapping isn't my strongest suit."

"That's OK," I say, trying to make a tear in the paper, but

it's impossible as it's covered in so much tape. "Er, does anyone have a knife?"

In the end, with the help of the pointy end of a bottle opener, I manage to get into the parcel. Inside is a beautiful hardback book of old black-and-white photographs of New York.

"I thought with you being into photography and all . . ." I can tell from the hopeful way he's looking at me that he really wants me to like it. "If you prefer more modern photography I can take it back and get it changed. I—"

"No, it's perfect. Black-and-white photos are my favorite— they're like little moments of history captured forever."

We look at each other and I feel that closeness again, that sense that we already know each other. I get the overwhelming urge to kiss Noah. If only we weren't surrounded by our families.

As if reading my mind, Noah gets to his feet. "Do you want to go get a soda?" he asks.

At least, that's what I think he says. I'm so overcome by the need to kiss him I can barely hear a word. I nod and follow him out of the room. Thankfully the others are way too engrossed in their gifts to notice.

When we get out into the hallway, Noah stops by the grandfather clock. The huge pendulum seems to be ticktocking in time with my pounding heart.

"Penny, I . . ." Noah begins. He looks into my eyes and for once I don't feel too embarrassed and look away.

"Penny," he says again, cupping my face in his hands.

And then we're kissing. And it feels as if my whole body, the entire world, has turned to stardust.

Chapter Thirty-Two

For the rest of Christmas Day, Noah and I take every opportunity to steal secret kisses. It's like we've invented a new
game—a kissing version of hide-and-seek—hide-and-kiss.
By the time I clamber into my bunk bed, I feel drunk with
happiness. This has been the best Christmas ever—apart
from . . . I have one last check of my phone—still no message from Elliot.

The next morning I'm woken by a gentle tapping on the
bedroom door. I creep down the ladder and out of bed.
Bella is lying on her bottom bunk tucked up between Rosie
and Princess Autumn, her ringlets fanned out on the pillow
like a halo. I creep over and open the door.

Noah is standing in the hallway grinning. "Get dressed—
we're going out," he whispers.

"What? But . . . what time is it?"

"Almost seven."

"In the morning?"

"Yes, in the morning! Put something warm on. And bring
your camera. I'll meet you in the kitchen."

I scramble into a pair of jeans and boots and my fleeci-est sweatshirt and I head down to the kitchen. Noah's over by the counter putting a couple of flasks into his bag. The beautiful smell of freshly roasted coffee is filling the room.

"All righty, let's get going," he says, as soon as he sees me. "Where to?"

"This morning is about the only time of the year when New York actually goes to sleep," Noah says, putting a note on the kitchen table. It reads, GONE FOR A WALK. BACK SOON, N & P. "I figured it would be the perfect time to show you some of the local sights." He takes hold of my hand. "I want you to know more about where I'm from," he says quietly. "Plus, I thought you might like to take some photos without a ton of other people getting in the way."

I smile at him. "Thank you."

It's a perfect morning outside. Everywhere is covered in a fresh blanket of snow and there's that weird muffled silence that it brings. Noah shows me his old school and his favorite café and the shop his mum used to take him to every Satur-day to spend his pocket money on comics and candy. Then he takes me to the local park. Apart from a man in the dis-tance, walking a dog, we're the only people there and ours are the only footprints in the blanket of snow. Noah sits on one of the swings and gets a faraway look in his eye.

"My dad used to tell me that if you swung high enough it was possible to shoot off into outer space," he says softly. "I used to believe him too!" He laughs. "Man, I used to swing my butt off trying to get into space." He turns to look at me. "Why do we believe everything our parents tell us?"

I sit down on the swing next to him. "Because we love

them? Because we want to? When I was little, my mum told me that my toys came to life every night while I was asleep. In the morning when I woke up I'd check in my tent and they'd all be in different positions to how I'd left them."

"In your tent?"

I laugh. "Yes. I used to have a tent made out of blankets at the end of my bed. It was my favorite place to play. It made me feel all cozy and safe. My mum must have crawled in there every night to move the toys around. I think it's good when parents tell us things like that. It makes life more magical."

Noah nods. "I guess. But when what they tell us doesn't come true . . ." He breaks off, a frown creasing his forehead.

"Then we have to find something else magical to believe in."

Noah looks at me and smiles. "Yes, I like that." He shifts his swing sideways till he's right up close to mine. "I believe in you, Penny," he says, looking into my eyes.

"I believe in you too."

We look at each other for a second, then Noah pushes his swing back.

"Come on," he calls. "Let's see how high we can go."

We don't quite make it into outer space but we do get high enough to see right across the park to the rooftop of Noah's house.

When we finally come back down to earth, we're flush-faced and giggling.

Noah runs over to a seesaw and jumps on top of it. "I'm the king of the castle!" he yells. He looks so happy and cute I instantly reach for my camera.

"I've got to get a picture of you," I call. "You look so funny."

"Hmm, funny is not exactly the look I was going for," Noah says with a frown.

"Really?" I say, taking the shot. "So what look were you going for?"

"Oh, I don't know." Noah leaps down from the seesaw. "Thoughtful? Mysterious?" He comes and stands right in front of me. "The kind of guy you might want to, you know, kiss?"

My heart starts beating so fast I can practically feel my rib cage vibrating.

"Oh, you're definitely all of those too," I say quietly.

Noah looks at me. "Really?"

I nod. "Yes."

The muffled snowy silence wraps itself around us like a blanket. And as he gently brushes the hair back from my face and leans in to kiss me, it feels as if we're the only people awake and alive on the entire planet.

It's not until the afternoon that I finally get a text from Elliot. As soon as I see it my heart sinks.

> Happy Christmas. Hope you had a good one

I stare at the screen. Is that it? The lack of exclamation marks, emoticons, and kisses immediately makes me think that something is very wrong. I have to call him. While the others all watch *The Wizard of Oz*, I sneak up to Bella's room and climb into my bunk. Thankfully this time, he picks up.

"Elliot, what's wrong?"

"What do you mean, what's wrong?"

"Your text—it was so blunt."

"Well, maybe if you'd just spent the Christmas from hell with the parents from hell, you'd be feeling pretty blunt too."

I feel a glimmer of relief that he might just be annoyed at his parents and not me. "Why didn't you call me back? Or text me?"

There's a long silence. It's so long I think we might have lost the connection.

"I didn't want to interrupt," Elliot finally mutters.

"Interrupt what?"

There's another silence.

"You told me he was just a holiday romance."

Now it's my turn to go silent.

"He—I—it's—I don't know what it is."

"You seem pretty clear about it on your blog."

"No, I don't. That's why I blogged about it, because I'm not sure, because I'm confused."

"So you'd rather talk to thousands of strangers about it than to me?"

"No! It's just—you're not here."

"No—I'm not."

"Oh, El, please."

"Look, we'll talk about it when you get home, all right?"

"All right. Well, I'll see you next week then."

"Yes. See you then."

As I finish the call, my eyes fill with tears. Why, why, why can things never go right? Why, even when something truly amazing happens, does something crappy have to happen too? I've never fallen out with Elliot—not even come close to it. And now it feels as if I'm losing him and I don't even know why. And then a terrible thought occurs to me. What if he doesn't want to be friends anymore when I get back home? I'll be miles away from Noah and I'll have no best friend. I'll have nobody. I hug my pillow to me and start to cry.

"Don't be sad," a squeaky little voice says, making me jump out of my skin. I roll over and see Princess Autumn hovering by the ladder at the end of the bed. Bella appears behind her and climbs up onto my bunk. "Every time you feel sad you should think of three happy things to chase the sad thing away," she says to me, propping Princess Autumn up next to her. "Noah told me that one time when I got sad about my mom and dad."

"That's a great idea," I say, wiping the tears from my face.

"So go on then," Bella says, staring at me.

"What?"

"What are three things that make you happy?"

"You," I say straightaway. "You make me very happy."

Bella beams at me. "OK, that's number one. What else?"

"Being here, in this house."

She nods. "And number three?"

"Noah," I mumble, my cheeks flushing.

"You make him happy too."

I look at her. "Really?"

"Oh yes. He was really grumpy last week but ever since he met you he's been all smiley again."

"Oh good." I really want to ask her why he was grumpy but that feels way too inappropriate.

"You make me happy too," Bella says to me shyly.

"Ah, thank you."

"And you make Princess Autumn happy, doesn't she, Princess Autumn?"

Bella picks up the doll. "Oh yes," she says in a squeaky little voice, waving the doll about. "She makes me very happy—even though she didn't give me a name."

I look at Bella and I laugh. Everything will be OK. I'll sort things out with Elliot as soon as I get home, but for now I have to make the most of my time with Noah—and Bella—and Princess Autumn.

31 December

It's the People, not the Place

Once, when my family ended up on a day trip to a place called Cow Roast and we realized that, despite its epic name, there wasn't really anything much there apart from a row of houses, a pub (that was shut), and a petrol station, my dad gave us a really cool piece of advice. He said that it doesn't matter what a place is like, what matters is the people you see that place with. If they are up for adventure then you can make anywhere fun. We made Cow Roast fun that day—playing hide-and-seek in some nearby woods and meeting an old lady who invited us into her cottage for tea and scones.

Even though New York is one of the least boring places in the world, seeing it with Brooklyn Boy has made it even more exciting. And the weirdest thing is that in the week I've been here, I haven't been to a single tourist attraction. Instead, Brooklyn Boy has been taking me to all of his secret favorite spots. Yesterday, we drove out to a beach in New Jersey and although it was deserted because of the winter weather it was magical. We wrote our names in the sand and drank hot chocolate from flasks and I took some great pictures of a boardwalk (which is an American promenade). *And* I survived the drive—there and back—without having a panic attack!

Another night, we visited an art gallery called Framed because Brooklyn Boy had heard there was a really cool photography exhibition on there. The theme of the exhibition was hope and all of the photographers had interpreted it in totally different ways. My favorite was a picture of a little girl with her face pressed up against a toy-shop window. But the best thing about the exhibition was going with Brooklyn Boy: because he's friends with the gallery owner, we got to go in at night when it was shut to everyone else. *(This was doubly good for me because it meant that no one else saw when I tripped over some rope on the ground. It turned out that the rope was a piece of modern art called* The Snake. *Personally, I think it should be renamed* The Health & Safety Hazard.*)*

So my dad was definitely right—it's the people you see a place with that really matters. Brooklyn Boy has shown me a really private and personal side of New York I never would have found on my own.

How about you guys?

How have the people you've been with made a place really fun and exciting?

Wishing you all a super-fun New Year's Eve—with super-fun people!

Girl Online, going offline xxx

Chapter Thirty-Three

In the olden days, people used to talk about time as if it were a person. They used to call him Father Time. According to Elliot, Father Time was an old man with a long white beard who carried an hourglass everywhere. I've decided that he also had a really mean sense of humor. Think about it. Whenever something horrible happens to you—like you're stuck in an algebra exam, or you're having a filling, or you fall over onstage and show your underwear—time goes by so slowly that every second feels like an hour, but whenever something really amazing happens to you—like you might actually be falling in love for the very first time—time goes by so fast you blink and an entire week has gone.

It's New Year's Eve morning. We're leaving tomorrow. We're leaving tomorrow and I'll be leaving the person I think I've fallen in love with. In the days since Christmas my list of evidence that Noah is my soul mate has grown and grown. I haven't put any more about it on my blog, though—there's no way I want to upset Elliot again. But, in my head, the list now includes things like:

- we both love to read books with killer twists at the end
- he takes me to special places I'd never find on my own
- I know exactly where I'd take him if he were ever to come to Brighton
- he loves my photographs and thinks I could exhibit in a gallery
- when he says this he makes me feel talented and confident and strong
- he hates selfies too
- we both love crunchy peanut butter
- he makes me say things like "we both love crunchy peanut butter"!

And tomorrow I'm going to have to leave him, fly across an entire ocean away from him, back to my phoney so-called friends and my barely-talking-to-me best friend. As I lie in my bunk and stare up at the ceiling, I feel hollowed out with sadness.

Unable to stand it anymore, I get out of bed and head downstairs. As I cross the hallway, I hear Sadie Lee's voice coming from the kitchen.

"Don't you think you should tell her?"

"No!" Noah's voice is so insistent it makes me stop dead. "I don't want to ruin it. It's been so cool—"

"Morning, Penny!" I jump and turn to see Dad at the top of the stairs. Argh! I hear the scraping back of a chair in the kitchen and Noah appears in the archway to the kitchen.

"Hey, Penny. Hey, Rob. You guys want some pancakes?"

"Is the Pope a Catholic?" Dad says, bounding downstairs. I force myself to smile at Noah but as I go to join him in the kitchen, I can't stop thinking about what I overheard. What were they talking about? Am I the "her" that Sadie Lee mentioned and, if so, what did she think Noah should tell me?

All day long the question bugs me, not helping my growing tension about leaving tomorrow. As I set about the horrible job of packing my suitcase, I start going over everything in my head, searching for clues that Noah might have been keeping something from me. In the whole time I've been staying in his house I haven't seen a single one of his friends. He hasn't seemed to have heard from anyone either, but then he is on his cell-phone detox. I'm still not entirely sure what he's been doing on his gap year either. He mentioned something about a part-time job in a store downtown but it was in the past tense. I sit down on my case with a sigh. Here I go again, searching for negative things instead of focusing on the positive. Noah took me to the art gallery. He introduced me to his friends there. He wouldn't have done that if he had something to hide. I don't even know that it was me Sadie Lee was talking about. The fact is, I only have a few hours left in New York. I can't ruin them with my stupid fears.

In the afternoon we all sit down at the kitchen table to play American Monopoly—well, all apart from Bella, who sits under the table playing with her dolls.

"Are you looking forward to Times Square tonight, Pen?" Dad asks as he hands out everyone's money. Dad's always the banker whenever we play Monopoly. He always wins too. I'm not entirely sure these two facts aren't related.

"Yes," I reply, but the truth is I'm not looking forward to it at all. We're going to Times Square to see in the new year, but as soon as the clock strikes midnight it will turn from the year

I met Noah to the year I have to leave him. I feel the overwhelming urge to cry, and begin studying the differences in the American Monopoly board to stop myself. But it's hard to be riveted by the fact that the stations are all called "railroads" when it feels as if your heart is breaking. Noah takes hold of my hand under the table. I look at him and smile.

"You OK?" he mouths to me.

I nod.

"I can see you holding hands," Bella calls out in a singsong voice from under the table.

Noah and I look at each other and laugh.

"You know, I was thinking," Noah says to Sadie Lee. "Why don't you all go out to Times Square with them and I'll babysit Bella."

"I don't need babysitting," Bella yells. "I'm not a baby!"

"OK, I'll *big-girl-sit* Bella," Noah says. "You deserve a night out, G-ma."

Sadie Lee stares at him. I stare at him. Why is he offering to babysit on our last night together?

"But what about Penny?" Sadie Lee says.

Yes, what about me? I want to yell.

"Well, I was thinking that Penny might want to babysit with me?" Noah looks at me hopefully.

I instantly grin. Spending my last night at home with Noah is way more appealing than being swamped by the crowds of people at Times Square.

"Big-girl-sit!" Bella yells, correcting Noah.

"Big-girl-sit," Noah says.

"But surely Penny wouldn't want to miss Times Square at New Year's?" Sadie Lee says, looking at me.

"I wouldn't mind at all," I say. "In fact, I'd prefer it."

"You would?" Dad looks at me and raises his eyebrows.

I pray to the God of Gullible Parents for a miracle.

"Are you worried about all the crowds?" Mum says, looking at me concerned.

I hardly dare breathe—could my miracle have been granted so soon?

"Yes," I say, and it isn't strictly a lie; I do hate big crowds.

"Maybe it would be best if we all stay home tonight," Mum says. "We have got to get up early for our flight tomorrow."

"No!" I practically yell. I take a moment to calm myself down. I don't want to give the game away. "I'd feel horrible if you just stayed in because of me and, anyway, there's no point feeling bad about it. I'd be way happier babysitting."

Bella emerges from under the table looking really cross. "I'm not a baby!" she says to me with her hands on her hips.

I laugh and pull her up onto my knee. "I know you're not. I'm sorry." Bella snuggles into me and I wrap my arms around her.

"I sure am gonna miss you, Penny," she says.

"I sure am gonna miss you too," I say in a fake American accent.

Everyone laughs, then Dad starts to nod. "OK then, if you're certain," he says.

I look at him and smile. "Yes, I'm certain." I don't think I've ever been more certain of anything in my life.

Once Mum and Dad and Sadie Lee and Sadie Lee's friend Betty have headed off to Times Square, Noah asks Bella what she'd like to do.

She tilts her head to one side and thinks about it for all of a second before answering, "Please can we play princesses?"

Noah laughs. "Oh man. Who do I get to be? Princess Noah?"

Bella shakes her head. "No, silly. You're the famous rock-star prince."

"Good role," I say, nodding my approval to Noah.

"Right," Noah says, looking distinctly unimpressed.

"And Penny is Princess Autumn and I'm Princess Bella the Third."

Noah looks at me and raises his eyebrows. "What happened to Bella the First and Second?"

"They were killed by an alien pig."

I bite down on my bottom lip to stop myself from laughing.

"Go and get your guitar then," Bella says to Noah. It suddenly dawns on me that I haven't seen Noah play the guitar since the day we met.

"And, Penny, you have to dress up like a princess."

"I don't think I've got any princess clothes."

"What about *the* dress?" Noah says. "The one you were wearing the night of the wedding party."

"Oh yes."

I run upstairs to Mum and Dad's room and find the dress in Mum's luggage. This time I don't put the shoes or headband on. I stay barefoot and let my curls tumble loosely over my shoulders.

When I get back to the living room, Noah is sitting on the edge of the sofa strumming a beautiful black guitar with a pearly white fret board.

"OK, still majestic," he says as soon as he sees me.

"Why, thank you, Prince Rock Star."

"You're welcome, Princess Autumn."

Bella, who has gotten changed into a gorgeous satin princess dress in deep purple, looks at me and claps her hands. "This is going to be so much fun!" She turns to Noah. "Play her the song."

"Which song?"

"*The* song," Bella says, looking at him pointedly. "You know, the one you wrote about her," she whispers loudly.

Noah's face flushes. "Oh, no, I can't, it's not finished yet. How about I do one from *Frozen*? Bella's seen the movie *Frozen* about seventy million times," he says to me with a grin.

Bella claps her hands together. "Yes! Sing 'Let It Go.' Please!"

Noah plays a few chords on his guitar, then starts to sing.

Bella starts dancing around the room with her teddy bear. "I love this song," she says to me breathlessly.

And as Noah carries on singing, I fall in love with it too. His voice is so beautiful, so soft and husky. The kind of voice that really makes you pay attention. I glance over at him and see that he's staring at me intently while he sings. Is he singing it to me? Does he actually mean the words he's singing? As the song builds and he gets to a line about overcoming your fears, he looks straight at me and I feel shivers run up and down my spine.

"Dance with me," Bella says, pulling me up from the sofa.

I hold her hands and we start spinning around and around, faster and faster. It's as if Noah's voice is carrying us and it makes me feel powerful, invincible, fearless, and free. It makes me feel head over heels in love.

Chapter Thirty-Four

After two hours of singing and dancing and acting out elaborate storylines involving beautiful princesses and rock-star princes and alien-pig invasions, Bella is limp with tiredness.

"I think somebody might be ready for bed," Noah says, putting his guitar down.

"No!" Bella cries, but it's really halfhearted and she rests her head in my lap.

"I tell you what, why doesn't Penny read you a bedtime story while I do a bit of clearing up down here."

Bella immediately springs upright. "OK!"

Noah looks at me and smiles. "Take your time," he says. "I've got a few things to sort out here."

I nod and pick Bella up. "Come on then, Princess Bella the Third."

Once I've gotten Bella in bed, I put Princess Autumn on the pillow next to her.

"I'm gonna be so sad when you go," Bella says in a tired little voice.

"I'm going to be really sad too," I say, smoothing down

her hair. "I was thinking—maybe Princess Autumn should stay with you."

Bella's eyes open wide. "For real?"

I smile. "Yes. I think she'd be happier here."

Bella nods. "I think you're right. And that way, every time I feel sad about you I can play with Princess Autumn instead."

"Exactly." I tuck Princess Autumn in next to Bella and start telling her a story about Prince William and Princess Kate and the day they had to rescue the Queen from an alien-pig invasion. Eventually, she falls asleep. I kiss her on the forehead and I'm just about to leave when Noah comes in.

"Good work," he whispers as he sees her asleep. "I'll just kiss her good night. I'll see you down in the basement."

I nod and a weird sensation of excitement and fear courses right through me to the soles of my feet. Finally, Noah and I are going to be alone together.

As I go down into the basement, I see some twinkling fairy lights at the far end. At first I think it's coming from a Christmas tree but it's the wrong shape. I go past the sofas and see that the lights are coming from the pool table. But it doesn't look like a pool table anymore because it's got blankets draped over it and fairy lights strung all around it.

I hear Noah coming down the steps behind me.

"I built you a tent," he says. "I remembered what you said about it being your favorite place when you were younger, where you felt safe and . . ." He breaks off, looking embarrassed.

Completely without warning, my eyes fill with tears.

"Was it a dumb idea?" Noah asks, looking at me. "Oh crap, you're crying. It was a dumb idea. I'm sorry, I—"

"No," I interrupt. "It's one of the nicest things anyone's ever done for me."

Noah smiles. "Seriously?"

"Yes." I look up at him. "Thank you for listening to me. For remembering what I say to you."

Noah frowns. "Why wouldn't I remember?" He grabs my hand. "Wait till you see what's inside."

Giggling, I follow him over to the tent. He's pinned a handwritten sign to one of the blankets.

THIS HERE IS PENNY'S TENT. KEEP OUT!
...unless your name is Noah.

He pulls back an opening in the blanket and gestures at me to go in. I get down on my knees and crawl inside. The entire floor is covered in different-colored cushions and the edges are lit by a string of fairy lights that are fading in and out. In one corner there's a tray of Sadie Lee's homemade mince pies. In another corner there's a tray with a jug of lemonade and a couple of glasses.

"This is amazing," I say, as Noah crawls in after me.

"Are you sure?" He looks at me with such intensity, as if he's trying to read my mind, to make sure that I'm telling the truth.

"Yes! It's way better than the tents I used to make. I never had fairy lights for a start."

Noah grins.

"Or a—" I break off, embarrassed.

"Or a what?"

He stares at me. We're so close I can feel his breath on my face.

"Or a handsome prince." I look down at the cushions.

"Penny?"

I look back up at him. He's looking really serious.

"Yes?"

"I really like you."

"I really like you too."

"No, I mean, *really* like you. I like you so much it might even be . . ."

I look at him, willing him to say it.

". . . love," he whispers.

I nod and take hold of his hand. "I like you so much it might even be love too."

He laughs. "You don't get lines that smooth in the movies."

I laugh too. "No. But smooth is very overrated."

And then he wraps his strong arms around me and pulls me close. "I'm so sad you're leaving," he whispers in my ear.

"Me too." I lean into him and rest my head on his shoulder.

"But this isn't it, you know?"

I pull back and look at him. His hair is tumbling in messy waves around his face. I fight the urge to reach out and touch it.

"I'll figure out some way to come visit you in the UK, and you can come back here whenever you want and until then we can hang out online. I'm even prepared to break my Internet detox for you," he says with a grin.

"I'm honored," I say.

"You should be," he says.

And then he starts to kiss me. Little kisses as light as butterfly wings all the way up the side of my neck. Then on my face, my eyelids, the tip of my nose, until finally our lips meet. And our kiss is so passionate and full of meaning I don't want it to ever end. But then something starts beeping. I pull away from Noah and stare at him in alarm.

"What's that?"

"Sorry, it's my watch. I set it for midnight so we wouldn't miss the new year." Noah pulls me back in toward him. "Happy New Year, Penny," he says.

"Happy New Year, Noah," I say, hoping with everything that I've got that it will be.

Noah gently guides me down so that we're lying on the cushions and, as he holds me to him, I silently beg Father Time to show some compassion and freeze all the clocks in the world so that our kisses will last forever.

Chapter Thirty-Five

It's official. I hate Father Time. I hate him more than I hate school bullies and exams and even pickled onions. In the end, Noah and I got about an hour together before the others arrived back home. An hour that flew by in a nanosecond. But I have discovered one small consolation. Whenever I close my eyes and remember what happened, my skin starts tingling where Noah touched me and it's like I'm with him all over again. I might not have been able to stop time but at least I'm able to time-travel back to the tent. I'm doing it now as I wait in the hallway for Mum and Dad to bring down their luggage. Sitting on my suitcase, eyes closed, remembering the way Noah stroked my hair and ran his fingers down my back.

"Penny for your thoughts."

I open my eyes and see Noah looking at me from across the hallway.

"I was thinking about the tent." My face starts to flush.

"Me too. I can't stop thinking about it." Noah comes over and takes hold of my hands. "Why don't you go down there and hide? I'll tell your parents you were abducted by alien pigs and they can go home without you."

I give him a sad smile. "I wish I could."

He puts his arm around me and I rest my head on his shoulder. It's a perfect fit. *We're* a perfect fit. This is so unfair.

"It'll be OK," he whispers in my ear. "It'll be OK."

But will it? How can it be, when we live so far apart?

All the way to the airport, I feel as if I have a ball of sorrow growing inside me like a tumor. Mum and Dad are traveling in Sadie Lee's car with Bella and I'm in the truck with Noah. Noah doesn't even need to do his running commentary of traffic maneuvers—I'm so numb with grief I can't even panic.

As we pull into a space in the terminal car park, Noah turns to me. "Listen, Penny, is it OK if I don't come in with you guys? I'm not very good at public goodbyes. I'd rather say what I have to say here—now—while it's just the two of us."

I feel a little stab of disappointment.

Noah reaches into the inside pocket of his jacket and pulls out a blank CD. "I have something for you. It's something I made—for you."

I take the CD and look at him hopefully. "Is it—is it the song that Bella was talking about?"

Color rises in Noah's cheeks. "It might be." He laughs. "OK, it is. I recorded it on my computer so the quality's not that great but I want you to have it. I want you to know how I feel."

I look at the CD player in the truck. "Can I play it now?"

Noah laughs and shakes his head. "No way!" He presses it

into my hands. "Save it for when you get home. That way it's like you'll have a message from me as soon as you get there."

The sorrow inside me starts to shrink a little. I take hold of Noah's hand. "Thank you. Oh, but I haven't got anything to give you."

"You've given me loads." He squeezes my hand. "You have no idea how much. Truth is, right before I met you, things had gotten a little—"

He's interrupted as Sadie Lee pulls into the space next to us.

"Never mind," Noah says with a sigh. He cups my face with his hand. "Penny, I like you so much it might even be love."

"I like you so much it might even be love too." My heart fills with hope. Doesn't love conquer everything? Isn't that what the song says? And if it does conquer everything then that has to include the Atlantic Ocean too.

I hear Sadie Lee's car door opening. Time is running out. Noah pulls me toward him and we kiss.

"I told you they love each other," Bella says in a loud voice right outside the truck.

All the way home on the plane, I cling onto that last conversation with Noah like an emotional life raft. Every time I feel anxious or upset I remind myself of how much has happened since I left the UK. It's almost as if I'm returning home as a totally different person. But this time I'm not having to pretend to be someone else—I don't need a superhero alter ego—this time I'm OK just being myself. Every time the plane hits some turbulence, I start running through a mental checklist of everything I've achieved since coming away: I've learned how to get my panic attacks under some kind of control, I've been the semi-official photographer at an American wedding, I've gone record shopping in Brooklyn, I've had my first ever American Christmas, I've fallen in love. *I've fallen in love!* And even as I watch the little plane icon on the screen in front of me slowly tracking its way farther and farther from America, farther and farther from Noah, I still feel OK. Somehow I feel certain that we'll make it work.

When we land in the UK, my relief at making it back safely combines with my newfound confidence, and even though I'm exhausted, I've never felt so determined. I'm going to sort things out with Elliot. I'm going to save up my money from my job at To Have and to Hold to pay for a flight back to New York. I don't care about the stupid video and I don't care about Megan and Ollie. I've shed my previous life like an old skin. I picture it drifting somewhere in the middle of the Atlantic Ocean.

We finally get home at just gone midnight. Everything looks different. Unfamiliar. The Christmas decorations look sad and dejected, and the house is freezing cold.

As Mum and Dad make some tea, I go straight up to my bedroom. I have to play Noah's CD. I plonk down onto my bed and straightaway I hear a knocking sound. Elliot! I hold my breath as I wait to decipher the code. One knock, followed by four knocks, followed by three: *I—love—you.* My body fills with relief. Since Christmas Day we haven't texted each other at all. It's the longest I've ever gone without having any contact with Elliot. Before I can respond he's knocking again. *Can I come over?* I quickly do the code for *Yes, come over right now.*

I can play the CD later. I need to get things back on track with Elliot first. I hear his front door shutting and I lie back on my bed staring up at the ceiling. I hear Dad letting Elliot in, the gentle murmur of their voices. Elliot's feet pounding up the stairs. My life is slotting back into its old patterns. I count the seconds till my bedroom door opens. One, two, three, four . . .

"Penny!" Elliot bursts in, breathless. "I'm so sorry. I've missed you so much. Are you—? Are we—OK?"

I sit up and smile. "Of course we are."

"Oh, thank God!" Elliot sits down on the end of my bed. "I'm so sorry I got so moody. But you have no idea the pressure I was under. It's been hell. Guess what my parents got me for Christmas?"

I shrug.

"A rugby season ticket. Rugby! They know I hate rugby. With a passion." Elliot throws his hands up in despair. "Why would you give your only son a present that you know he actively hates with a passion? Why? And they actually thought it would be a good idea for us to have a cheese fondue for Christmas dinner. I mean, hello! The seventies called—they say they need their kitsch back."

I shake my head in disbelief. "Oh, Elliot."

"I know. They're beyond help. Or hope." Elliot looks at me and sighs. "So go on then."

"What?"

"Tell me all about Prince Charming."

"Seriously?" I study Elliot's face for any sign that he doesn't really mean it.

Elliot smiles. "Yes, seriously."

So I give Elliot a watered-down version of my week with Noah, leaving out anything too corny that I think might make him feel jealous. When I finish, I look at him nervously.

Elliot's expression is unreadable. "But how do you feel now? Now you know you can't see him again?"

"It'll be OK—we'll work something out."

Elliot frowns. "But how? He's in New York and you're in Brighton."

"Yes, I know that." I fight hard to stay positive. "But we can visit each other."

Elliot nods but there's something about his gaze that looks really doubtful and it makes a chink in my armor of positivity.

We both fall silent and I start to really regret having said anything.

"So, do you have a picture of him?" Elliot asks, breaking the silence.

I nod and take my phone from my bag and scroll through to the picture of Noah in the park. "This was on Boxing Day morning, when he took me on the tour of his neighborhood."

As Elliot studies the picture, I study his face for a sign of approval. I so badly want him to like Noah and to be supportive. He gives a curt nod. "Very nice," he says, but I can detect a slight undercurrent of tension. "He looks kind of familiar. Must be those Johnny Depp cheekbones." He hands the phone back to me. "So, listen, how do you fancy coming into town with me tomorrow? I've decided to buy a plaid shirt, to go with my new cowboy hat."

And that's it—conversation about Noah, over. As Elliot

carries on talking about how it's time to "Americanize his look," I feel so disappointed. Surely your best friend should be happy for you when you meet someone? Surely they should want to hear all about them? I just don't understand what Elliot's problem is. Especially now that I'm home and thousands of miles away from Noah.

I'm thousands of miles away from Noah.

Just as I'm about to be engulfed in a wave of sadness, my text alert goes off. While Elliot is still talking, I dive for my phone and open the message.

> Hope you're home safe. But wish you were still here. I miss you, Inciting Incident

I grin with relief.

"Should I go?" Elliot says, looking pointedly at the phone.

"What?" I say, distracted as I start composing my reply to Noah in my head.

"Do you want me to leave?"

"Oh. Well, I am pretty tired—from the flight."

Elliot gets up. "'OK. See you tomorrow then."

"Sure."

As soon as Elliot has gone I send a reply to Noah.

> Yes, home safe but miss you too and wish I was there too. Just about to play your CD xx

I light the orange-and-cinnamon candle that Sadie Lee gave me for Christmas and put on my fairy lights. My text alert goes off again.

Gulp! I hope you like it

I open the case and take out the CD. I suddenly get an attack of nerves. I've been imagining it as a heartwarming ballad but what if it's something jokey and silly? What if it's about how much I love crunchy peanut butter? *Get a grip*, I tell myself as I put the CD into the stereo and press play. I needn't have worried. Right from the very first gentle strum of the guitar, I know that it's going to be beautiful. As I lean back against my bed, I spot a little folded-up note inside the CD case. I open it as Noah starts singing. At the top of the page is the title "Autumn Girl." Beneath it are the lyrics. I read them as Noah sings.

AUTUMN GIRL
Autumn Girl
You changed my world
You made my winter golden

When I was lost
You made me found
Your loving smile
Turned my life around

Autumn Girl
You changed my world
You made the moon shine amber

And now you're far
Away from me
I close my eyes
And still I see
Your sunset hair
Your glowing skin
The arms I long
To be held in.

Autumn Girl
You changed my world
You changed my world
You changed my world

By the time the song's finished playing, my entire body is glowing like my cinnamon candle. Noah wrote that for me. He wrote those beautiful words for me. About me. I grab my phone and send him a text. I go overboard with kisses at the end, because I know he won't mind.

I love it! Thank you ☺xxxxxxxx

Straightaway he replies.

> Seriously?

> Yes!!! It's beautiful Xxxx

> So are you

I'm about to reply when he sends another text.

> The most beautiful inciting incident in the history of inciting incidents

> Ditto xxx

That night, when I go to sleep, I play Noah's song on repeat and I imagine myself back in the tent, surrounded by the warm glow of fairy lights and with Noah's arms wrapped tight around me. For the first night in ages I don't have any nightmares.

HAPPY NEW YEAR!

Hello!

I hope you all had a great Christmas.

So, I'm back home. And as it's the start of a whole new year I thought it would be fun to do a post about new year's resolutions.

On the plane on the way home I read a magazine article that said you should only choose three new year's resolutions because that way there's way more chance of you actually achieving them.

This is so true!

I used to be so into new year's resolutions I'd write pages of them and then, by February, when I'd only done about one of them *(and never the one about eating less chocolate)* I'd feel all crap about myself and not bother anymore.

So this year I'm only going to have three and I think it would be really cool if you guys each chose three too and posted them in the comments below and then we can keep up-to-date with each other's progress—just like on the fear post.

So I'll start. This year my three resolutions are:

Number One: To be happy

Number Two: To face my fears

Number Three: To believe in myself

OK, I just realized something as I was typing.

If it wasn't for Brooklyn Boy I wouldn't be posting those resolutions at all.

The truth is he's already helped me to start achieving all three of them.

I'm missing him SO much right now but your comments on my previous post have really helped me.

Thank you so much to everyone who said that things will work out between us. If I could add on a sneaky extra resolution it would be to believe in that too.

And thank you to everyone who posted about the fun people who've made the weirdest places interesting. I loved hearing about them.

And to all of you who have asked me to post a picture of Brooklyn Boy, I'm really sorry, but some things just need to be kept private. I hope you understand.

Happy New Year, everyone—I can't wait to read your resolutions!

Girl Online, going offline xxx

★ ᴄ𝒽𝒶𝓅𝓉𝑒𝓇 𝒯𝒽𝒾𝓇𝓉𝓎-𝒮𝒾𝓍 ★

As soon as I've posted my blog, I sit down at my dressing table and start getting ready to go out with Elliot. It's almost midday and Mum and Dad have gone to the supermarket to do a mega-shop as there's hardly any food in the house. Tom is back home and downstairs doing some last-minute work on a uni assignment. Everything around me is going back to how it was before New York—but I'm not.

As Noah's song plays in the background, I look at my reflection in the dressing-table mirror. On the surface I'm the same person—the same sprinkling of freckles on my nose and the same auburn hair—but how I see myself is totally different. It's a bit like when you watch a movie with a killer twist at the end and you discover that the goodie is actually the baddie. But in this case the twist is that I've discovered that I'm not embarrassing and ugly after all. I've discovered that the things I thought were ugly actually make me look like autumn—and sunsets. I don't need to conceal my freckles with a layer of foundation anymore. I don't need to tie my hair back to hide its redness. I can leave it down and show it off.

Seeing myself through Noah's eyes has helped me to see the truth. I look at the photo of Noah pinned to the top of my mirror. I printed it out as soon as I woke up this morning so that I'm still able to see him whenever I want. "Thank you," I whisper to his smiling face.

I'm just about to brush my hair when the text alert goes off on my phone. My first thought is Noah but as I click into my messages my heart doesn't just sink—it plummets. It's from Megan.

> Hey, Penny! Are you back home? It would be lovely to catch up xoxo

I stare at the screen. And then I realize that this is one of those "put your money where your mouth is" moments. If I truly have changed I have to prove it with my actions, starting right here, with Megan. I click on reply and text back.

> No thanks

As the text alert goes off my heart pounds so hard it actually feels like it might come bursting up through my throat.

> What?!!!

I take a deep breath and start to type.

> I don't want to catch up with you because
> I've got nothing to say to you

I sit tapping my fingers on my dressing table waiting for her response. I picture her throwing her hair back over her shoulder and pouting. She seems so silly now—so childish. It's as if going halfway across the world has allowed me to see everything so clearly; it's like it's given me a bird's-eye view of my life and everything that needs to change. My phone goes off.

> I can't believe you're being like this!
> And after all I've done for you!

What?! I stare at the phone. All she's done for me? This time I feel no nervousness as I type my reply. This time I'm fired up by anger.

> What, like posting that video of me on Facebook
> and constantly putting me down? I can do
> without that kind of friendship, thanks. Don't
> contact me again

I press send and, although my hands are shaking like crazy, I feel really proud. And then I realize that I just managed to achieve all three of my resolutions in one go. I faced my fear of Megan, I believed in myself, and it's made me feel incredibly happy. I refresh the page on my blog and see that I've already got two comments.

Hi Girl Online,

Happy New Year!

My three resolutions are:

1.   To be proud of how I look

2.   To read more books

3.   To cut down on sugar

Amber xx

I quickly post a reply to her.

Thanks, Amber. Good luck—especially with the sugar one! Xx

I scroll down to the next comment and what I see makes me freeze.

I just have one resolution this year—to make sure I never put the online world before the real one.

But it isn't the comment that's making me feel so sick, it's the username: Waldorf Wild. Elliot has posted on my blog.

He never posts on my blog. It's a kind of unwritten rule we've had from the start, to make sure that it stayed anonymous. And it has to be me he's talking about. I stare at the screen as I try to work out why he would write that. It must be because I blogged about Noah again. But what does he expect me to do when he keeps acting so weird about it all? At least my readers are supportive. At least they want to hear about it.

I hear the doorbell ring downstairs. Elliot's not supposed to be calling till one. I feel a glimmer of hope. Maybe he's feeling bad about the blog post. Maybe he's come around early to apologize.

I hear Tom and another male voice talking, then the sound of footsteps on the stairs and a knock on my bedroom door. I put my laptop on my dressing table and take a deep breath, trying to mentally prepare myself as I call out, "Come in." But no amount of deep breathing could prepare me for what happens next. The door opens, and Ollie walks in.

"Ollie!"

"Hi, Penny." He shifts uncomfortably from foot to foot and runs his hand through his tousled blond hair. "I hope you don't mind me coming round like this. Your brother— he told me to come up."

"Oh." I stare at him for a moment, not having a clue what else to say. Why is he here, in my house? He looks so awkward and embarrassed, like he isn't sure why he's here either. "Come in, sit down," I say finally, gesturing at my armchair.

Ollie comes in and stands by the chair. He really does look embarrassed. He's holding a flat package wrapped in Christmas paper. He sees me looking at it and holds it out. "I—er—I got you a gift."

"Really?" I'm barely able to conceal my shock. I take the present from him and put it on the bed. "Sit down—if you want?"

Ollie sits down. "You look really different," he says, "really great. Not that you didn't look great before of course."

OK, what is happening here? Then I get a horrible sick feeling. Has Megan sent him around? Is this all part of some elaborate trick to get back at me for my texts? But it can't be. Ollie got here way too quickly. And he looks way too shy.

"Thank you," I mumble.

"So, did you have a good time?" he says.

"Yes, it was amazing." And just the thought of New York and Noah makes me feel calmer again. This situation is very weird but it's OK. I can handle it.

"Good." Ollie looks down at the floor. "Look, I—the reason I—I wanted to see you before we go back to school is to say that I'm sorry."

I stare at him. "What for?"

"For what happened after the play—not that I posted that video or shared it or anything," he adds quickly.

I nod, remembering his comment that he thought I looked cute.

"But I'm really sorry it happened. And that you had to stay off school because of it."

I study his face for any sign that he might be lying but he looks completely genuine and really concerned.

"The thing is—I like you, Penny."

I become aware that my mouth is now actually hanging open in shock.

"I need to go to the toilet."

I don't know why I say it—well, I do—it's because I have to get out of there for a moment to try to make sense of everything that's happening, but still.

"Oh. OK." Ollie nods and takes a step back.

"I'll be right back." Before he can say another word, I race from the room.

Once I'm safely locked in the bathroom, I start pacing up and down—which is pretty difficult as the room's only about six feet long.

Ollie likes me. *Pace, pace.* What does he mean he likes me? As in *like*, likes me? Oh no! I actually groan out loud as I think back to my conversation with Noah. Everything really has changed since I've gotten back from New York, because for years I've dreamed about Ollie saying something like that to me. So many nights I've lain in bed, running through Ollie-telling-me-he-likes-me scenarios in my head. But I never, ever thought it would happen. And I never, ever thought that if it did by some miracle happen, I would end up feeling . . . nothing. All of the scenarios I played through in my head ended in a passionate kiss. But meeting Noah has made me realize that my feelings for Ollie were only a crush. They weren't based on any reality. They were all based on my fantasies.

But this isn't a fantasy. This, right now, is very, very real and I have to deal with it immediately. I splash my face with some cold water and look at myself in the bathroom mirror. *You can do this*, I tell myself.

When I get back into my bedroom, Ollie is, rather worryingly, sitting on my bed.

"Please tell me you don't have a crush on him too," he says, nodding toward the picture of Noah on my mirror.

"What?"

"Noah Flynn. Megan won't stop going on about him and that stupid "Bridge" song. I keep telling her that he's madly in love with Leah Brown but she won't listen."

Just like the moment before the car crash, everything starts happening in a weird slow motion. I hold on to the back of my chair to steady myself. "What did you say?"

Ollie nods at the picture again. "The singer Noah Flynn. Have you got a crush on him too?"

⋆⁎ Chapter Thirty-Seven ⁎⋆

I focus my gaze on Ollie and try to ground myself. The world hasn't just turned inside out and upside down. There has to be some kind of explanation for this. "I—I know him."

Ollie smiles. "Yeah, right."

"I do. I met him in New York."

I sit down at my dressing table, my brain going into overdrive. What did Ollie mean, do I have a crush on him? And why did he say Noah was madly in love with Leah Brown? Leah Brown is a mega-famous pop star.

Ollie leans forward, looking really impressed. "Seriously?" I nod.

"Wow, Megan's going to be so jealous when you tell her. What was he like?" Ollie's now looking at me so wide-eyed, it's like I just said I met the president.

"He was—is—really nice. I don't get what you said before, though—about him and Leah Brown . . ."

"Oh, they're dating. And apparently he's written a track for her next album or something."

Ollie says this so casually it almost makes me want to laugh.

This is all so ridiculous. So unbelievable. Or is it? I feel a horrible sense of unease as the conversation I overheard between Noah and Sadie Lee pops into my head. Was this what she was saying he ought to tell me? But it can't be. This is way too big. There's no way Noah could be famous, and have a girlfriend, let alone a world-famous drop-dead-gorgeous girlfriend, without me knowing about it. Ollie must have the wrong person. It must be a coincidence.

"Are you sure it's him?" I say.

Ollie gets up and studies the picture. "Yeah, definitely. He's got the same tattoo on his wrist." He turns and stares at me. "Why are you asking that? You must know it's Noah Flynn if you met him."

"Yes, I . . ." It suddenly dawns on me that Noah never told me his surname.

"I—I'm not feeling too good," I say, sitting down on the bed.

"Oh no." Ollie puts his hand on my shoulder, making me wince.

"Really, I think you should go."

"What—but—you were fine a minute ago."

"Yes, but now I'm not." I don't care how rude I sound. I just need him out of here. I need to get to the bottom of this.

"Oh. OK. But I was going to—I wanted to ask you if . . ."

How can Noah be a famous singer? It doesn't make sense. Yet in a horrible way it does. His incredible voice. The song he wrote for me. But why would he write a song like that for me if he was with someone else?

"Would you like to come out for a pizza or something?"

"What?" I look at Ollie, horrified.

"It's all right, Penny—I know how you feel about me," he says. "I've known for years. Megan told me."

OK, now I feel as if I'm trapped inside a horror story that just keeps on getting worse and worse with every twist.

"And I think I might—well, I think I might finally feel the same."

Finally? Seriously?

"I need you to go," I say abruptly.

"OK, but is that a yes?" Ollie looks at me hopefully.

"No! It's a no. I'm sorry. Please can you leave?"

Ollie looks at me for a moment and there's a terrible silence. "Right," he says curtly. "See you in school then."

"Yes." I can barely think straight as I practically bundle him out of the door.

As soon as he's gone, I go straight over to my laptop, click out of my blog, and Google the name Noah Flynn. This has to be some stupid mistake. I don't know how or why, but Ollie must have been mistaken.

"Oh no!" I clap my hand to my mouth as a load of results come up. There's an image next to the second one. It's Noah, holding a guitar. I click on the link feeling sick to my stomach.

Sony Signs Internet Sensation Noah Flynn, the headline reads. I click on the article, overcome with shock and disbelief. Apparently, about two years ago Noah started posting songs on YouTube. He ended up getting over a million subscribers to his channel. Then a couple of months ago the record label Sony signed him. I feel a burst of pride as I read a quote from an executive at the label talking about Noah's "raw talent" and how excited they are to be producing his first album.

But then I remember what Ollie said about Noah and Leah Brown. Surely that can't be true. Leah Brown is a major star. A "travels in a private jet, headlines big festivals, and sells out arenas" kind of major star. Tom and his friends saw her at the Isle of Wight Festival last year. Hands trembling, I type *Noah Flynn* and *Leah Brown* into the search engine. A page of results fills the screen, mostly from American gossip sites. All of them are from about a month ago and all of them say the same thing: Leah Brown and Noah Flynn are an item. I'm so tense now I can barely breathe. About halfway down the page I see a result from Leah Brown's Twitter page.

Chillin' with @noahflynn at venice beach

I click on her page, my heart pounding. Her most recent post is wishing her fans a happy new year. Then there's one plugging her new single. And then . . . I shudder as I read it.

Merry xmas @noahflynn so looking forward to seeing you when I'm back from LA Xo

I scroll down again. It's like I can't stop now, no matter how much it hurts.

With my baby @noahflynn at the sony xmas party Xo

This one is attached to a photo of Leah Brown standing behind Noah with her arms draped around him. It's dated the day before I met Noah. Seeing this actually makes me retch.

I go to Noah's Twitter profile in search of more incriminating evidence, but he's only ever made three tweets and all of them are about his record deal. I look up at the photo of him on my mirror and my eyes fill with hot, angry tears. How could he have done this to me? How could he have lied so convincingly and so coldly, all the time knowing that he had a girlfriend? And not just any old girlfriend—a world-famous girlfriend who is madly in love with him. And how could Sadie Lee have let him do that to me?

My text alert goes off. I have a moment of horror at the prospect of it being Noah. What am I going to say to him? What am I going to do? I pick up the phone with trembling hands. But it's from Elliot.

> Not in the mood for going into town. Think I'll
> stay in and do my math homework instead x

I stare at the screen. So he isn't sorry at all for writing that comment on my blog. He doesn't even want to see me. I bet he would if he knew this latest twist. I suddenly feel overwhelmed by anger. I'm glad Elliot doesn't want to go into town. I'm glad I don't have to tell him what's happened and see the look of pleasure on his face. And then it feels as if all of the foundations in my life have started to crumble. All of the strength I'd built up while I was away begins to dissolve.

I get into bed, burrow right down under the duvet, and start to sob. And once I start I can't stop because I keep on thinking of more things, more evidence that Noah was lying to me. The girl who'd kept staring at him when we went to the vintage store to get the tiara. What was it she'd said into her phone? "*It is*"? It is what? It is him? And the way she'd started coming over toward us when we got in the truck. And the way Noah had sped off. Had he realized she'd recognized him? But then he'd taken me to the art gallery and introduced me to his friends. Why would he do that if he was lying to me about everything? But even that takes on a more sinister meaning now. When the woman we met in the corridor said well done to him, she must have been talking about the recording contract. It hadn't been to do with not having a girlfriend at all. He'd barefaced lied to me.

I feel feverish with shock and embarrassment. But I can't stop the awful realizations from coming. The way he'd cut Antonio off in the café and hurried me out of there when we'd finished our lunch. I squirm as I remember how happy I'd been, thinking that he'd wanted to spend more time alone with me, but it had actually all been to protect his lie. I think of him hugging me in the darkened corridor and how special that moment had felt, and my embarrassment is replaced with fury.

"Liar!" I yell, getting out of bed. I go over to my dressing table, tear the picture off the mirror, and rip it into pieces. "Liar! Liar! Liar!"

I sink down onto the floor, sobbing my heart out. I'd actually thought I'd escaped my curse; that I could be myself and be accepted and loved. But it was all based on lies and deceit. And to think I'd actually blogged about it. I actually told the world I'd fallen in love and met my soul mate. What was I thinking?

I spend the next few hours lying curled up in my bed. Unable to move. Unable to do anything apart from cry into my pillow. Thankfully, Mum and Dad think I'm sleeping off my jet lag so they've left me alone.

Finally, when the day has turned to night and my room is back in darkness, I feel able to face the world again. Well, my bedroom at least. I peel back the duvet and stare out into the darkness. The fact is, much as I might want to, I'm not going to be able to stay in my bed forever. I've got to face up to what's happened. I turn on my phone and the text alert immediately goes off. A text from Noah. I feel a chill run through my body.

> Hey, Inciting Incident, wassup? I miss you. Bella misses you. Sadie Lee misses you. Let me know when you're awake and you feel like skyping

I stare at the text in disbelief. How has he got the nerve to be so blasé about it all? How can he send me messages like that when he has a girlfriend? But I have no energy left to get angry. I feel totally drained. Shaking and crying, I start writing a reply.

> I don't think this is going to work out and I think it's probably best if we don't contact each other again. Sorry

I frown at the text. Why have I written "sorry"? Why the hell should I be apologizing to him?! I delete the word "sorry" and send the text before I have time for any second thoughts. Then I turn the phone straight off again and get back into bed.

As I burrow down under the duvet, I remember what Bella said to me the time she caught me crying over Elliot. Whenever you're sad, you should think of three happy things to chase the sadness away. I rack my brains. In the end, all I can think of is my blog. Right now, it's the only thing that makes me feel remotely happy. At least on my blog I have people who understand me. At least on my blog I can totally be myself and everyone loves and supports me. I feel a tiny glimmer of hope. In the morning I'll blog about what's happened. I won't go into the details but I'll tell them that Brooklyn Boy turned out to be a total sham. My readers will know what to do and what to say. They'll help me get over this. They have to.

Chapter Thirty-Eight

When I wake up, it's still dark and I feel disoriented. What time is it? What day is it? What country am I in? And then a horrible nauseous feeling churns in my stomach. Something really bad has happened but I can't remember what.

The sick feeling reaches the tips of my limbs as I remember: Noah. I close my eyes tight and will myself to go back to sleep just so I can forget about it again. But it's no good. Horrible memories crowd into my mind. Noah lied to me. About everything. He's a professional musician. He has a record deal. And a girlfriend. A girlfriend who used to have pride of place on my brother's wall—not literally, of course, that would be really weird, but in poster form.

It all feels so strange and unreal. I'm just a schoolgirl from Brighton. The closest I've ever come to a celebrity was the time Elliot and I walked past Fatboy Slim in Snooper's Paradise and I sneezed and my chewing gum flew out of my mouth and landed on his coat. I do not get romantically involved with American YouTube sensations who also happen to be going out with Leah Brown. How has this even happened to me?

I sit bolt upright and stare into the darkness. Was nothing real? Had Noah just been using me? Was I just some entertainment for him while Leah Brown was out of town? It doesn't make sense. Either he has to be the world's worst liar or there's some kind of explanation. Then I remember the text I sent him. How will he have responded? I fumble around for my phone and turn it on. Both my text alert and email notification go off. I think of the happy-new-year blog post I wrote and I cringe. Then I think of having to tell my readers that Brooklyn Boy was a big old con artist and I cringe some more.

I take a deep breath and click on my text messages. Two from Noah. The first one was sent right after I sent mine telling him I didn't want any more contact with him.

> What the hell? This is a joke, right? Call me!
> I can't get through to your phone

The second text was sent at 5:30 a.m.—I check the clock on my phone—less than an hour ago.

> I hope whatever they paid you was worth it.
> Damn right there'll be no more contact.
> I've changed my number and email address.
> I never want to hear from you again.
> I trusted you

What the hell?! I click out of the message and back in again, to make sure I wasn't seeing things, but it's right there in front of me. Why is *he* so mad at me? And what does he mean, *he* trusted me? I'm not the one who's been lying. I'm not the one with a girlfriend. Too angry to think straight, I start typing a reply.

> YOU trusted me?! What about my trust? How could you have lied to me like that? How could you have thought I wouldn't find out? Didn't you care?

Adrenaline courses through my veins as I click send. Almost immediately the text notification goes off. Message failed. I look back at his text. He must have changed his number already. He's cut me off completely. But why . . . ? And then I get it. He realized I'd discovered his lies and he's gone on the defensive. Wow! I sit back on my bed, stunned at how wrong I'd been about him. He's probably worried that Leah Brown might find out. Like I'm going to call her and say, "Hey, Leah, you don't know me—in fact, I'm just some random school-girl from Brighton—but while you were spending Christmas in LA I was busy falling in love with your boyfriend in New York."

My anger and indignation fade into sorrow. How has this even happened? How can the Noah and I who saw in the new year together in that magical tent now be so completely cut off from each other? I feel a weird stabbing ache inside my rib cage, like my heart has just been torn in two.

Hoping for a distraction from the tears welling in my eyes, I click into my email account. I have 237 new messages. I feel a tiny shot of happiness. People must have been posting their new year's resolutions on my blog. But when I go to my inbox I see that at least half of them are Twitter notifications. I immediately feel uneasy. I only opened a Twitter account to share my blog posts and follow a few of my favorite photographers and other bloggers. I never get this many notifications. I click on one out of curiosity.

@girlonline22 you make me sick

What?! I click on another one.

@noahflynn cheats on @leahbrown with UK blogger @girlonline22. WTF?!!

Panic starts rising inside of me. Who are these people? Why are they saying these things? How do they know?

I go straight to my Twitter account and start scrolling through the notifications. There are a few from regular readers of my blog all saying things like: "Is it true? Is Brooklyn Boy Noah Flynn?" And a few saying, "Who is Noah Flynn?" But the rest are from total strangers and they're horrible.

omg, like @leahbrown has anything to worry about? @girlonline22 is an ugly dog

Trying to get your 5 minutes of fame @girlonline22?

I hate people who kiss and tell @girlonline22 #noclass

On and on they go. Finally, I get to a tweet from the American gossip site *Celeb Watch*.

I click on the link to their website and read the article in horror.

CELEB WATCH EXCLUSIVE!

While Leah Brown spent Christmas in LA with her folks it looks like her new love interest Noah Flynn found someone else to smooch beneath the mistletoe—UK blogger Penny Porter, better known as Girl Online.

I stare at the screen in horror. They know my name. How do they know my name?

Giving him the pet name Brooklyn Boy, Penny has been blogging all about her time with Noah, not caring at all that he's currently in a relationship with Leah Brown. I guess some folk will do anything for their moment in the spotlight. Well, we wouldn't like to be in Noah's shoes when Leah gets back in town!

There are fifty-six comments beneath the post. I scroll down to the first one.

What a skank!

Someone has replied to it.

I don't think she's in it for the money. I think she sounds kinda sweet. He's the skank, cheating on his girlfriend while she's out of town.

Yeah but she must have known he had a girlfriend

How do they know what I sound like? I look back up at the article and see that they've linked to my blog. I click on the link and it takes me to the first post I wrote about Noah. I cringe as I reread my words, now knowing the truth. I look down at the most recent comments.

Yeah, but Prince Charming wasn't a cheater and Cinderella wasn't a ho.

Numb with dread, I scroll down and read more of the same. Then a couple of my regular readers posting "Is this true?" And finally, at the bottom of the feed, there's a post from Pegasus Girl.

Dear Penny,

I know you probably don't care what I think but I had to say something. The reason my parents' marriage broke up and my mum started drinking was because my dad went off with another woman. I was so happy that you'd found someone and fallen in love but getting involved with someone else's boyfriend isn't good. It causes so much pain. Sorry, I know it's none of my business but I feel so strongly about this subject I couldn't not say anything.

I don't think I can read your blog anymore.

Pegasus Girl

My email notification goes off again. Five more messages telling me that total strangers have mentioned me on Twitter. I click on one and see the word "hate" and quickly click out again.

I sit on the edge of my bed, staring at my phone in terror.

I picture people all over the world reading about me, posting hate-filled messages about me. People I don't know. People who've never even met me. But they know who I am. They know my name. And they know my blog. What if they find out where I live? What if they come to this house? My body starts shaking and tears start streaming down my face. What am I going to do? I have to go back to school tomorrow. How will I face everyone?

My throat tightens. I can't swallow. I can't breathe. I feel as if I'm shrinking. Tinier and tinier. I need help. I need someone to help me. But I can't move. My limbs feel as heavy as stone. I look at the door. It seems so far away. So unreachable. What am I going to do? I picture a mob of people marching down the road to my house. Setting up camp on the driveway. Throwing stones up at my window. Waving placards filled with abuse. I have nowhere I can feel safe anymore. My readers will all hate me. Everyone will hate me. Tears are pouring down my face now. I've never felt so frightened or so completely and utterly alone. Pressure keeps building in my head, like it's being clamped in a vise. I can't swallow. I can't see. I can't breathe.

Chapter Thirty-Nine

"Penny! Penny! What is it? What's wrong?" Mum races into the bedroom and turns on the light.

I'm lying curled up in a ball on the floor. Why am I on the floor? What's happened?

"Rob! Rob! Come here!" Mum yells. Then I feel her crouching down beside me and her hands clutching my arms. "It's OK, darling, it's OK."

I'm wailing now. I can hear myself but I feel disconnected somehow, like it's not really me, like I'm not really in my body.

"Can you sit up?" Mum says gently.

I hear feet pounding up the stairs.

"What's going on?" Dad says. "Oh no, Pen, what's happened?"

I feel his arms around me, big and strong. I somehow find the strength to ease my way into a seated position and lean into him. I can't stop crying. I want to cry and cry my way back to being a baby again so that I don't have to worry about anything anymore.

"What happened?" Dad says again softly.

"Is it . . . ? Did you have another panic attack?" Mum says. I hear her moving about behind me, then I feel her wrapping my duvet around me.

I nod, unable to speak. My teeth are chattering like crazy.

"What caused it?" Dad says. He hugs me tightly. I want to stay like this forever, snuggled in a Dad-and-duvet cocoon.

How can I even begin to tell them? Noah lied to me about everything and now the whole world hates me. Or *will* hate me, once they've all found out.

"I don't know," I mumble. "I was just stressing about going back to school."

I feel Dad tense. "Has there been any more nonsense about that video? Because if there has I—"

"No. It's all cool. I was just being silly. And tired. I'm probably still jet-lagged." I start grabbing at excuses.

"Hmm." Mum doesn't sound too convinced.

But one thing I do know for sure in all my panic and confusion is that I can't dump this on them. I can't freak them out. I have to try to find a way to sort it myself.

"Do you want a cup of tea?" Mum says.

"Yes please."

"And how about some breakfast?" says Dad. "Shall I make you some pancakes?"

I nod, even though I'm not at all hungry.

Once they've tucked me up in bed and I've reassured them that I'm OK, they both head downstairs. I grab my laptop and log on to my blog and delete all of the posts about Noah. Then I change the settings so that no one can post comments. Instantly I feel a tiny bit better, like I've managed to shut a door on the haters.

I go back onto my Twitter account. I already have over twenty new notifications. I don't check them. Instead I fumble around in the settings and finally find the option to delete my profile. A message pops up: *Are you sure you want to delete your account?* I click down hard on YES. Another door shut.

I go to Facebook and take my account offline, once again ignoring all the new notifications.

Then I shut my laptop and stare at the wall in front of me. As the brain fog from my panic attack begins to lift a little, I start searching for answers. How has this happened? Who told *Celeb Watch* about me and Noah? Who told them about my blog?

My first thought is Ollie. He's the only person who knows that Noah is Noah Flynn. But I only told him that I'd met him. I didn't tell him that anything had happened between us. And there's no way Ollie knows about my blog. The only person who knows about that is Elliot.

I get a queasy feeling in the pit of my stomach. Surely Elliot wouldn't have done something like that. But he's been acting so weirdly about Noah. And he posted that snarky message on my blog yesterday. I never thought he'd do something like that so maybe . . . But Elliot didn't know Noah's true identity. Or did he . . . ? I think back to when I showed him the photo of Noah. He'd said something about him looking familiar. Had he recognized him then but not said anything? Is that why he changed the subject so abruptly? Oh my God, did Elliot leak the story? I stare at my bedroom wall, picturing Elliot on the other side, sending an anonymous message to *Celeb Watch*. It's all beginning to make a horrible kind of sense. Elliot was jealous of Noah and my blogging about him. Then he saw his picture and realized who he was and he saw the chance to ruin things for good. He must have canceled going out with me yesterday because he already had it planned. And he hasn't contacted me since. It's unheard of for Elliot to go so long without knocking on the bedroom wall at least. And he must have seen what's been happening online. I think of how he reacted when Megan posted the stupid knickers video. How he'd sent me a text to warn me and come around straightaway. But this time I haven't heard from him at all.

As the terrible truth dawns on me, I feel as if I've been punched in the stomach. First Noah and now Elliot. At least I'd only just met Noah—at least I can put what happened with him down to an appalling error of judgment. But Elliot? Elliot and I have known each other forever. He's my best friend. Or was.

I'm just about to start crying again when Mum comes in with a mug of tea. She places it on my bedside cabinet and sits down on my bed. "Are you sure there isn't something more specific troubling you, sweetie? Something you want to talk about?"

I shake my head, not daring to talk in case a sob escapes.

"OK, well you know where I am if you change your mind."

I nod and focus what little energy I have left on forcing my mouth into a smile. After she's gone, I sit with my eyes closed until Dad arrives with a plate of pancakes.

"I used Sadie Lee's special recipe," he says with a grin.

I feel another blaze of pain as I think of how much I'd liked Sadie Lee. But she's just another person who betrayed me.

After Dad's gone back downstairs—having made me

promise to yell for him the second I need anything—I put the pancakes down and stare into space. I feel so numb and so exhausted. All I want to do is stay in bed until this all blows over. If it ever does blow over.

Every time the email notification goes off on my phone I feel a stab of fear. In the end I turn my phone off and put it and my laptop in the bottom of my wardrobe, buried beneath a mound of clothes. For a while, this makes me feel safe, like no one can get to me anymore. But then I start picturing a mountain of abusive messages piling up inside my wardrobe, just waiting to engulf me as soon as I open the door.

And once again panic starts to take hold of me. But this time I remember what to do. This time I close my eyes and picture it inside my body: a large black ball of fear inside my rib cage. *It's OK*, I tell it—and myself. *It's OK.* And instead of panicking and trying to block it from my mind, I make myself picture it, right there inside of me. All black and dense and scary. I take a deep breath in through my nose. And another. "It's OK," I whisper out loud. And the fear starts to shrink a little. And as it does, I realize that it really is OK; it's not going to kill me. And then another thought pops into my head—what's happening to me won't kill me either. Yes, it's terrifying and yes, it's hugely painful, but it's not going to kill me. *It's OK.* I take another breath. The fear shrinks again. Now it's about the size of a tennis ball. And it's slowly fading, from black to grey, to white, and now gold. I take another breath. Outside a seagull squawks. I think of the sea and I actually manage a weak smile. *It's OK.* I can control this. I picture myself sitting on the beach, my entire body filling with golden sunlight. *It's OK.*

I sit like this for at least an hour, with my eyes closed, focusing on my breathing and listening to the seagulls. Then there's a knock on my door.

"Pen, can I come in?" Tom says.

I open my eyes and sit up straight. "Sure."

As soon as he walks into the room, I know he knows. I've never seen him look so worried.

"I've just been online," he says, sitting on the end of my bed. "Is it true? Did you and Noah Flynn . . . ?"

I look down at my lap.

"Is he the Noah Mum and Dad have been going on about? The one you were staying with?"

I nod, then I look up at Tom. "But I didn't know who he was, honestly. I'd never heard of him before. Had you?"

Tom nods. "Yeah. I'd heard on a music site that he'd been signed to the same label as Leah Brown and that they were an item. Didn't he tell you?"

I shake my head. "No! I'd never get involved with someone who had a girlfriend."

Tom frowns. "So he lied to you?"

I nod. "How did you find out?"

"It's all over Facebook. And Twitter. And Tumblr. And—"

"OK, OK."

"Have you seen what people are saying?"

I nod again and hot tears start burning my eyes. "I don't know what to do, Tom. I'm so scared."

Tom takes hold of my hand. "It's all right, sis. We're gonna sort this. How did that website find out?"

"I don't know. Someone must have told them."

"But who?"

I shrug. There's no way I can tell Tom I think it was Elliot—not until I'm absolutely sure.

"OK, well that doesn't matter for now. What matters is getting your side of the story out there."

Instantly, I start to panic. "Oh no. I can't. I can't go online again. No way."

Tom looks me straight in the eye. "Do you remember when I started secondary school and that kid Jonathan Price started picking on me and starting rumors about me?"

"The one who used to take your lunch?"

"Yeah. And do you remember how I'd pretend to be sick and beg Mum and Dad not to make me go in?"

"Yes."

"And then one day you said to me"—Tom puts on a squeaky high-pitched voice—"*But if you don't ever go back to school, no one will realize that he's lying.*"

"Did I say that?"

Tom nods.

"But I didn't sound like a Smurf."

Tom smiles. "Oh, yes you did. But you were right. And it was the one thing, out of everything that everyone said to me back then, that I actually listened to. It was the one thing that made me go back to school."

I stare at him. "Really?"

"Yes. Because you were right. If I hadn't gone back and kept hiding away in my bedroom, everyone would have believed him." He grins. "And they'd never have got to know what a truly incredible, gifted, and wonderful person I am."

I smile. "Not to mention modest."

"Yeah, that too. But it's the same for you now. If you hide

away and let them say all that crap about you, then they'll never get the chance to see what an amazing person you are."

My eyes fill with tears. "Tom!"

"It's true. You are. And you know that I'll stick up for you always, but I really think you should say something. Tell your side of the story." Tom pulls his fierce face, the one he always used to pull when he had play-fights with Dad. "Then I want you to give me Noah Flynn's address and I'm going to go around there to New York or wherever and I'm going to kill him."

I laugh.

"I mean it, Pen—well, the bit about telling your side of the story anyway."

"OK, I'll think about it."

"Don't just think about it—do it. You'll feel way better. I know I did when I went back to school and told Jonathan Price where he could shove it." Tom gives me a hug. "Love you, sis."

"Love you too. Please don't tell Mum and Dad about what's happened, though. You know what they're like about the Internet. I don't want them worrying."

Tom nods. "OK. I'll put off going back to uni for a couple of days, just in case you need me."

"Really? But won't you get into trouble?"

"Nah, I never get into trouble." Tom grins at me and I feel overwhelmed with gratitude. I might have lost Noah and Elliot but I'll always have my family. The best family in the world.

Chapter Forty

As soon as Tom's gone, I put my laptop back in my wardrobe and go to run myself a warm bath, rummaging through my basket of bath bombs until I find one called Chill Out Bliss. As the warmth of the fragrant soapy water soaks into my bones, I feel a weird kind of calm. I'm still hurting and sad but I no longer feel helpless. I dunk my head right under the water and feel my hair floating out around me.

"You remind me of a mermaid." Noah's words from the underwater corridor echo around my mind, causing me to sit right up. As I squeeze the water from my hair a chorus of hows fills my mind. *How could he seem so nice and so genuine? How could he lie so easily? How could he do that to me?* But I force myself to block them out. It doesn't really matter how. The fact is he did.

I get out of the bath and slather myself with my favorite moisturizer. Then I wrap myself in my coziest dressing gown and go back to my bedroom. I turn on my fairy lights—and immediately I think of the tent Noah made for me on New

Year's Eve. I turn the lights off and put on my bedside lamp. Next door, I hear Elliot's bedroom door slam.

To stop myself thinking painful thoughts about Noah, I think angry thoughts about Elliot. He must have seen what's been happening online by now but still there's been no knocking on the wall and no texts or calls. Unless he tried contacting me while I was in the bath. I feel a glimmer of hope and go over to the wardrobe to retrieve my phone. When I see that there are no messages, my hope turns back to anger. It must have been him. I think of what Tom said to me earlier and I know what I have to do. I can't hide away in my bedroom. I have to go around there and have it out with him.

It's only when I'm marching up Elliot's driveway that I realize I haven't set foot in his house for years. I can't even remember what the doorbell sounds like. As I press it, a loud *ding-dong* rings out. I feel gripped by nerves. I hear footsteps on the wooden floor inside and the door opens. His dad looks at me like I've just interrupted him doing the most exciting thing in the world. He looks at everyone in this way, even Elliot, all the time.

"Yes?" he says questioningly, like he doesn't even know who I am.

"Is Elliot there, please?"

He sighs. "Just a moment." And then he pushes the door to, leaving me out in the cold.

"Elliot!" he bellows. "There's someone at the door."

I hear Elliot's voice muffled, but can't work out what he's saying. The door re-opens and his dad reappears.

"I'm afraid he can't come to the door at the moment."

"What? But . . ."

"Thank you. Goodbye." And that's it. The door's shut and he's gone.

By the time I've stormed back home and up to my room, I'm in a fury. I stare at the bedroom wall, wishing Elliot and I had a secret knocking code for *I hate you, you stupid coward!* But we don't have anything even close because we've never needed anything like that. We've never, ever fallen out. Until now.

I sit down on my bed and look around the room in despair. Why would Elliot do something like this to me? Why would he do something so horrible, and then hide away from me like this? But he can't hide away from me forever. I consider keeping watch at my window so that I can ambush him the second he leaves his house. But that would be nuts. I contemplate drilling a hole in the wall to punch him through, but that's even crazier. In the end, I get my phone from my wardrobe and send him a text.

> I can't believe you would do that to me.
> Some best friend!

As I press send, I feel a fresh wave of sorrow. *I'm not alone*, I remind myself, thinking of Mum and Dad and Tom. *I'm not alone.* But all I feel is loneliness and loss.

I stare at my phone, waiting for a reply. But there's nothing. I get more and more frustrated. How dare he and Noah hurt me like this and then hide away from me? And then I do the worst thing I could possibly do. I get my laptop out of the wardrobe and go online.

First, I check Elliot's Twitter to see if he's updated lately. I'm not sure what I'm looking for really—proof that he's been online, a hateful comment about me . . . But his last tweet was on Christmas Day.

@ElliotWentworth Worst. Christmas. Ever.

I can't check his Facebook without reactivating my account so I leave that and check his Instagram. He hasn't posted since his last day in New York—a selfie of me and him at breakfast, grinning over a bottle of maple syrup. For a moment, I wish I could magically transport myself back to when the picture was taken so that I could stop things from going so horribly wrong. But then I feel a stab of anger. I wasn't the one who made everything go wrong in the first place.

And then I do something really stupid. I go onto Google and do a search for Noah Flynn. Now all of the top results are to do with me. I see a new headline from the *Celeb Watch* site: *Noah Flynn Had Breakdown Over Parents' Death.*

I click on the link with trembling fingers.

Noah Flynn must really be regretting the day he decided to play away from home with UK blogger Penny Porter aka Girl Online. Another of the revelations to come from Penny's blog is that Noah had a breakdown after the tragic death of his parents four years ago. Could this explain his less-than-wise choices over the holidays? Is he still struggling to deal with his loss? A spokesman for the new star declined to comment. Leah Brown

There's a link at the bottom of the post to another article, titled: *Girl Online Reveals Noah Flynn's Favorite NYC Hangouts.* I don't click on it. I can't. I'm too shocked by what I've just read. What are they talking about? What breakdown? Can they really just make stuff up like that? Then I think back to the post I wrote about facing fears and how I talked about the exercise Noah shared with me. My face flushes red-hot. But I didn't say that he had a breakdown. I didn't even mention his parents. I just said he'd lost someone close to him. I stare at the screen in disbelief. How can they do this? How can they twist things like this?

I click back to my search, swinging between feelings of guilt and anger. I scan through the list of results until I see one that fills me with dread: *The Girl that Noah Flynn Cheated on Leah Brown for—yes, really!*

I click on the link and it goes to the YouTube video of me falling over onstage. How have they found that? But it doesn't take a genius to work it out. A simple search for my name would have thrown it up. The sad fact is, apart from my blog, my entire Internet presence before today was that stupid video. Thousands of people have now posted comments. I tell myself to shut the laptop, to put it back in the wardrobe, but it's like I'm on some weird kind of self-destruct and I automatically start scrolling down. "Ew, gross" and "What a state" are the nicest comments on there. The rest are so horrible I can barely believe what I'm reading. Clearly

Leah Brown's fans have embarked on a major hate campaign against me.

"Penny, come and have some dinner," Mum calls up the stairs.

I groan. I think about saying I'm not hungry but then that will only make them worry. So I drag myself downstairs, my head buzzing with thoughts of Elliot. I must have really hurt him to make him do what he's done. To make him end our friendship in this way. I go into the kitchen and sit down at the table.

"Are you OK?" Mum asks the question, but she, Dad, and Tom are all staring at me, concerned.

"Yes. Yes, I'm fine."

"I've been asked to do another job in New York," Mum says, sitting down next to me. "A Valentine's Ball." She looks at me excitedly. "I've been trying to get through to Sadie Lee to see if she'll do the catering but she's not picking up."

"I bet she's not," Tom mutters.

I frown at him and shake my head.

"What?" Mum looks at him questioningly.

Tom looks down at his plate. "Nothing."

Mum looks back at me. "It's great news, isn't it? We can all go over there again."

No, it's not! I want to yell. *It's actually the worst news you could possibly tell me. If I set foot in America right now I'll probably be lynched!* But I somehow force myself to nod.

As Mum and Dad talk excitedly about how these American jobs have really turned the business around, I focus on making myself eat some lasagna without having a choking fit. It's so weird to think that when Megan posted that video of me, imagining the whole school seeing my underwear felt like the worst thing ever. But now the whole world's seeing it. Now, thanks to Elliot, I truly have gone viral. Just like the Black Death. Or smallpox. Great.

I manage to eat half of my dinner before the need to get back to my bedroom becomes overwhelming. Thankfully, Mum and Dad are still engrossed in a chat about Valentine's Day themes so they don't notice the food left on my plate. As soon as I get back to my room, I go straight to my phone to see if I've had a reply from Elliot but there's nothing.

"Fine!" I say to the wall crossly.

But then that weird self-destruct urge kicks in again and I start scrolling through the photos on my camera. When I get to the one of Noah, my finger hovers over delete. But for some weird reason I can't bring myself to do it. I keep on scrolling through until I get to the photos of my room in the Waldorf Astoria. At first it feels as if it was all a dream; that I never even stayed there. But then little details start catching my eye. The blanket on the chair. The orange moon. Princess Autumn on top of my pillow. These things did happen. They were real. Even if Noah was lying, I wasn't. I was in that room. And I sat in that chair. And I felt for the first time, that my life was my own.

Then I have an idea. I remove the memory card from my camera and slot it into my laptop, removing the pictures of the hotel room and sending them to the printer. Then I stick them around the edge of my dressing-table mirror like a frame.

I look at each of the photos in turn. The way I felt back in that hotel room was only partly down to Noah. But most of it was down to me. I chose to face my fear and fly to New

York. I chose to believe in myself. I chose to trust Noah and fall in love. I am a good person. It doesn't matter what anyone says about me online. I know the truth because this is my life story, not theirs. And OK, so it hasn't turned out to be the perfect love story, but that doesn't mean that I won't have one, one day. My life can be anything I want it to be—as long as I keep on remembering that it's mine. Not theirs.

I catch my reflection in the mirror. I look really, really tired and my eyes are bloodshot from crying. But I take my hair down and shake it out. I still love that it's red. That love is still there, even if Noah's kind words about it were all lies. I turn off my laptop and phone and I get into bed.

Chapter Forty-One

The first thing I do when I get up the next morning is go and sit at my dressing table and stare at the photos again, absorbing the positive memories like a battery recharging. After about ten minutes, I feel ready to go downstairs. Tom is already up and sitting at the table.

"I'm going to give you a lift to school," he says as soon as he sees me. "And I'm going to wait outside in the car all day, in case you need me."

"What? You can't do that!"

"Oh, yes I can."

"But won't you die of boredom?"

Tom grins. "Probably. I'm going to bring my laptop and finish off my uni assignment."

I smile back at him. "Thank you."

Tom puts his arm around me. "You can do this, you know."

As I walk into school, I keep reciting his words like a mantra. *I can do this. I can do this.* I feel like I have a neon sign above my head saying SILENCE because everyone I walk past stops chatting within seconds. But I don't mind silence. Anything's better than the abuse I was getting yesterday. Even when people nudge each other and stare at me, I don't mind too much. It's really weird because I've spent most of my school years feeling invisible, living in the shadow of Megan's spotlight. But not anymore. Now, everywhere I go, people seem to notice me. Even kids in other years seem to know who I am. As I walk down the corridor to my form room I think of Tom, parked outside school in Dad's car. I'm so glad I didn't persuade him to go home.

As soon as I walk into my form room, everyone stops talking and stares at me. But that's OK. It's like the walk through the school was a warm-up for this moment. And at least I won't have to face Megan and Ollie until drama, as they're in different form groups. I go to the table next to Kira and Amara. They're both looking at me like I've grown another head.

"Hi," I say as calmly and confidently as I can.

"Oh, hi," Amara says. "How are you?" She looks genuinely concerned.

"OK." I pull my chair back and sit down.

"Are you sure?" Kira says, leaning across to me.

I nod and bite down on my lip. Their obvious concern is giving me the urge to cry.

I become aware of everyone else looking at us and my face starts to burn.

Kira pulls her chair even closer to me. "Is it true? Did you . . . ?"

I shake my head. "No."

"It's not?" Amara whispers. She and Kira exchange glances.

"No. Someone told a load of lies to that website."

"So you're not Girl Online?" Amara says.

"Yes, I am. I was. But the rest of it isn't true. Not the way they're saying."

"I can't believe you're Girl Online. I love Girl Online," Kira says, smiling. "I found it when I was doing a Google search for Snooper's Paradise. That post you did about potholes was hilarious!"

"I love it too," Amara says, nodding enthusiastically.

"Really?" I feel a prickle of hope. They're being so nice. They don't seem to be judging me at all.

The twins move their chairs so they're right up to my table.

"So, was Brooklyn Boy someone else then?" Kira asks.

I take a deep breath. "No. He was—is—Noah Flynn but"—I fight down a wave of embarrassment—"I didn't know who he was. He didn't tell me he was a musician and I'd never heard of him before anyway."

"I hadn't either," Amara says.

Kira shakes her head and sighs. "So he lied to you?"

I nod. I wonder how long it will take before I can acknowledge this fact without feeling sick to my stomach.

Amara places her hand over mine on the table. "That's so horrible."

I swallow hard. I mustn't cry now. Not with everyone looking.

"We couldn't believe it when we found out," Kira says. "I told Megan there was no way you would have done something like that. I didn't even believe that you were Girl Online. But then it went all over the Internet and—"

"All right, you horrible lot, holiday's over. Let's have some order, please." We all turn to see our teacher, Mr. Morgan, standing in the doorway.

The twins take their chairs back to their table and fumble in their bags for their planners. But I sit there motionless, with Kira's words on repeat in my mind. *"I told Megan there was no way you would have done something like that. I didn't even believe that you were Girl Online. But then it went all over the Internet . . . But then it went all over the Internet . . ."*

I barely register a single thing during form period. All I can think is, how did Megan know about my blog before the news broke online? Ollie could have told her I'd met Noah but he didn't know anything about my blog. For a second, I have the crazy notion that Elliot must have told her, but that is truly insane. But if Megan somehow knew about the blog and Noah before it got out online, could she be the one who leaked it? Form period goes torturously slowly but as soon as the bell finally rings, I'm over at the twins' table like a shot.

"When did Megan tell you about the blog?"

"On Tuesday night," Kira says, putting her things back in her bag. "We were at Costa and she showed us it on her phone. She didn't realize we were already subscribers!"

"I hope you're going to carry on blogging," Amara says. "You know, once all the fuss has died down. I love the things you write about."

I give her a weak smile. "And what did she say about— about Noah?"

"She said that he'd cheated on Leah Brown with you."

"I had a right go at her when she said that," Kira says, giving me a shy smile. "I told her there was no way you'd do something like that. Not intentionally, anyway."

I smile back at her. "Thank you."

"To be honest, I'm not really sure I like Megan all that much anymore," Kira says. "I couldn't believe she posted that video of you on Facebook after the play."

I feel the sudden urge to hug Kira but I'm way too scared it will make me cry.

"Come on, ladies. Haven't you got lessons to go to?" Mr. Morgan calls to us from the front of the class.

"See you at lunchtime?" Amara says.

I nod.

"Don't worry, we'll take care of you," Kira says.

"Yeah. You're Girl Online," Amara adds. "We're your biggest fans."

The glow from my conversation with the twins lasts as long as it takes me to get to the drama department—about two minutes. As I walk down the corridor toward my class, the thought of seeing Megan and Ollie has my stomach tied in knots. I'm late getting there and everyone has gone in, but there's no sign of either of them.

"Pen!" Call-Me-Jeff exclaims as soon as I walk in. "How are you?"

I can tell immediately that he knows and I feel twenty-something pairs of eyes boring into me. I picture my room in the Waldorf. I remind myself that this is my life, not theirs, and I know the truth.

"I'm fine," I reply, and as I go to sit down I feel as if I almost mean it.

By lunchtime I'm feeling even more relieved. Megan and Ollie are both off sick and all the people I thought would give me the most grief about what's happened are actually show-ing me a grudging respect. Maybe it's that they don't quite know how to handle it, or maybe Leah Brown just doesn't have too many fans here. Either way, Kira and Amara are lovely and everyone else leaves me alone. Before I go back for afternoon lessons, I pop out to see Tom. He's fallen asleep over the steering wheel. I knock on the window to wake him up.

"What's happened?" he says, instantly looking panicked.

"It's OK—you can go home," I tell him.

He rubs his eyes. "Are you sure?"

"Yes, everyone's being fine. Seriously. Go home. Get some proper sleep—in a bed."

Tom frowns. "OK, well, I'm going to leave my phone on so if you need me just call and I'll be straight back down here."

I smile. "Will do."

I watch Tom drive off and I'm about to go back into school when I feel my phone vibrate in my blazer pocket. I take it out and see that I've got a text from Elliot. My heart starts to pound as I open it.

> Please don't hate me. My dad confiscated my laptop and phone and I only just got them back. We were in the middle of a massive argument when you called and I couldn't face seeing you. PS: I've run away

I study the text for clues as to whether Elliot leaked the story about me. When I don't find any, I send a reply getting straight to the point.

> Did you tell that website about me and Noah—
> and about the blog?

> What website? No, but I feel terrible about
> the comment I posted on your blog. It's been
> so horrible at home, I wasn't thinking straight.
> PS: I'VE RUN AWAY, AS IN RUN AWAY FROM
> HOME!!

Elliot didn't do it. He didn't leak the story. I feel overcome with relief that he didn't, and guilt that I ever thought he could.

> What do you mean you've run away?
> Where are you?

> On the pier

You've run away to the pier?!!

No!!! I've run away and I happen to currently be at the pier. I need to see you xxx

I start walking down the road away from school, texting as I go.

I need to see you too! xxx

Can you come and meet me? Please? I'll even play that stupid 2p game . . .

On my way

⋆ ⋆ *Chapter Forty-Two* ⋆

As soon as I see Elliot leaning against the 2p game in the arcades, I know there's something seriously wrong. He's wearing an enormous burgundy Puffa jacket, a huge pair of green wellies, and a Russian-style fake fur hat, and for once he has not managed to make a weird combo look cool.

"What's happened?" we both say at exactly the same time.

"Jinx!" we both say at exactly the same time. We look at each other for a second before we burst out laughing. Then Elliot hugs me as the laughter quickly turns to tears.

"I can't breathe," I splutter, trying to remove my face from the humongous Puffa jacket.

"Sorry. Sorry." Elliot takes a step back. "Oh, Pen, I'm so sorry."

"What for?" I say, a last trace of suspicion flickering in my mind.

"For that stupid comment I made on your new year's resolution post. I've been such an idiot, but so much has been going on at home I need to explain."

I look at him. "Have you really run away?"

Elliot nods gravely. "'Fraid so. As of tonight, I am a man on the street, a man of no fixed abode, one of our nation's lost souls."

"But it's the middle of winter. You're going to freeze."

"Why do you think I'm wearing this getup?" Elliot gestures at his bizarre outfit. "I'm not dressing like a chavvy Russian fisherman for fun, you know. I'm trying to avoid hypothermia!"

"But why are you running away?"

"My dad's said he'll disown me if I ever get a boyfriend." Elliot turns and stares into the 2p machine. The flashing lights cast patterns on his face.

"What?" I stare at him, horrified.

Elliot looks back at me. His eyes are glistening with tears. "He said that there's no way I can keep on living under his roof if I ever became"—Elliot mimes a pair of speech-marks—"'a practicing homosexual.' And then yesterday morning the whole thing escalated and he took away my laptop and phone."

"What? But why?"

"Because he'd gotten it into his head that I'd met someone while I was in America and he didn't want me contacting them."

"But why did he think that?"

"Remember my campaign to ruin my parents' Christmas?"

I nod. "Hank the Hell's Angel?"

"Yep. You could say it backfired slightly."

"Oh no."

"I said to my dad, 'You can't take away a teenager's online access; it's like taking away their right to breathe.'"

"What did he say to that?"

"He's a lawyer. He just quoted a load of laws at me until I lost the will to live. I think that's when you turned up at the door." He frowns at me. "Why didn't you knock on the wall? And why did you send me such a stroppy text? Was it the comment on the blog? It was, wasn't it? I'm so sorry. I've been so jealous and it's been horrible."

I stare at him. "What do you mean? Jealous of what?"

"Of Noah. And of you." Elliot looks away, embarrassed.

"Why are you jealous of me?"

"Because it's so easy for you. You meet someone you like and your parents are fine with it. They're like, 'Hey, let's go and spend Christmas with him!' You can fall in love and live happily ever after just like Cinderella. But if I ever meet my Prince Charming I'm going to be disowned."

"Oh, Elliot." I hug him to me, my eyes filling with tears. The whole time we were away it never occurred to me that Elliot might be feeling like this, and how difficult it must be for him.

"And I hate myself for taking it out on you," Elliot sobs into my shoulder. "You're my best friend. My only true friend, and I wasn't able to just be happy for you. But I was so scared, Pen. I'm so scared of losing you to him."

I can't help a sarcastic laugh when he says this.

Elliot frowns at me. "What?"

"There's no danger of that happening."

"Why not?" Elliot wipes the tears from his eyes and studies my face.

I sigh. "I take it you haven't seen what's happened?"

"Seen what?"

"Online?"

"No. I told you, I only just got my stuff back. I broke into Dad's study while he was at work and stole them back."

"It turns out that Noah is a musician."

Elliot looks at me blankly.

"A famous musician. Well, famous in America anyway and—" I break off, barely able to bring myself to say it. "And he's in a relationship with Leah Brown."

Elliot's mouth drops open. "What? Leah Brown, as in the chart-topper Leah Brown?"

I nod.

"Leah Brown, as in singer of the bestselling 'Do You Wanna Taste My Candy?' Leah Brown?"

I nod again, my eyes filling with tears.

"But that's insane!" Elliot stares at me and I notice that there isn't a trace of pleasure on his face, only shock and horror, and once again I feel terrible for doubting him. "Oh, Pen. Oh my God. But how—how did he manage to keep that from you?"

So I tell him all about the little clues that were there all along but I just didn't notice. The girl by the vintage store, the overheard snippet of conversation with Sadie Lee, the fact that Noah barely went anywhere with me in public.

Elliot can't stop shaking his head. "But what about the things you said on your blog—about him being your soul mate?"

"I was wrong." A sob wells up inside of me as I say it. "And now the whole world knows because someone leaked it to a celebrity website. And everyone knows about my blog."

"But how? Had you told Noah about your blog?"

320 · Zoe Sugg

"No. I hadn't told anyone—apart from you."

Elliot stares at me. "Wait a minute." He takes his phone from his pocket and starts scrolling through his messages. "You thought I did it!"

"Only because you were the only one who knew. Or at least I thought you were . . ."

"But who else could know?"

"Megan."

Elliot's eyebrows shoot up so high they almost reach his hairline. "What? How would she know? You didn't tell her, did you?"

"No. But maybe she saw something when she stayed over that night or maybe . . ."

"What?"

"Maybe Ollie told her."

Elliot frowns. "How would Ollie know?"

"He was round at mine on Tuesday—in my bedroom. He could have seen my blog on my laptop."

Elliot's eyes are now practically popping out of his head. "OK, from now on can you please just assume that my response to anything you say is prefixed with a 'WTF'!"

I nod and laugh.

"WTF was the Walking Selfie doing in your bedroom?"

"He came around to see me. He brought me a Christmas present."

"A Christmas present? What was it?"

"I don't actually know. I never got around to opening it. Ollie was the one who told me that Noah was a musician. He saw a photo of him on my mirror and he recognized him."

"What—but—oh my God." Elliot grips hold of my arm.

"OK, I'm sorry but I think we need to be seated for this conversation. Seated in front of two chocolate milkshakes so that I don't actually pass out from the shock."

"Choccywoccydoodah?" we both say together. "Jinx!"

I link arms with Elliot—or attempt to link arms with the enormous Puffa jacket—and we walk out onto the pier. But despite the biting sea breeze, I feel a growing warmth inside of me. My worst fears from yesterday were all unfounded. I'm not alone at all. I've got my family and the twins and I've got my amazing best friend back.

✦ Chapter Forty-Three ✦

By the time we get to the café, I'm feeling even better. None of the nightmare scenarios I'd been afraid of happening yesterday have happened. We've walked right through town and not a single person has recognized me and there hasn't been a single abusive comment. As long as I can avoid the Internet for the next year, I should be fine.

We order our milkshakes and find a table at the back. Normally I like to sit facing the door so that I can people-watch, but not today. Today, I instinctively sit with my back to the rest of the room, just in case.

"You know what, Penny, it's Noah's loss," Elliot says, unzipping his Puffa jacket. "You'll get over this eventually and move on, but if he's the kind of guy who can be so deceitful then he'll never be truly happy."

I nod, wishing that I could believe him. "Thank you. I'm so glad I've got you. And you know what? No matter what happens in the future—even if I do one day, by some miracle, meet a genuine Prince Charming—no one could ever replace you. I'll always need my best friend."

I look at Elliot hopefully but he's frowning.

"Well, well, well," he says, pursing his lips the way he always does when he's really annoyed.

At first I think he's looking at me but then I see that he's actually looking at something over my shoulder. I turn and see Megan and Ollie walking over to the counter, huddled in conversation. I feel a sudden burst of panic. What am I going to say to them? What am I going to do? But it turns out that I don't need to do a thing because Elliot is already on his feet.

"Hey, Mega-Bitch?" he calls over to Megan.

Megan and Ollie turn and look over at us and in that instant I know for sure that they're behind the Internet leak. As soon as they see me, they both look so guilty.

"Why don't you come and join us?" Elliot says.

"Oh, no, it's OK—we were just going," Megan calls back, looking really flustered.

"That's funny, because I could have sworn you'd just arrived." Elliot starts walking over to them. I get to my feet and hurry after him.

"Hi, Penny," Ollie mutters, not even able to make eye contact with me.

"Did you leak the story?" I ask, staring at Megan. She refuses to make eye contact with me too, staring at the floor. I take a step closer to her. "I said, did you leak that story about me?"

"About you *what?*" Megan hisses. "About you cheating with someone?"

"I didn't cheat with anyone," I hiss back. "I didn't know who he was. I didn't know he was with anyone."

"Yeah right." Megan looks at me scornfully. "If you didn't want anyone knowing about it, why did you put it all over your stupid blog?"

"That blog is anonymous. Well, it was until you found out." I turn to Ollie. "Did you see it on my laptop when you were in my room?"

Ollie doesn't say anything, but his face flushes bright red.

I stare at him in disbelief. "You were snooping on my laptop?"

"It was right there," Ollie says. "I just thought I'd have a read while you were in the bathroom."

"I don't think you've got any right to be judging anybody right now, Penny," Megan says haughtily.

"Tell me," Elliot says, turning to her, "do you go to night school to learn how to be such a bitch, or does it just come naturally?"

"I've got nothing to say to you," she says snidely.

"That's good, because I've got plenty to say to you and it'll be so much better without any interruptions." Elliot takes a step closer, so that his face is just inches from hers. "You have to be one of the most vacuous (look it up), inane (look it up), stupid (you should know that one) people I have ever met. And if it wasn't for the fact that you have just really, really hurt my best friend, I wouldn't even be wasting a single pascal (look it up) of breath on you."

Megan turns to Ollie. "Are you going to let him talk to me like that?"

Ollie looks at her blankly.

Elliot laughs. "Oh, please. He's probably too busy wondering whether this is a good time for a selfie." He turns to

Ollie. "It's not, by the way; it's a very bad time. But anyway—what was I saying?" He turns back to Megan. "Ah yes, you are easily, without a shadow of a shadow of a doubt, one of the ugliest people I have ever met."

Megan visibly recoils.

Elliot nods. "It's true. You're so bitter and fake it actually oozes out of your pores. Just like pus!"

Megan gasps.

At this point, the waitress comes out of the kitchen holding the tray with our milkshakes. "Oh," she says, when she sees us standing by the counter.

"It's OK. We can have them over here," Elliot calls, "with our friends."

I look at him and he gives me the tiniest wink. The waitress puts the tray on the counter, then disappears back into the kitchen.

"Ready?" Elliot says to me quietly as we turn to pick up the glasses.

"Ready," I reply.

We both pick up our drinks and we turn and we throw them over Megan and Ollie. And if there was an Olympic event for synchronized milkshake throwing, we would have just won gold. Megan and Ollie stand there gasping in shock as sludgy brown milkshake drips down from their heads.

"OK," Elliot says to Ollie. "Right now? This would be an excellent time for a selfie." Then he turns to me. "I think we'd better go."

I nod. "Yep." But before I leave I lean in close to Megan. "You're pathetic," I say. "And I'm not the only person who thinks so."

Then Elliot and I turn and we run.

We don't stop running until we're up by the station. I clutch my side and try to catch my breath.

"Oh my God, that was epic!" Elliot gasps. "Even my favorite revenge fantasies aren't that good."

"You have revenge fantasies?"

"Oh yes. But they were nothing compared to that." Then suddenly his face clouds over.

"What's wrong?"

"I'd totally forgotten that I've run away." We both look over at a homeless man lying in a doorway next to the station. His face and clothes are black with grime.

"There's no way you're sleeping rough tonight," I tell him. "You're coming home with me. I'm sure Mum and Dad won't mind you staying over. They were only saying yesterday how much they've missed you since New York."

"Really?"

"Yes. And then maybe we can get Dad to talk to your parents. You know how good he is in a crisis. He'll know what to do."

Dad knows exactly what to do. As soon as we arrive home and tell him what's happened, he tells Elliot that he's welcome to stay for as long as he likes and then he goes around to have a word with his parents. It turns out that Elliot's mum had been really distraught when she read his farewell note— apparently his farewell note was five pages long so it was more of a farewell *essay* really—so she said she was going to have a serious talk with his dad when he got home.

We spend the evening eating pizza and watching old episodes of *Friends* and every so often turning to each other and whispering, "Oh my God, the milkshakes!" and dissolving into fits of giggles. It feels so good to have this kind of normality again. But all the time I'm aware of a nagging sadness deep inside me that no amount of pizza or laughter is able to heal.

At about eight o'clock, Elliot's dad calls around, asking to have a chat with him. While they talk in the kitchen, I wait nervously in the living room. But there are no raised voices and at one point they even laugh. Elliot finally emerges with a nervous smile on his face.

"I'm going to go back home," he whispers. "He's said I can keep my laptop and phone."

"But what about . . . ?" I give Elliot a pointed look.

"Apparently he's going to go for 'counseling'"—Elliot mimes some quotation marks—"to help him come to terms with 'my sexuality.'"

"Wow. Oh well, at least he's trying."

Elliot laughs. "Yes, very trying!" He hugs me tight. "Love you, Pen."

"Love you too."

Once Elliot's gone, I make a mug of camomile tea and take it up to my bedroom. What a day it's been. I think back to how I'd been feeling yesterday and I breathe a massive sigh of relief. Tom was right; it felt great being able to face the world again and stand up to Megan and Ollie like that.

I look down at the floor at the unopened Christmas gift from Ollie. I wonder what he got me. I pick the present up and tear off the wrapping paper. Inside there's a framed photo—of Ollie. It's one of the ones I took of him down at the beach.

328 · Zoe Sugg

I can't help laughing. What kind of person gives photos of themselves as a gift? I immediately think of Noah and the presents he gave me. Princess Autumn, the photography book, the song. All of them were about me, not him—the way presents should be. Once again I feel that crushing sense of pain and disbelief. He seemed so genuine, so caring.

I throw Ollie's picture in the bin and go over to my CD player. It doesn't make any sense, but that doesn't matter; the fact is it happened and I have to deal with it. I eject the CD from the stereo and put it back in its case, along with the handwritten lyrics. I hold it over the bin. But for some reason, I can't let go, so I take it over to my wardrobe instead and bury it under my mound of clothes.

As I'm shoving the CD to the very back of the wardrobe, my hand brushes against my laptop. Can I truly say that I'm facing the world if I'm still too scared to go online? I pull the laptop out and stare at it for a moment. *Come on, you can do this*, I tell myself, thinking of Ocean Strong.

I take my laptop over to my bed and log on to my email account. Because I'd deactivated my Twitter and Facebook, and disabled comments on my blog, I hardly have any new emails at all. But I do have one from *Celeb Watch*. My stomach starts to churn as I open it.

From: jack@celebwatch.com
To: girlonline22@gmail.com
Subject: HUGE INTERVIEW OPPORTUNITY—EXCLUSIVE

Hey there!

As you're probably aware, we've been featuring your friendship with Noah Flynn on our website recently and we'd really love to share your side of the story with our 5.3 million readers. For an exclusive interview with *Celeb Watch* about your relationship with Noah Flynn we'd be willing to pay $20,000 and obviously the exposure on our site would massively increase your profile, not to mention the potential for sponsorship deals via your blog.

I stare at the screen, unable to believe what I'm reading. So now they want my side of the story, after telling a load of lies about me? And they seriously think I'd want their money after what they've done! I'm about to type a furious reply to them but then I have a better idea. I log out of my emails and into my blog.

4 January

From Fairy Tale to Horror Story

Hello,

As most of you probably know by now, in the past couple of days, this blog and I have become the focus of A LOT of online attention.

A lot of very negative attention.

For the past couple of days, I've had total strangers posting lies and abusive messages about me all over the Internet.

And I've had celebrity gossip sites writing articles about me without even bothering to check their facts.

These people don't know me.

None of you know me.

None of you know the truth about what really happened to me.

And yet you all think you have the right to post an opinion or call me names.

I've only ever been completely honest on this blog. That was the whole point of it—so that I had somewhere I could totally be myself.

Everything I've ever written here has been the truth.

Or the truth as I've been led to see it.

I didn't know Brooklyn Boy's true identity. I knew he was called Noah and I knew he liked music, but I didn't know that he had a record deal and I definitely didn't know he was in a relationship with someone else.

If I'd known that I never would have gotten involved with him.

I was lied to.

I've had my heart broken.

And, on top of all that, someone found out about this blog and leaked my identity.

When it all happened, it felt as if my world had ended.

For so long this blog has been my safe place—the one place I felt I could talk about my innermost feelings and not be judged.

But in the past couple of days I've seen how shallow the online world can be.

It's a world where people think it's OK to hide behind their screens and their usernames and say poisonous things about a person they don't even know.

And even websites like *Celeb Watch* think it's OK to print a story without checking the facts first.

Today, *Celeb Watch* contacted me for the first time since running their story on me.

They asked me if I'd like to do an exclusive interview with them about my "relationship with Noah Flynn."

They told me they'd pay me $20,000 for it.

They also said that it would be great for raising the profile of this blog.

Like I want my profile raised by a bunch of liars.

The fact is I would never sell a story on anyone, let alone someone I love.

Even if they really hurt me.

So, to finish my last blog post on this site, I've got just one more thing to say.

Every time you post something online you have a choice.

You can either make it something that adds to the happiness levels in the world—or you can make it something that takes away.

I tried to add something by starting Girl Online.

And for a while it really seemed to be working.

So, next time you go to post a comment or an update or share a link, ask yourself: is this going to add to the happiness in the world?

And if the answer's no, then please delete.

There's enough sadness in the world already. You don't need to add to it.

I won't be posting on here anymore.

But to everyone who added to my happiness while I did, thank you so much—I'll never forget you . . .

Penny Porter aka Girl Online xxx

Chapter Forty-Four

The next morning I'm woken up by Elliot hammering the *Can I come over?* code on the wall.

I knock back *Yes*, rub my eyes, and look at my alarm clock. It's only 6:30 a.m. My heart sinks. What could have gone wrong now? Still half-asleep, I stumble downstairs to let him in.

"OK, I know you said you were never going to blog again," Elliot says, pushing past me into the hall.

"Ever," I say.

"Yes, never ever, whatever," Elliot says, waving his phone about excitedly. "But there's something I really think you ought to see."

I stare at him. "Is it to do with what happened with Noah? Because if it is, then no I don't."

Elliot grins. "It is, kind of, but it's so good. Seriously."

I sigh. "OK, it better be." I take the phone from him. The screen's displaying Elliot's Twitter notification feed.

"You've got your very own hashtag!" Elliot says breathlessly.

"What?" I look at the tweets. They all have the hashtag #WeLoveYouGirlOnline after them.

"There's also #BringBackGirlOnline and #WeWant GirlOnline," Elliot says proudly. "Since you posted last night it's gone crazy."

I start reading the tweets. They're all saying really lovely things about how much they're missing my blogs and how I should ignore the haters. Then I see one from @PegasusGirl.

I'm sorry I judged you. Please come back #WeLoveGirlOnline

Elliot looks at me. "Isn't it great?"

"Yes. No. I don't know." And the truth is I don't. What happened before has left me so scared of the online world that I truly don't know if I want to go back there—especially now that I don't have the anonymity of Girl Online to hide behind.

"You said that the online world isn't real, but some of it is," Elliot says. "Your blog is." He points to his Twitter feed. "And this is. They really love you."

For all of Friday and Saturday I deliberate over what to do with my blog, with Elliot giving me regular updates on the hashtag campaign. On Sunday morning, I'm wide awake as soon as the seagulls start squawking. In the end, I decide to do the one thing guaranteed to help me get my head straight—go out and take some photos. I meet Dad in the kitchen as I'm about to head out.

"Oh, are you going somewhere?" he says, looking at me, surprised.

"Yes, I thought I'd go and take some photos down at the beach, while it's still empty." I grab a banana from the fruit bowl and stuff it in my pocket.

"How long do you think you'll be?"

"I don't know. About an hour, maybe two."

Dad frowns. "OK, and then you're coming straight back home?"

"Yes. Why?"

"Oh, I was just wondering when I should start Sunday lunch." He disappears back behind his paper.

I'm just turning to leave when Mum appears. "Penny! Why are you up so early?"

"I couldn't sleep." I frown at her. "Why are *you* up so early? You do realize it's Sunday?" Mum never normally gets up before ten on a Sunday; it's the one day of the week she's able to have a lie-in.

"I couldn't sleep either."

I shrug. "OK, well see you guys later."

"How much later? Where are you going?" Mum asks.

"To the beach, to take some photos. I'll be back by midday."

"OK, well let us know if you decide to go anywhere else," Dad says, peering at me over his paper.

"Will do. See you later."

It's only when I've gotten outside that I realize they're probably still really paranoid about my last panic attack.

I send Dad a quick text.

Going to go down to the old pier

I guess it will make him feel a little better if he knows exactly where I'll be.

The beach is completely deserted when I get there. It's one of those bleak January days where the whole world seems to be painted in shades of grey. I kind of like it, though. I like being by myself with the sea and feeling as if the beach is my own private garden. I sit in the shelter of one of the shingles and watch the waves rolling out. And all of a sudden I'm engulfed by sorrow. It's like now that I've finally stopped thinking about everything else—Elliot, my blog, school, Megan and Ollie—it's left a space in my head for memories of Noah to rush into. I sit there for ages, rerunning everything that happened. I don't feel angry anymore. I just feel sad. Finally, I force myself to get up. I need to think about something else. Something pain-free. I pick up my camera and head down to the old pier.

I love the old pier in Brighton. With its blackened, crumbling frame it looks like something from a spooky old film. And it looks even more atmospheric today with the wind whipping around it and the waves crashing at its legs. Behind me I hear a sharp whistle, like someone whistling for their dog.

I crouch down and zoom in on the pier thinking how cool it would be if I spotted the pale outline of a ghost hovering. I hear the whistle again, longer and more insistent this time. Maybe someone's lost their dog or maybe it's gone swimming in the sea. I turn around but I can't see anyone. Then I spot a flash of color on top of the shingle where I was sitting. A flash of auburn. I instinctively train my camera on the object and zoom in.

"What the . . . ?"

I blink and look back through the lens.

Princess Autumn is sitting on top of the shingle. But it can't be. I left her with Bella in New York. I start striding back up the beach, the pebbles crunching beneath my feet. There must be some explanation. I must have made a mistake. However, the closer I get, the more certain I become that it is her. I can see her blue velvet dress and the creamy-white color of her face and her hair billowing in the wind.

When I get within a few feet, I stop walking and look around. This has to be some kind of trick. But who's playing it? And how? And why? Did Mum and Dad bring the doll home with them? Have they put it there? But why would they do that? It doesn't make any sense. I turn and scan the length of the beach right down to the sea but there's no one in sight at all. Then I hear a crunch on the stones behind me and I spin around.

"Oh my God!"

Noah is standing next to the shingle. He must have been crouching behind it. He's wearing his leather jacket, black jeans, and scuffed boots, with the hood of his sweatshirt pulled up over his head.

"Bella told me she was missing you," he says, nodding at Princess Autumn.

I'm actually unable to say a word. I'm so sure that I must be hallucinating, that this cannot be real.

Noah takes a step toward me and I instinctively take a step back.

"I need to speak to you," he says with real urgency in his voice.

"But—I don't understand." A fresh gust of wind hits me straight in the face and snaps me back into reality. "Why did you—why did you lie to me?"

Noah looks down at the stones. "I'm sorry. I wanted to tell you the truth but I didn't want to ruin everything."

What?! Now my shock is giving way to anger. "Yes, I guess telling me you already had a girlfriend would have that kind of effect."

Noah digs his hands into his jeans pockets. "I don't have a girlfriend. I didn't."

"Oh my God." I'm feeling really angry now. "Have you seriously come all this way just to carry on lying to me?"

"No—I—I'm not lying."

"Yes, you are! I've seen it all online. All the tweets and the articles and the—"

He interrupts me. "It's all crap."

"What? Even Leah Brown's tweets about you?"

"Yes! Especially those."

I glare at him. How can he lie so brazenly to me? And how can he expect me to believe him? "What do you mean 'especially those'?"

Noah finally manages to look at me. "Her last album bombed. The record label was panicking. So, when they signed me, the marketing people said they wanted to orchestrate some kind of phony romance between us. They said it would help both our album sales. I didn't want to go along with it but they said all it needed was a few staged photos and tweets. Although I couldn't bring myself to do that bit," he mutters. "It felt so sketchy. I hated it. I even thought about turning the deal down but I couldn't; I'd signed a contract. I was locked in. So I figured, what the hell, it wasn't as if I was actually going out with anyone. And then you came along."

I stare at him, trying to compute everything he's just said. "So you and Leah aren't . . ."

"No! We never were."

"So, she hasn't been hurt by what's happened?"

Noah laughs. "No. She was a bit pissed at first cos she said I made her look like an idiot but then her record sales went through the roof because everyone felt so sorry for her so she got over it pretty quick."

"But I can't believe a record company would make you do something like that."

Noah shrugs. "I know. But apparently it happens all the time."

I feel my anger beginning to fade. "So why didn't you just tell me?"

Noah sighs. "I wanted to. And Sadie Lee kept on begging me to but I was scared."

"Of what?"

"Losing you." He looks out to sea. "Who wants to go out with a guy with a pretend girlfriend? And it's so hard to find someone . . . who doesn't just want their moment in the spotlight too."

I can't help laughing now, and as I do, hope starts fizzing inside of me. Noah is here. In Brighton. On the beach just a few feet in front of me. He hasn't got a girlfriend. He isn't going out with Leah Brown. He never was. But . . .

"Why did you get so angry at me? Why did you change your phone number?"

He starts shifting from foot to foot. "I thought you'd sold a story on me. I thought it had all been to get publicity for your blog."

"But I didn't even know who you were. Hardly anyone's heard of you in the UK—apart from my brother, but then, my brother's into all kinds of obscure music."

"Thanks!"

"No, I mean . . ."

Noah smiles. And just the sight of those dimples makes me feel all fluttery inside. "It's OK. I just didn't know what to think and I guess I freaked out. And then when they started saying that I'd had a breakdown after my parents . . . and revealing all my favorite places. I'm a really private person. I felt totally under attack."

I nod. "Yeah, I know that feeling."

Noah instantly looks concerned. "How have you been dealing with it?"

"OK. Well, OK once I went on an Internet detox."

He laughs. "So I guess you haven't seen my new YouTube video?"

I shake my head.

"Do you want to come here and I'll show it to you if you like?"

I suddenly feel overwhelmingly shy. Noah is here. He's actually here. And nothing is how I thought it was. Everything is OK. I think. We sit down behind the shingle and Noah takes his phone from his pocket. He clicks on a YouTube video and presses play. A tiny image of him appears on the screen.

"There's been a whole bunch of crap written about me

lately," Video Noah says, "and as I'm not one for Twitter and all that, I'll stick to what I know best instead. This song is going to be the first single from my new album. It's called 'Autumn Girl' and it's about the only girl I've ever loved." Then he starts singing the song. My song.

Next to me, Noah coughs and shifts on the stones. "I'm so sorry I didn't tell you," he mutters.

"It's OK."

"Is it?" He turns and looks at me.

I look right back at him. "Yes."

"When I read your last blog post, I felt like such a fool."

"What do you mean?"

"For thinking that you could have ever sold a story on me. I guess when it all went crazy, my fear kicked in and I wasn't thinking straight."

I nod. "Mine too."

"So."

"So."

He puts his hand over mine. It feels so warm and strong. "Can we start again?"

"As friends?"

He shakes his head. "No, as inciting incidents."

I laugh. "Yes."

Noah grins at me. "Because, you know, I don't say 'I like you so much I think it might be love' to all the girls."

"Not even to Leah Brown?" I say, grinning back at him.

"Never to Leah Brown!"

He shifts closer to me. "Can I kiss you?"

"Yes. Please."

Noah cups my face in his hands. "Man, you British chicks are so polite."

We kiss but it feels shy, apprehensive.

"How did you get here?" I ask.

"I flew."

"No, to the beach."

"Oh. Your dad gave me a lift."

"Oh my God, did they know you were coming?"

Noah nods. "Uh-huh. I told them I wanted it to be a surprise."

"It was definitely that!"

Noah looks at me nervously. "They know what happened. I'd told Sadie Lee not to say anything to them at first. But then, when I'd calmed down and realized what had happened, I called your dad to ask if I could see you and it all came out. I'm really sorry—I assumed you'd have told them."

"It's OK. It's all sorted now. Isn't it?" I look at him and he nods.

"Can we walk for a bit?" he says.

"Yes, that would be lovely." But as I start getting up I lose my footing and slip and fall—right over the shingle. If I'd been doing a stunt in an action-adventure movie it would have probably looked spectacular but in the context of a romantic makeup it looks totally ridiculous.

"Are you OK?" Noah calls over to me.

I scramble up, my face red with embarrassment.

"That was an awesome body roll. I wanna try." Noah takes a step back before hurling himself over the shingle. He crashes into me and we land on the beach in a tangled heap.

And as we laugh our heads off, the very last traces of tension between us disappear.

"I've missed you so much, Inciting Incident," he whispers.

And this time when we kiss it's not apprehensive at all. This time when we kiss it feels like coming home.

* * *Acknowledgments* *

I want to thank everyone at Penguin for helping me put together my first novel, especially Amy Alward and Siobhan Curham, who were with me every step of the way.

Huge love to my manager Dom Smales (Dombledore), who is the most supportive and caring man ever, and who has helped turn me into a more confident woman and stood by me through this whole journey with its many ups and very few downs.

I also want to acknowledge Maddie Chester and Natalie Loukianòs, my talent manager and talent producer, who have kept me up to speed with all my deadlines in a loving and friendly manner (even when I am being very slack and disorganized).

I also have Alfie Deyes to thank for putting up with all the nights I chose to write and re-read this book over and over again, and who gave me cuddles when I got a bit stressed.

I also want to mention my family too—Dad, Mum, my Broseph, my adoring Nannies, and my loving Grandpa, who have all been so supportive and stood by my every decision with big grins across their faces. I hope I've made them all very proud.

I also want to acknowledge all my friends too, new and old, online and offline. Each one of them inspires me every day to carry on doing the things I love, and I am so very grateful to have them in my life.

I want to thank my Chummy Louise for keeping a big smile on my face for four years as we went through this crazy journey hand in hand, through the fun times and the tough times.

There are so many people who have come together to help me on this journey, and I will at some point hug you all and tell you how splendid you all are (even if that takes me a very long time).

BIG LOVE,
Zoe Sugg